Copy

All rights reserved

The characters and events portrayed in this book are fictitious. Any similarity to real persons, living or dead, is coincidental and not intended by the author.

No part of this book may be reproduced, or stored in a retrieval system, or transmitted in any form or by any means, electronic, mechanical, photocopying, recording, or otherwise, without express written permission of the publisher.

THE HOLY BIBLE, NEW INTERNATIONAL VERSION, NIV Copyright 1973, 1978, 1984, 2011 by Biblica, Inc. Used by permission. All rights reserved worldwide.

ISBN: 9798838830159

Cover design by: Tracy Morand
Editing by: Jo Morand

Printed in the United States of America

This book is dedicated first and foremost to God who has given me the ability to write and the passion to do so. Without Him, this book would have never come to pass.

And to my parents who have read, re-read, edited, brainstormed, listened to all of my ideas, and supported me through everything.

FOREST DWELLERS
The Exile

S.G. Morand

S. G. MORAND

PROLOGUE

Exiled...banished... a traitor
In just a matter of days, Leif's whole life had been turned upside-down.

Two days ago, he had been walking through the town gates bearing the most important news of his career. Now, he was leaving in disgrace, told never to return. First the poacher, then the camp in the forest, then the riot and exile. Where had it all gone wrong?

PROLOGUE

CHAPTER 1

Three months later...

Brier reclined at the base of a tall oak tree. From her position atop a hill, she looked out over the small camp below her.

It was a rare moment of peace.

The last few months had been chaotic. And disheartening. First the riot, then the exile. They journeyed from town to town being rejected at each as soon as their situation as exiles was found out. After all, who would want criminals dwelling in their midst? Whenever they stayed in a village for longer than a day, rumors would start to spread, nasty rumors that Brier knew her father, Leif, tried to hide from her. Despite his best efforts, she had caught bits and pieces. *Trouble. Can't be trusted. Should have been executed instead.* From this rejection came an alliance born from necessity. The dozen or so families that were exiled banded together and turned their backs on civilization just as it had turned its back on them. They retreated into the forest far from any towns, far enough that they wouldn't be forced to leave. And they formed their own home, deep in the forest.

Brier's father and the other outcasts were considered guilty of treason, an offense punishable by death. The duke had supposedly had mercy by exiling them instead, Brier wasn't so sure exile could be considered merciful.

Their situation and their sentence were all because of the riot. Brier could still taste the dust kicked up high into the air, could still feel the fear of the crowd. She could still smell the scent of blood and sweat. Even though she had seen the battle from a distance, it had implanted a bitter memory forever in her mind.

The story which spread was that those who were exiled had taken part in the riot. They had attacked the duke's knights and tried to storm the castle. Brier had never believed that story. When she went to her father demanding answers, his only response was, "It was all a misunderstanding. It wasn't the duke's fault. I just pray that God will open his eyes." The answer was cryptic and Brier wasn't satisfied with it.

It had taken time for her to learn the rest of the story. Or at least, most of it. She got her answer in bits and pieces. "The riot was overwhelming, the dust in the air was so thick that it choked me and there were so many people that it seemed like the whole town was present. The crowd was suffocating, I can still remember it," Leif told her. She'd asked him why one of the outcasts ran off during the afternoon meal. Everyone had been crowded around the fire and the children had taken to dancing, kicking up dust, and laughing raucously.

"I was attacked by a group of men during the riot," he explained one evening when Brier's mother was inspecting the scar on his right shoulder, "There were six of them."

Some of Brier's questions were answered

unintentionally. "It's as cold as the castle dungeons in here," Leif announced jokingly when he entered their tent one night.

Then there were Leif's unusual mannerisms. He would flinch and spin around whenever someone came up behind him. He would always carry his longbow strung and ready for action. He was suspicious of everyone he did not know and only let himself relax around his family and his friend, Warren. Brier could tell by his nervous behavior that he was keeping something from them all.

She started to grow frustrated at his lack of answers and finally confronted him fully. "Why were you exiled?" She asked, catching him off guard.

Leif looked at her with what Brier could only interpret as fear. Then he went back to sharpening his knife and Brier thought he might ignore her. At length, he spoke, "I was just trying to help the knights. There were many people, and the duke's forces were outnumbered. The main street was so crowded, that I was forced to take an alley. I was cornered and had to fight. I did what I had to in order to defend myself. When I stood trial, the duke wouldn't believe my story. He said I was a traitor."

Brier started to form a clearer image of the riot and her father's exile. She had seen the chaos which had taken place; she could imagine the panic her father must have felt as he was surrounded. She could picture him sitting in a cold, dark dungeon all night waiting to be judged then standing before the duke and being sent into exile. Righteous fury seeped into her bones. Her father had served the duke of Mac'tire faithfully for years, sacrificing so much.

Brier might have been young but she had seen her father's dedication.

She had seen the minor injuries he had sustained from poachers who wouldn't give up without a fight and wild animals that had attacked him while he was doing his job. Her father had always been faithful to the duke and how did the man repay him? With disbelief. They had not betrayed the duke; the duke had betrayed them. Still, her father defended Duke Orion. He claimed that it was all a misunderstanding. He even blamed himself for what had happened, "If only I had demanded to see the duke and made my report. I could have prevented this all. If only I had warned him."

Brier maintained her anger. They didn't deserve the lot they were given. It was all the duke's fault.

Her father trusted that they would be okay, but Brier wasn't so sure. "God will provide and protect us," Leif often said. Brier trusted her father but she couldn't help wondering why God hadn't protected them from being exiled.

Despite the unfair situation thrust upon them, the outcasts moved on. They adapted. Three months had passed since their exile and they had established a dwelling in the forest. There were elders who made decisions and settled disputes and permanent structures were slowly replacing tents as winter quickly approached. The outcasts were speedily becoming accustomed to their new environment. Brier detested what the duke had done to them but she enjoyed life in the forest nonetheless. While some still held out the hope that one day they would return to Mac'tire, Brier prayed that they never would.

She looked out at the camp that was now her home.

So much had changed in the last three months.

In the forest, positions melted away, and everyone was treated as an equal.

In Mac'tire, people were regarded based on the situation they were born into. In the forest, they were respected for showing capability and skill.

Brier's family was especially respected. Her father patrolled the gathering to ensure the outcasts were safe from wild animals and he hunted to provide food for the community.

The expectations of staying apart from others based on station in life were nonexistent. The pressure of society had disappeared.

Her father had always told her stories of his adventures catching poachers and bandits and rounding up dangerous animals. From her childhood, the imagery of the forest had been ingrained in her mind. Brier had always craved adventure, now she was living it.

The night after they were exiled. She heard whispers between her father and his friend Warren, a once-trusted knight of the duke. They stayed up late into the night talking about what they had lost, what they had experienced, and what they would do next.

They all lost something in the riot, their homes, their families, their friends. Leif had lost his friend and fellow forester, Rowan. He had received the news in a shocking way as Rowan's son Reid ran up to them as they were being led to the town gate. He had barreled headlong into Leif, sobbing about his father's death and begging to be brought along. Blood coated his hands and face and his eyes were filled with horror.

Reid's mother had died from an illness several years

back. His father's death made him an orphan. Leif had comforted the distraught boy and agreed to bring him along. The incident had made Brier incredibly uneasy.

She was faced with a crying boy the same age as her, dealing with an event that Brier could not begin to fathom. Reid willingly followed them into exile and Brier was forced to accept that she was no longer the sole focus of her father's attention.

After the exile, Warren had lost something too. More than just his home and his position, he had lost his honor. Warren was once the duke's most trusted guard. Brier's father had never been overly fond of knights. He'd thought them proud and arrogant. Never had he mentioned Warren's name when he discussed such things. Warren was a kind man and he shared her father's faith in God. They talked often about God's blessings in their lives. Warren loved to serve the duke and he was loyal to a fault. After the exile, he was nothing more than a traitor.

Kept awake by Reid's muffled sobs, Brier had overheard their conversation. "I'm worried about Corvus," her father said.

Warren sighed, "If the duke trusts him then we should too. And we should trust that God's will is being done." Their voices were suddenly indistinguishable over the crackling of the campfire. Brier wondered who this Corvus was. She heard Warren again, "I was wrong Leif, what happened was my own doing."

"He can't be trusted," Leif argued.

"We have to focus on our own problems now," Warren insisted, "The duke can handle things. We must pray that God will protect him and the dukedom since we could not."

Leif gave a frustrated sigh. Brier couldn't help but agree with her father. The duke could not be trusted to handle anything.

He had been foolish to exile those who were loyal to him. He had been foolish about many things. Brier could see the pain in Leif and Warren's eyes. She hated the duke for everything he had done. He had taken away everything from them, their home, their positions, and their honor. She looked over at Reid, crying out in his sleep for a father who was dead. She looked at her mother, Rachel, a short distance away, a frown of worry on her face even in sleep. She clutched an embroidered handkerchief to her chest, the last possession she had taken with her into exile. The scene on the handkerchief was bittersweet, a little row of trees. Her father had always told her she was quick to anger and that she liked to hold grudges. He told her that anger and hate were a sin. But Brier could feel nothing else when she thought of all that had been taken from them.

Despite what they had lost, they were rebuilding in new ways. Leif and Warren were the first to suggest a group of elders to govern the outcasts. They volunteered as members along with nine others.

At that very moment, as Brier sat peacefully under a tree, the elders were shut up in a stuffy tent discussing 'important' matters.

Brier was grateful that her father was able to play such an integral part in the camp, but he was often busy and unable to spend time with his family.

His duties were great and Brier understood the importance of them. Unfortunately, that left her with two options as to how to spend her time, neither particularly appealing. She could either help her mother with household chores or interact with the other children in the camp.

Brier didn't fit in with the other children. Although she was only twelve, almost thirteen, Brier was mature for her age. Being the daughter of a forester, she knew that life was not all fun and games. Her father dealt with criminals every day, or at least he used to.

They all had tasks around camp but during their free time, the children were left to their own devices. Brier was more rough and tumble than the other girls. She had spent much of her childhood going on walks through the forest with her father.

By all accounts, her father had raised her almost like a son. If not for her mother, Brier probably would have been even more unorthodox. She preferred to spend time with the boys, who fought with sticks mimicking swords, and who played good-natured pranks on the adults. But although Brier shared many of the same interests as the boys, they did not appreciate her presence. Much to Brier's chagrin, they were all reaching the age where boys and girls started to see each other as an entirely different species and treated each other accordingly.

Then there was Reid.

Brier was convinced that he truly was a different species.

After Reid had unexpectedly joined their family, Brier was encouraged to treat him as a brother and friend. Her parents tried to welcome him as if he had always been there but Brier couldn't adapt so easily.

She didn't know what to make of Reid. He was silent to the point of being eerie and stayed mostly to himself. Occasionally she would forget he was there and be caught off guard by his presence. Her father said Reid had just been through a lot and needed time to process. Brier knew this, and she was sure she would never truly understand what it was like for Reid.

She was still frustrated though. Reid never started a conversation, and when she tried to talk with him, he was almost like a statue, unresponsive and cold. She tried, at first, to include him and treat him as a friend but before long she didn't bother. Reid didn't seem to mind. He would disappear for hours on end and Brier left him alone, as he obviously wanted to be.

Today, Brier was taking a lesson from Reid's book. She had originally gone to see what the boys were up to but realizing that they were fighting, she quickly left. Because she was a girl, she would never be invited to take part in such an activity. And if she came home covered in bumps and bruises her mother would make her wish she had avoided the fight. So, Brier decided to spend the afternoon alone. She climbed the hill to her favorite tree that overlooked the camp and made herself comfortable. Very few people knew about the spot and that was how Brier liked it. It was difficult to get to and few would make the attempt, but Brier knew it was worth the effort. From this location, a person could see the whole camp and the mountains in the far distance.

A light breeze rushed through Brier's simple tunic and pants but it was a pleasant feeling. She brought a hand up to push the flyaway hairs away from her eyes and let out a sigh of contentment.

Her simple clothes and sturdy boots were another benefit of her new life. She and Reid had been given hand-me-down clothes not long after the exile.

Reid had been forced to leave with only the clothes

on his back and Brier had begged her mother and father to let her wear something other than a dress now that she was out of Mac'tire. The clothes were a little big, but she didn't mind.

She sat under the tree, considering the beautiful view of the mountains. Those mountains were the last bit of Mac'tire they had left. The town and castle were hidden behind the peaks and the only way to access them was through a pass that was several days' ride away.

As Brier studied the camp, she noticed something was different. It took her a while to realize what had caught her interest. She sat up and peered closer until the oddity became clear. Brier gave a start of surprise. Near a small grouping of tents, there was a large, gray shape moving. It took Brier a moment to realize it was an animal, and not just any animal.

"A wolf!" Brier exclaimed.

She was to her feet in an instant, moving to the edge of the hill to better see the creature. She was filled with panic but also a sense of curiosity. She had never seen a wolf before, only heard stories about them. Her father often said, "Out of all of God's creatures, only the snake is more dangerous than the wolf."

Brier's curiosity was quickly replaced by a sense of urgency. She needed to warn everyone.

Brier started running.

Smaller animals had wandered into the camp before, but this was the first time a large, dangerous predator had ventured in.

There was shouting up ahead. The wolf must have been spotted. Brier ran at full speed down the steep hill. She stumbled once and slid a few feet, only catching herself at the last minute.

Her hand burned as it scraped against the rocks and she winced when she saw specks of blood. She kept moving, gravel sliding down all around her. Her racing heart made it difficult to keep her footing on the slick terrain.

They had been fortunate to not have any deaths in the camp so far. Brier feared that if the wolf went unchecked that may soon change. At Brier's breakneck speed, it wasn't long before she reached the outskirts of the camp. Brier turned sideways to walk on flatter terrain, then turned again and got her first good glimpse of the wolf. It was a hideous creature of incredible size with a rough fur coat. It snarled and moved at a crouch, ready to attack. A shiver ran up Brier's spine.

A group of people was standing nearby looking on in horror. So far no one was willing to get close enough to kill the creature. The wolf moved closer to the onlookers. Its hackles raised. Brier felt a thrill of disbelief and fear. Why wasn't anyone doing anything?

The elders were gathered in a tent on the other side of the camp still unaware of the danger.

Until someone warned them or the wolf made its move, this standoff would continue. Brier took off towards the council tent.

As she drew to a stop outside the tent, Brier paused and gasped for breath. The image of the wolf made her heart beat erratically.

After she had regained control of her breathing, she pushed inside.

Normally her bursting into a meeting without any notice would result in a strong punishment. But this was an emergency. The elders, who were gathered around a table, looked up at her appearance.

"What is the meaning of this, Brier?" Leif asked, upset at her disturbance.

"There... There's a wolf in the camp," Brier gasped out.

At this news, all eleven elders started talking at once. Brier found herself overwhelmed by questions she couldn't answer.

"How did it get here?"

"How large is it?"

"Has anyone been hurt?"

"What's being done to stop it?"

Brier stood frozen. The elders, seeming to sense that she wouldn't speak, started to move. Some grabbed for their weapons while others fumbled with their cloaks trying to quickly throw them on.

Then there was a surge of movement as everyone tried to exit the tent at once, nearly running over Brier in the process. Finally, the elders stumbled through. They ran off without even bothering to ask Brier what direction to go. Leif hung back.

"Go home, and stay there until I return," he instructed her.

Brier wanted to argue but Leif held up a hand to stop her.

"Understand?"

She dropped her gaze and nodded.

Satisfied, Leif pushed past her out the door. With his longbow in hand, he headed for the wolf. Brier followed after him.

She ran along at a half-crouch, careful to keep in the shadows as much as possible. Her father would be furious if he found out she had followed him. But she couldn't stand to sit back and wait for news.

As she neared where the wolf was, she could hear shouts and screams. Climbing slightly uphill, she could see the whole scene as it took place.

The elders took turns approaching the wolf then as the beast snarled, they would hurriedly back away. Armed with knives and wooden clubs they couldn't get close enough to attack. Warren got the closest but couldn't get in range to swing his sword. Brier held her breath as she watched him. She had seen Warren and his family often after the exile and had grown to be good friends with Warren's son, Flint. She could hardly breathe as she watched the action unfold. Suddenly, Brier remembered what her father had always told her to do when she was scared. She prayed. She asked God to protect the elders and the other onlookers. And she prayed for the wolf to be stopped. As Brier finished her prayer, Warren was forced to retreat. Brier wondered how much longer they could hold out like this. Surely the wolf would attack.

Leif stepped forward. His lips were pressed in a tight line and there was a furrow of worry between his brows. He looked at the wolf with a sense of fear like none Brier had ever seen him express. He swallowed hard and Brier watched as his fear was pushed aside and his posture straightened.

"Everyone, back away!" He shouted.

Those gathered quickly stepped back, parting to create an opening. Leif brought up his longbow, reached back to his quiver for an arrow, nocked it to his bowstring, and drew back. He waited a moment, making certain the wolf wouldn't move, then released.

The heavy draw weight of the bow propelled the arrow forward and it slammed into the chest of the wolf sending it reeling. The creature collapsed, dead.

There was a blur of movement as many people surged forward to examine the wolf and make sure it was truly finished.

"Wait!" Warren shouted, stopping the crowd. He approached the wolf's carcass and thrust his sword into its side. Brier watched breathlessly.

"It's dead!" Warren announced.

The crowd broke into wild cheers and gathered around Leif giving him slaps on the back and congratulating him on his good shooting. Brier realized then that from her position just out of sight if Leif's arrow had missed the wolf, it would have flown right at her.

CHAPTER 2

Leif stood in the shadow between two tents.

A plan had been forming in his head for some time. He was finally preparing to move forward with it. After much prayer and consideration, he realized that it was the right choice. Still, he was plagued with doubts. The large, canvas package in his hands seemed to mock his indecision. What he was planning was crazy, but after the events of this morning, it was also necessary.

The wolf attack had made his greatest fears come to light. Leif was a forester, or at least he had been. He knew how dangerous the forest could be. He had encountered his fair share of dangerous animals and conditions while doing his job but never had he imagined his daughter would face the same. Part of the reason he was a forester to begin with was to protect her. Now they were exiled and he realized that he couldn't always watch over her. It was a heartbreaking realization and one that tore Leif apart. He wanted to protect her more than anything but he couldn't. Being exiled had proven that. He trusted that God had a plan for them but he couldn't help but feel like he had failed as a father. It was time he finally consented to his plan.

He had already talked with his wife, Rachel. It seemed she had been doing some thinking and praying of her own. Leif expected her to call him crazy and reject the plan outright. However, Rachel only said, "She needs to be able to protect herself."

When Leif tried to argue with her, realizing he had been counting on her to talk him out of it, Rachel grew serious, "I want to protect her too but we can't always be there. She needs this, Leif. We all do."

It was settled. He spent hours creating the object in his hands. He had Rachel's blessing. Still, it was difficult. He took a deep breath and he prayed. "Lord, please don't let this be a mistake. Please protect my daughter and let her never be in a position of danger."

Leif knew that the prayer was unrealistic. He couldn't keep Brier from danger forever. The world they lived in was filled with it.

The sky was dark with clouds. It wouldn't be long before winter came. It was already cold and the days were growing shorter. Winter would bring its own challenges; challenges he could not fix. The camp of outcasts had just found a place to call home. They hadn't had time to prepare. With the snow, hunting would become more difficult and the animals would be more cautious. There was no dried meat or vegetables stored up for the harsh winter months. In their current state, Leif feared there would be a shortage. They also needed more permanent structures. Tents would not keep out the cold winter air or protect against the snow. Worst of all would be the illnesses that were sure to spread once the cold and damp arrived. Winter would be a challenge. Leif could only hope God would see them through and they would be able to overcome it.

He couldn't do much about that problem but he could help Brier. He realized he was stalling. Leif sighed and stepped out of the shadows.

Brier stood a few feet away talking with Flint, Warren's son. The two had become close friends after the exile and Leif was pleased.

Flint seemed like a good boy. He was obedient to his father, eager to please, and loyal to a fault. Flint was determined to be a knight like his father had been. He was a year older than Brier but there were times when his actions made him seem younger. He could be impulsive but his heart was in the right place. He believed in God just as his father did and Leif was glad Brier had picked Flint as a friend. The two bonded after the exile, most likely from the close friendship between their fathers. They were both athletic and fun-loving and once they got to know each other better they became fast friends. Due to their exhausting jobs back in Mac'tire, Leif and Warren hadn't been able to arrange for their families to meet very often. Leif regretted not introducing Flint and Brier to each other sooner.

Leif's one concern was that Brier didn't include Reid. Leif worried about how distant he was. They were all trying to make the best out of a truly terrible situation but it *was* difficult. Brier had tried talking with Reid and inviting him to participate in activities with her and Flint but as time progressed, the attempts became few and far between.

Reid was quiet at the best of times and completely unresponsive at others. He was completely withdrawn and emotionally cold. Brier was uncomfortable around him and with all the changes going on, Reid's presence was even more overwhelming. Leif had to keep reminding himself that Reid had only just turned thirteen.

It would take time for the boy to adjust to not having his father. Still, Leif worried. There was little he could do to comfort Reid. He could only pray with and for the boy. He hoped Reid would allow Brier into his life before the chance was lost for good.

Rachel was the only stable presence anymore. She somehow managed to keep all of them together and functioning. She kept Brier out of trouble and helped Leif as he tried to make everything right again. She interpreted Reid's emotions with ease and was a calming presence for everyone. Leif wasn't sure what he would have done without her. He had thought so before and now he was certain that God had truly blessed him with Rachel as a wife.

He was happy Brier had been able to find a friend in Flint, but he hoped Reid would soon come out of his shell and join them. Leif shook his head, knowing that he was stalling once again.

As he walked towards Brier, Leif had the brief notion to turn back and abandon his idea altogether. He quickly pushed all such thoughts away. This had to be done. Flint noticed Leif first and nudged Brier to get her attention. Brier turned to look at her father.

"We need to talk," Leif told her, gesturing to the spot between the two tents.

Brier looked apologetically toward Flint then followed Leif. As Leif gathered his thoughts, Brier shifted nervously from foot to foot. It seemed to take all of her self-control not to speak.

Leif finally put her out of her misery, "I know you snuck back to where the wolf was."

Brier looked away, ashamed. She opened her mouth to make an excuse but Leif held up a hand to silence her,

"It's alright. I knew you would."

He was more than aware of Brier's curious personality and while he had hoped she might listen to his instructions; he hadn't been surprised when she didn't. Brier might think she was good at staying unseen, but Leif had spent years as a forester.

He was used to noticing the presence of animals and poachers who could remain undetected far better than her. He was only glad that she hadn't been in any real danger. He'd been forced to take a quick step to the side angling his bow to make sure that if he missed his shot the arrow wouldn't hit her. The small alteration hadn't been too much trouble.

"That's it?" Brier asked, shocked to be let off so easy. Leif was fairly certain Rachel would not have been so lenient in punishment but he had other matters to deal with. Leif offered Brier the package he was holding. It was too late to change his mind now.

Brier looked at it curiously, "What is it?"

"Open it," he instructed.

Brier turned the package over in her hands once, then started to unwrap the covering. When she uncovered a long, curved piece of wood and a string, she looked up with a question in her eyes.

"It's a bow," Leif explained.

It looked different from his longbow especially unstrung but it would be easier for a beginner to handle. Brier's eyes brightened as she picked up on the word "bow".

Leif reached for the weapon, gently taking it from her.

She was reluctant to let it go now that she knew what it was. Leif quickly strung the bow and then handed it back to her. It wasn't as large as his but was nonetheless a powerful weapon.

"I was hoping I wouldn't need to give it to you," Leif remarked.

Brier's eyes grew wide, "To me? You mean this is mine?"

"After the wolf attack, I did a lot of thinking," Leif continued, "You need to be able to defend yourself if something like this happens again. I suspected for a while that this might be necessary. The wolf attack was the final straw."

Brier looked at the bow in her hand contemplating what Leif was saying. He could see her taking in every curve and wood grain. To most, the small bow would seem simple and weak but Brier was a forester's daughter. She saw past the seemingly unimpressive exterior and determined the bow's true qualities. She had always wanted to learn archery.

"Really?" Brier asked, "You're serious. You'll teach me?"

Leif nodded. He could tell that Brier was trying very hard to control her emotions. She rocked back and forth in excitement. Now was the hard part.

"There's more," he said in a casual tone.

Brier looked at him expectantly.

"Reid will be training with you."

Immediately a look of distaste and disappointment crossed Brier's face. Leif had been expecting as much. Brier had given up on Reid. Now she mostly avoided him.

Leif suspected something other than mere annoyance between them. Comforting Reid through his grief had taken a lot of time and effort. That attention used to be solely focused on Brier. With everything happening, Leif hadn't had a lot of time to spend with his family.

Leif suspected Brier was starting to grow jealous of Leif's divided attention. Where she might see Leif's attention toward Reid as favoritism, in reality, he was just trying to keep an eye on him.

The loss of his father deeply affected the boy. Even worse was the fact that Reid had been forced to watch his father die. Leif hadn't heard the whole story; Reid wasn't strong enough to tell him everything that happened. He did know that Rowan was attacked and killed the night of the riot and Reid had held his father in his arms as he died. Along with his mental scars, Reid also carried a constant reminder in the long, jagged scar running down his cheek. The wound was ugly and fresh and Leif winced whenever he imagined how it might have happened. Leif worried that the traumatic experience would forever separate Reid from the other boys at camp. Reid was already regarded as an oddity among the other children. He was quiet, keeping mostly to himself, with a scar on his face and, in addition to everything else, Reid was left-handed. This made it difficult for him to practice swordplay with the other boys and made him even more of an outsider.

"Why?" Brier asked, annoyed, "Why does *he* have to train with me?"

Leif sighed and didn't answer. He had decided to train Reid in archery before he had considered teaching Brier. He had even constructed a special left-handed bow. Rowan had begun to train Reid in the ways of a forester and Leif intended to finish his friend's work. It was what Rowan would have wanted.

Brier probably thought he favored Reid. Leif could only hope that this training would allow her to realize he cared for both of them equally.

It was a difficult road ahead but they needed to learn to defend themselves. Brier needed the time with her father, and Reid needed the distraction.

He regretted the fact that he had to train Brier at all. The idea that he wouldn't be there to protect her all the time was a blow to his pride as a father. He had already failed to protect her once when he had been the cause of their exile. Now they were all facing the consequences of his actions. Most of all he was worried about what would happen when he put a weapon in her hands. She was still young, much too young to be worrying about such things. Leif didn't want her to grow up too quickly. Using a weapon required a tremendous amount of responsibility and once she started her training, she would be entering an environment akin to adulthood.

Then there was the possibility of what might happen if she was forced to defend herself. Even killing an animal for the first time left a mark on a person. Leif remembered the first time he had killed.

He remembered the dull glassy and lifeless look in the animal's eyes. It had turned his stomach to think about the power he suddenly possessed, the power to take away a life.

Only God should have that power. And he shuddered to imagine her ever having to end the life of a person. Leif could still see sandy brown hair and a scar on a relatively young face. The stiff, lifelessness. He told himself he hadn't had a choice. It was either his life or the mercenary. But what gave him the right to end a life? What gave anyone that right?

He couldn't imagine his little girl, the same little girl he had told stories to and laughed with, ever being a killer.

When he put that bow in her hands and trained her to use it, he was giving her that power. If anything happened because of that decision then it was his fault.

Leif regarded Brier with a sad expression. The years had gone by so quickly.

Brier groaned, realizing she wouldn't get a response. Without any further argument, she started to walk away. After a few steps, she spun around to face him again.

"When do we start?"

"Tomorrow."

CHAPTER 3

Brier stood with her arms crossed as she watched Reid shoot his bow.

When she had arrived early in the morning for practice, Reid had already been in the clearing. A full set of ten arrows had been loosed before Brier was noticed. When Reid finally finished, leaving to gather his arrows, Leif finally turned around and registered Brier's presence. The fact that her father had started the lesson without her hurt. His not noticing her arrival hurt more. However, she was willing to put it aside and move on.

That hadn't been the worst part of her day.

Not even close.

She started the lesson by learning how to use her bow. Brier spent the first five minutes trying to hold it correctly, something she thought would be much simpler than it was. The fact that her hand was sweating from nerves and frustration didn't help. There was seemingly endless instruction regarding how to bend her elbow and where to place her fingers. Then her father forgot to warn her that she needed to wear a leather strip on her arm to prevent the bowstring from hitting her upon releasing an arrow. She ended up with an angry red welt on her forearm that stung like crazy and made her drop the bow in shock. She was sure she would never find the arrow that had been lost somewhere in the trees.

Leif *had* tried to warn her, but at that point, Brier was so eager to start loosing arrows that she proceeded before he could utter a word.

She couldn't have known that such protection was necessary, Leif himself had stopped using an armguard years ago.

Properly chastened by her throbbing arm, Brier was more willing to listen as Leif gave her his lecture on proper handling and safety. "Never point your weapon at anything you aren't prepared to kill," he warned her, "If someone is down-range from you, don't loose any arrows. As you've already learned, there is some necessary equipment required before you get started. The armguard is to protect you until you're used to holding the bow properly."

"What do you mean?" Brier asked, "I thought I *was* holding the bow properly."

"You are, but you'll have to bend your elbow slightly so the bowstring won't graze your forearm. It takes practice and the armguard will save you from a lot of discomfort until you get used to it."

Brier nodded, she understood now what a bowstring slapping against your arm felt like and she was not eager to experience the sensation again.

"Lastly," Leif said, hoping to wrap up his lecture before he lost Brier's focus, "You must understand what wielding a weapon like this means."

Brier looked at him, confused, "It means protecting myself, right?"

Leif placed a hand on her shoulder, "It means more

than just protecting yourself. When you hold this bow in your hands you have the ability to hurt someone... more than just hurt someone."

Leif left the words unspoken but Brier understood his meaning.

Having a weapon like this meant she would have the power to kill. She swallowed hard, struggling to maintain eye contact.

Leif grasped her shoulder, "Just understand the responsibility I'm entrusting you with when I teach you this. Okay?"

Brier managed a nod.

Leif offered a strained smile, "Then let's begin."

With her bow held properly, her armguard in place, and Leif's stern lecture echoing in her mind, Brier was finally ready to start her training.

She learned quickly that the flawless way her father used his bow did not mean that using the weapon came with ease. Her first arrow missed by so much it hit Reid's target. Reid, who had been steadily firing arrow after arrow, each hitting its mark, stopped at this disturbance and glared in Brier's direction. She glared back all the harder. She hadn't asked to take lessons alongside him. Besides, it was partially his fault she had missed. The sound of his arrows hitting the target was beyond distracting.

As the day progressed, Brier's arrows slowly got closer and closer to the target. Some of them even hit the edges. Her frustration only grew.

"Don't aim at the target," Leif instructed as he adjusted Brier's hand, "Look where you want the arrow to go then release."

Brier sighed, confused at his directions but not

wanting to seem incompetent next to Reid's natural talent.

When her arrows kept missing, Leif repeated his instructions, sometimes adding, "You'll get there, it's only your first day after all."

His reassurances would mean a lot more if Reid wasn't making it all look easy, hitting his target with every arrow loosed.

"Don't aim," Leif started to repeat after another of Brier's failed shots. Brier felt her face flush red with anger and frustration.

"I'm not aiming!" she yelled, throwing her bow down and storming away. Honestly, the instructions made no sense, she was looking at the target, she had told him that already. How could she look without aiming?

Brier walked a few paces into the forest, noting how Reid had stopped firing arrows for a moment. He was probably worried he would hit her, even though all his arrows hit the target anyway. Brier heard footsteps behind her and turned to see her father. She crossed her arms. She didn't want to hear any more of his nonsense directions, she just wanted to be left alone to wallow in her self-pity.

"Brier!"

Brier slowly came to a stop, knowing she would only get in more trouble if she ignored him.

"I know you're frustrated but you can't just throw your bow away and storm off. If you want, we can call it a day. Or you could come back, clear your head, and try once more."

Brier knew his reasoning was sound and she had already started to feel ashamed of how she had acted.

She regretted losing her temper but she wasn't sure she was ready to go back.

Brier vaguely wondered if Flint became so discouraged in his sword fighting lessons. She doubted it. Flint practically worshiped the ground his father walked on.

He was constantly telling her all about the new strikes and parries he learned. He was desperate to become a knight.

Ridiculous.

They had been exiled with no hope of returning to Mac'tire, much less having a future there.

Brier desperately wished that Flint would stop talking about becoming a knight but she couldn't bring herself to point out the minor detail he had missed and crush his dreams. She hoped in time he would realize it himself and find a new dream, one far more practical. Still, she envied his determination. If sword fighting was half as frustrating as this, then she didn't see how he could do it every day.

Brier kicked a tree root sticking out of the ground and then yelped, jumping up and grabbing her foot. She could feel her father's disapproving gaze. She sighed.

"Okay... I'll try again," she reluctantly agreed.

Approaching the one-hour mark of practice, the aches set in. First in her forearm then her shoulder and neck followed by her entire lower back. She couldn't remember ever being so sore and in so many places. The welt on her arm stung and her fingers were turning purple.

They had taken a short break earlier to walk around and stretch but it had done little to quell Brier's pains.

Leif noticed her discomfort and called for an early

stop to the practice. Brier sighed in relief and quickly retrieved her arrows.

She collapsed gratefully to the soft grass and lay on her back groaning as her muscles screamed in protest. Much to Brier's chagrin, the difficult training hadn't seemed to affect Reid at all.

He didn't appear tired or sore. He walked over to a tree and sat down beneath it, stretching his arms leisurely above his head and closing his eyes like he hadn't a care in the world.

Brier was sore and discouraged and upset but by far, the worst part of her day came when her father approached Reid first.

Leif went over to Reid and placed a hand on his shoulder. Brier could not hear what was said but she was sure he was whispering praises. Anger boiled up. How could he approach Reid first? She was his daughter! To add salt to the wound, Reid didn't even react to what Leif was saying. He sat still with his eyes closed, not seeming to care.

Reid's carefree, effortless attitude throughout the day surely didn't deserve praise. He had barely pushed himself and his arrows had still been on target. Brier had worked hard... so hard. Her fingers were bruised and every muscle ached. But her father had walked right past her to Reid. She forced back the angry tears that sprang to her eyes. She shouldn't cry. It wasn't worth it. She was very aware of her childish behavior earlier and she was determined to not repeat her mistake. She waited with clenched fists until Leif finished with Reid and made his way toward her.

He smiled and lowered himself to sit beside her on the cool grass.

"Good job today, Brier. You worked very hard. I know it seems difficult but you'll get the hang of it. I'm proud of the progress you've already made."

Brier didn't listen. His words washed over her like a swift breeze. She didn't want to hear anything he had to say. He hadn't cared enough to talk to her first.

Besides, she couldn't believe that he would be proud of her for the horrible job she had done.

She knew she wouldn't master archery right away but that didn't make it any less discouraging. She wanted so desperately to prove that she was just as good as Reid.

She wanted to make her father proud. This was supposed to be her opportunity to do so. Yet, at every turn, Reid was only gaining more of her father's attention and affection.

"God sees the amount of work we put into things," he told her, "And I can tell that you tried your hardest, too. It takes time to learn this type of thing, trust me, I know. Don't be discouraged." Leif gave her a quick pat on the shoulder before heading home with a sigh.

Brier sat there for a long time contemplating his words. This was going to be far more difficult than she'd thought.

CHAPTER 4

Leif's words caught Reid off guard.

He thought the practice had gone fairly well; all things considered. He hadn't broken down as the memories of practicing with his father came flooding into the forefront of his mind. He thought he had controlled his emotions well. Even if he hadn't though, it wasn't likely it would have been noticed, what with Brier. Her frustration was understandable. He had felt similar when he'd first begun to learn how to shoot a bow. However, her angry behavior was embarrassing. He didn't mind though. He was grateful that it had distracted Leif because Reid couldn't hold himself together much longer.

Every time he raised his bow, he remembered his father's strong and calloused hands gently lifting his arm a little higher as he taught him. Whenever Leif gave him a word of praise, Reid remembered his father's kind voice instructing him to relax and reminding him that he was doing a great job. Whenever he went to retrieve his arrows, he could see the overwhelmingly proud smile on his father's face the first time his arrow found its way to the middle of a target.

It had been an exhausting day.

His muscles were already conditioned to the draw

of the bow, so he wasn't physically tired, but his heart ached. He wanted to lie down in a corner somewhere and cry himself to sleep.

He rarely cried anymore. He had shed enough tears for a lifetime in the days following his father's death.

That had been months ago. He didn't cry now. The only pain left was the aching loneliness. He knew his father was in a better place but that knowledge did nothing to appease the pain Reid felt.

When Leif called an end to the practice, Reid laid his bow aside and collapsed under a tree. He needed time to think, to reinforce the wall he had built around his emotions. He was tired of the pity, tired of feeling like he was helpless. So, he blocked people out. He found that he liked being alone.

He closed his eyes, trying to picture his father again. Reid worried sometimes that he would forget what his father had looked like. His memories of his mother were sometimes hazy. He feared his father's face would become the same. In quiet times, he would picture his father and he would find peace knowing that he could still see him clearly in his mind's eye. He had just begun to picture Rowan's kind smile when a hand touched him gently on the shoulder.

Reid started in surprise, then, seeing that it was only Leif, relaxed. He appreciated the former forester who had once been so close to his father. He knew he was a burden to Leif and his family. They had just been told they would have to live as outcasts when a blubbering twelve-year-old ran headlong into them saying his father's last instruction was to follow them. Leif had taken it in stride and quickly started to treat Reid like he was part of their family.

More than anything, Reid was grateful for the late-night talks Leif had with him when they were gathering firewood for the camp.

They would find a small clearing and sit down on a log. Then Leif would ask him how he was handling things. Sometimes Reid would reply, sometimes he wouldn't. Leif would listen if he wanted to talk, or simply be the strong fatherly presence that Reid so missed. He would try to comfort Reid with scriptures and assurances that God would give him comfort in his time of grief. The first few times, Reid cried, letting all his pent-up emotions out. Leif would rest a gentle hand on his shoulder and comfort him as he shook with the unfairness of it all. As time progressed, Reid started to heal, if it really could be called that. Maybe he had just gotten better at controlling his feelings.

The conversations with Leif started to become less frequent and shorter in length, but they never stopped. Leif had a way of sensing if something was bothering Reid. He likely didn't know he possessed such a skill.

Perhaps he thought he was useless at helping others with their grief. However, Leif had aided Reid more in that aspect than he would ever know.

Reid remembered one occasion not long after the exile. It had been his birthday. He hadn't told anyone, not wanting to cause any more trouble for Leif and his family or draw attention to such an insignificant event. With everything going on, Reid himself had nearly forgotten.

He woke that morning feeling an unfathomable emptiness. Leif found him outside curled in a ball, clutching at his arms and desperately trying to silence his anguished sobs.

It had taken several minutes for Leif to calm him down enough to get some answers.

Reid finally managed to explain the problem though he couldn't explain his reaction.

Even as he sobbed uncontrollably, Reid didn't know why. Leif sat with him, comforting and consoling. Reid realized then why the tears wouldn't stop. He wanted his family back. He wanted them back more than anything. And there was nothing he could do. Reid tried to do as Leif advised and turn to God when he felt lonely and full of grief. Sometimes he would feel a hint of peace and perhaps that was what allowed him to hide his emotions but often he still felt hollow. For so long it had been just Reid and his father, and when it mattered most Reid hadn't been able to save him. He tried to remember that he wasn't truly alone, that God was with him but when his grief rose, he was overcome with despair and powerless to stop it. Leif was the only one who could help Reid during that time. Just the act of being there for him had helped Reid overcome his grief enough to carry on with life even when it was difficult. When Leif sensed that Reid was upset, he would seek him out and ask him if he wanted to gather some firewood.

Even though he shut everyone else out, Reid never shut out Leif. Perhaps it was because his father had trusted Leif so much, or maybe it was just Leif's kind nature and steady presence.

When Reid thought about it now, he realized those conversations deep in the forest were the only thing that had kept him from sinking long ago into the deep, dark pit of despair that constantly beckoned to him.

It would be so easy to give up completely and let the

grief overwhelm him but Leif helped him overcome it.

The only times Reid truly felt at peace were when Leif prayed over him. Leif had once told him that he believed Reid's constant grief and inability to overcome it were a result of the devil.

"You're being attacked, Reid," Leif had said on more than one occasion, "God is trying to give you healing but you have to accept it. You cannot listen to the devil's lies. You are not alone." Reid thought that maybe Leif was right. After all, he did feel like he was in a constant battle.

Now, Leif stood with his hand on Reid's shoulder.

"You did well today," Leif told him, "Your father would be so proud."

Tears were forming in the former forester's eyes. Reid quickly squeezed his own eyes shut, and nodded curtly. That short sentence meant more to him than Leif could ever realize. Right then, when he was missing his father so much, they were the words he needed to hear.

With his hand still on Reid's shoulder, Leif spoke, "We're running low on firewood. Maybe you'd like to help me gather some tonight?"

CHAPTER 5

Brier released another arrow.

It must have been the hundredth one.

She had been practicing all day. Her shoulders ached and her fingers felt like they were ready to fall off. Leif was walking back and forth between her and Reid making minor adjustments to their technique and urging them to keep trying. Brier was far from encouraged. She glanced at Reid's target and saw that five of his eight arrows were grouped towards the middle. The other three lay in the outer range. In contrast, her target only had four arrows in the outside rings while the others had missed altogether.

How had Reid picked this up so fast?

She was ready to give up. At the same time, she wanted so desperately to be better than him. Every time she looked at his target, she felt herself start to shake with suppressed anger. Every time he fired an arrow, she hoped he would miss.

Reid released another arrow quickly and Brier tried to determine how he was making them fly so smoothly. The motion as he laid an arrow to the bowstring, drew back, waited for half a second then released was fluid and graceful. Brier was still struggling not to jerk her hand as she released.

Brier turned back to her target and hesitated. She couldn't help looking at Reid out of the corner of her eye. Because he was left-handed and she was right-handed, their stances were facing each other.

She didn't just see his back like she would if she were shooting with her father.

She saw every move Reid made. He noticed her staring and met her gaze with a questioning look. Brier quickly turned back to the target. She felt her father standing behind her, and could feel his gaze as she brought an arrow to the bowstring. She looked at her target, trying to remember everything she had learned. She tried to picture her arrow flying straight and landing in the center of the carved circle. She drew the bowstring back, noticing Reid doing the same. She waited a moment, her arm starting to shake with the strain. She heard Reid's arrow hit the target. Brier released her bowstring but didn't hear the sound of impact.

She groaned. She felt the overwhelming desire to storm away in frustration. She turned her gaze toward Reid's target, which now had an arrow sticking through the middle of it. He set his bow aside, glanced in her direction to make sure she wasn't going to shoot, then moved to retrieve his arrows.

Brier scowled. She walked to her target and inspected her progress. She was not impressed. This was only the second day, but still, she had expected to be doing a little better. She'd managed to hit the target more, but her improvement was too slow for her liking.

Brier stormed off to hunt for her missing arrows. She pushed through the foliage, kicking leaves out of her way as she went. It was cold and damp and her fingers were numb. She knew it would only get colder. It was almost winter. She reached down to pick up one of her arrows and stared at the shaft. It was bent.

She wouldn't be able to use it anymore. She stuffed the arrow in her quiver. *Of course*, it was broken.

It was only natural that she couldn't even release an arrow without destroying it. Her hands started to shake.

Brier stalked further into the forest in search of her other missing arrows. As she was walking, she sensed someone behind her. Looking over her shoulder she saw her father jogging to catch up. When he did, he gently grabbed her arm and pulled her to a stop.

"Brier," he said.

Brier didn't turn to look at him. She didn't want to talk. She just wanted to gather her arrows and get back to practice. She had to get better. She had to show him that she could be just as good, if not better than Reid. She kept silent but when her father didn't release her arm, she reluctantly turned to face him.

"What?" she snapped.

"What's wrong?"

Brier took a deep breath.

"What do you mean?" she asked, trying to keep her tone neutral.

"You're obviously upset."

She clenched her fists and Leif let go of her arm. She pushed past him to pick up another arrow. The shaft of this one was completely ruined. She had to be careful just to pick it up. Brier roughly stuffed it in her quiver alongside the bent arrow.

She thought she had gotten better at hiding her anger and frustration. Apparently, she hadn't done a good enough job. Brier didn't face him. It was obvious he was expecting an answer but if she spoke now her anger would get the better of her.

"I'm fine," she finally said.

Leif's sigh was audible.

"I can tell you're discouraged, but keep at it. It takes time to get good at using a bow. You're already doing great. With some more practice, you'll be an expert in no time."

Brier looked at him with an expression of distaste. "You mean like *Reid*."

She knew she must sound childish, but she couldn't help feeling like everything was always about Reid. Her anger started to bubble over. Reid was practically a prodigy. After only two days he was already hitting every arrow on the target. She doubted she would ever catch up.

A look of understanding crossed Leif's face. He smiled. Brier started to stomp away. She still had one more arrow to find.

"You don't understand," Leif remarked.

Brier swung around, "Don't I?"

"No, you don't." Leif ran a hand through his hair.

"I know Reid is just *so* great at everything, but I'm trying and I will be better than him. Just wait."

"Brier, Reid's father started to teach him how to use a bow when we were still in Mac'tire. He's been doing this for a while now. That's why he hits the target more, that's why he seems so far ahead. It's not because he's naturally better than you. He's just had more practice, that's all."

"Oh," Brier said. She felt herself blush in embarrassment. Brier found her last arrow and yanked it out of the ground; at least this one was still usable.

"Perhaps you *will* surpass Reid's abilities one day. Just remember something. It's not all about skill or practice. Sometimes it's about dedication and desire."

Leif paused giving Brier a brief moment to process the words, "Reid learned how to shoot a bow from his father, now that his father's gone, it's one of the few connections he still has. Maybe the real reason Reid has such an edge is because he's practicing for the right reason. If you truly want to succeed, then you need to find your right reason."

Leif started to walk away, "Retrieve your arrows then let's call it a day. We'll pick up again tomorrow, but for now, you both need a break."

Brier stared at the arrow in her hand, trying to make sense of everything she had just learned.

"And Brier," Leif called over his shoulder, "I am proud of you."

Brier felt a surge of warmth flood through her and she turned away to hide her smile. She placed the arrow carefully into her quiver and started back towards the clearing. Her father's words rang in her ears chasing away some of the negative thoughts. *He was proud of her.* She hadn't given him much cause to be proud of her lately. Perhaps that would be her right reason. She would give her father a real reason to be proud.

CHAPTER 6

Sometime late in the night, Leif jerked awake.

He wasn't sure what had woken him, but he was instantly alert for trouble. He ran a hand through his hair and sighed. He wouldn't be able to get back to sleep until he made sure there was no threat. He stretched his sore muscles, looking around his small home for any signs of danger. Rachel was still asleep so Leif tried not to disturb her as he pushed through the curtained-off section that served as their bedroom. Though he supposed since they didn't technically have a bed, it could hardly be called such. He missed his nice warm cottage back in Mac'tire at times like these.

The small hut that was their new home consisted of one large room curtained off in various sections to give each resident a sense of privacy. Living in the forest with the other outcasts made privacy a rare commodity. They ate together, lived in very close proximity, and saw each other every day. Their huts were the only place they could be alone and even then, each family was packed tightly into a small space. Leif's hut was still not fully finished. The basic structure was set and the logs, which would serve as cross pieces were in place. The other outcasts needed homes too, so Leif had insisted his hut could wait. As a result, the wooden siding was incomplete and several tarps served as walls. They had started to insulate the inside of the hut with mud but some of the cold night air still managed to seep through.

Leif peeked inside the curtained-off sections that were Brier and Reid's rooms. Reid was sound asleep, curled up with his blanket pulled high up to his chin.

His face was peaceful, and Leif dared not wake him for fear that his peaceful expression would disappear. Quietly, he let the curtain drop back into place and made his way towards Brier's room. He pulled back the curtain and saw a small lump under the blankets. Not a single sound came from the sleeping form.

Leif shook his head, wondering what had woken him. Maybe it had been some noise coming from outside. He reached for his cloak hanging by the door and almost unconsciously, for his dagger. He would look around the perimeter of the hut to make sure there wasn't any trouble, then perhaps, he could get back to sleep.

The air outside was cold with a biting wind. Leif pulled his cloak tightly around him and looked towards the mountains. A snow cloud was forming. It was probably snowing in Mac'tire right now. Leif imagined the crisp white powder blanketing the town rooftops. Mac'tire had always been beautiful in the wintertime.

He held his knife in front of him as he carefully paced around his home. The moon provided the only light. Leif could see nothing out of the ordinary. There were no broken branches or animal tracks. No signs of human presence other than his own. Apart from the wind howling, it was quiet and peaceful.

His hut was a little distance from the other homes

so whatever had woken him hadn't been one of the other outcasts. He looked toward the other huts regardless.

There were no signs of anyone awake and moving around.

He had requested to build his home on the outskirts of the camp. He liked having some distance between himself and the others. It reminded him of his cottage in Mac'tire. He had lived near the town gate to better suit him as a forester. Now, of course, the location of his home served no practical purpose. He missed his life back in Mac'tire. He missed serving the duke and the feeling of purpose he had felt every time he grabbed his bow and made for the forest.

What was happening in Mac'tire now? Leif felt like he had left quite the mess behind him when he was sent into exile. He had spent many an afternoon discussing such matters with Warren. Leif was concerned and wanted to help but also feared the consequences of doing so. Warren, on the other hand, was plagued with uncertainty as to whether he was truly innocent. Warren wanted to return to Mac'tire just as much as Leif did, if not more, but he feared that perhaps the duke had been right to exile him. Warren's part in the chaos of that day had been much different from Leif's. More than anything, Leif was worried about Corvus. What was the duke's advisor's role in all of this? What power had Corvus gained since the exile?

Leif quietly laughed. It was ironic that even after being exiled, Corvus still wouldn't leave him alone. His thoughts were constantly filled with uncertainties and his distaste for the duke's advisor had only grown. If only Leif had told the duke what he had found in the forest the day before the riot. Maybe then, they would all still be in Mac'tire.

The huts rested peacefully around him. There were far too many.

Too many innocent people had been exiled because of the riot. Too many lives had been ruined.

The duke had been fooled and deceived. Leif couldn't help but feel that it was partially his fault. If there was any possibility of setting things right, Leif would take it.

He took a deep breath and prayed, *God please, allow me to fix this. Open the duke's eyes and let him see that we're innocent. If it's your will, please let us return to Mac'tire.*

He sighed and reached for the door to his hut. "Looks like I woke up for nothing," he muttered to himself. Maybe he could get a few more hours of sleep before morning. Just as his hand brushed against the door, the wind shifted direction and Leif heard a noise.

A dull smacking sound came from the trees up ahead. Through those trees lay the practice field where Leif taught Brier and Reid. What sound could be coming from there in the middle of the night? His mind conjured up the image of a wolf. He almost laughed at his own ridiculousness. Wolves growled; they didn't make a smacking sound.

Yet, try as he might, Leif couldn't get the image of yellow eyes out of his head. Maybe he should go back for his bow. But if he did, he might miss the source of the noise, whatever it was.

Holding his dagger in a defensive position, Leif started to follow the trail. He would risk having only his knife. It would protect him a little. Even if it wasn't a wolf making the sound, it could still be dangerous. Leif tried to decipher the noise but he couldn't form a connection.

The howling wind distorted the sound. He kept an eye on the ground, careful not to stumble in the uncertain lighting. Tree roots snaked along the path and bushes pressed in on the sides. It was all he could do to keep his footing in the dark.

The knife in his hand was comforting but it did little to quell the unease rising in his chest. The noise gradually grew louder and more distinct as he neared the clearing. The *Twang...Thump* repeated itself. Suddenly he knew what it was he was hearing.

It was a sound he had heard countless times over the years, a sound that had brought him confidence and strength. It was the sound of an arrow hitting a target.

Leif slowed to a stop. Who would be shooting arrows this late? Brier and Reid were safely in bed and, as far as he knew, any of the other outcasts who could shoot a bow did so only as a hunter. Surely a hunter would not be shooting at wooden targets this late at night.

Leif stayed in the shadows and took another step closer. The trees around the clearing were thick, protecting the mysterious archer from Leif's view but also protecting Leif from his. He was getting close. Soon he would be able to see who was there. He took a deep breath and stepped around the last of the trees.

A small, cloaked figure reached back for an arrow from the quiver that hung around its shoulders. The shadowy figure placed the arrow on their bowstring, drew back to full draw, and released.

The arrow, indistinct in the night sky, arched

upward and then landed an inch or so from the middle of the target. The figure, frustrated, flung back the hood of their cloak.

It took Leif a moment to recognize the shoulder-length hair and lightly freckled face illuminated by moonlight. It took him a moment longer to accept who it was.

"Brier," Leif whispered.

How? Brier had been asleep in her room when Leif left the hut. She couldn't have snuck past him. Leif's mind flashed back to the misshapen lump under her blankets, and the soundlessness of her sleep. Suddenly he realized what she had done. He shook his head at her trick. He was ashamed of his skills of perception mistaking a pillow stuffed under a blanket as his sleeping daughter.

Brier walked across the dark field to retrieve her arrows. Leif noted with pride that all of them had hit the target. Never had he seen such excellent accuracy from her. Brier, though, did not seem so happy with her less than perfect results.

Had he been too hard on her during practice? Perhaps he had seemed to expect perfection from her. It was obvious to him that she was capable but it would take time to reach mastery. What had driven her to sneak away in the middle of the night to practice?

While he was pondering this, Brier resumed her stance and fired another set of arrows. Her form was graceful and Leif was surprised that this was the same Brier who struggled through the basic aspects of archery just a few days ago.

A sense of pride washed over him. Her determination to learn and perfect was admirable. He just hoped she wasn't working herself too hard. The practice sessions for her and Reid were rigorous and taxing.

The only way to keep pace was if they were able to rest their bodies and minds. Brier would need a good night's sleep before repeating the routine tomorrow. More than that, it could be dangerous to practice in the dark.

She could hurt herself, or someone else if they snuck up on her. And there were wild animals in the forest, and the cold air would surely make her fingers ache. Yet... Leif couldn't bring himself to interrupt her.

Her movements were fluid and smooth and she looked relaxed and focused. Again, he was struck by how different she seemed now as opposed to during practice. With no one distracting her, she could truly flourish.

Eventually, her movements became sluggish and her shoulders sagged with exhaustion. She gathered up her arrows one last time. She struggled to remove them with her arms weak and the arrows deeply embedded in the wooden target. Again, not a single arrow had missed.

She replaced the arrows in her quiver, grabbed her bow, and started back towards the hut. Leif, standing in the shadows in the direction she was heading, quickly backtracked so she wouldn't know he had been watching. He didn't know why he did it. He didn't know why he didn't confront her and ask why she was doing this. He had the feeling that a responsible parent would put an end to this right away. However, the image of her peaceful and focused practicing wouldn't leave his mind.

He would let her keep this up for now. He wouldn't punish her for her motivation. Besides, he didn't think he could stop her if he tried.

CHAPTER 7

Winter had arrived.
With it came cold, illness, and despair.
The first snow had been lovely, unobstructed by the manmade lines of Mac'tire. It was a light, pleasant dusting that sparkled in the treetops and spotted the ground in white. But it kept snowing.
Soon the light dusting was a heavy blanket that covered the forest floor and the still unfinished huts. Damp seeped through incomplete roofs and chilled the residents to the bone. The cold was bitter and unending. In Mac'tire one could escape by retreating to their homes. In the forest, it was simply going from one cold to a slightly lesser one.
The wind howled, sending gusts through the trees that shook the snow from their branches onto unsuspecting passersby. The fall clothes the outcasts had worn upon exile proved to be insufficient. There was no way to overcome the cold. They were caught unprepared.
The elders met every day to discuss plans. They gathered in a small supply hut. Everyone in the outcast's camp hurried to complete projects, which should have been done long ago. All hands worked together to finish the huts. Even the children helped by

insulating the inside of the buildings with mud.

There hadn't been enough time to gather food for the winter and the outcasts struggled to provide for their families.

Each meal became uncertain and portions shrunk as the weeks went by.

The elders solved this problem by rationing food for each person. Still, there was not always enough.

Brier and Reid's training nearly ground to a halt. They were assigned tasks to help out around the camp instead. They helped finish the huts, gathered branches for firewood, and looked for any edible plant life. In between meetings with the elders, Leif showed them how to create traps and they lined the forest floor with snares for any unsuspecting rabbits.

Still, whenever they had the opportunity, Brier and Reid could be found loosing arrows at wooden targets. Their fingers would grow numb in the cold and their cheeks turned red from the wind but the repetitive motion was their only break from the despair and panic around them.

Occasionally Leif would find the time to take them for a hunt. Brier and Reid were still beginners but every extra hunter was appreciated. Brier's chest swelled with pride when she shot her first deer and was able to provide food for all the outcasts. Even the deer hides were tanned and used for clothing.

The first month was hard. It was cold and filled with grueling work and scarce commodities but the worst was yet to come.

CHAPTER 8

"Another death today," Rachel announced.

Leif sighed as he pulled off his cloak and hung it by the door. He had just returned from a trying meeting where the ever-present food shortage was discussed. He had been hoping when he got home there would be some good news.

Rachel was leaning against one of the hut walls with her hands clasped tightly in front of her. Leif noticed with concern how dry and worn her hands were starting to look. She had been working with a group of women as healers these last few months. It was a fitting job for her. Rachel had always been strong. She was often filled with worry that one day an animal would attack Leif or a poacher would fight back and he wouldn't make it home. It was part of being married to a forester. He had been in danger before, even dealt with minor injuries, but he had always come home to her. Until the day of the riot when he very nearly hadn't. He remembered that day clearly when he had told her they would be exiled.

Leif wasn't proud of the way he acted.

He had to be dragged from the courtroom and the castle, fighting all the way.

The restraining knights led him to his home,

stopping at the door. Those who were to be exiled were given an hour to gather any personal belongings they could carry before being forced to leave town.

The duke had established this rule to give exiled criminals a chance of survival.

The knights kept hold of Leif's arms for several minutes to ensure that he wouldn't try to run, not that he had anywhere to run to. If he tried to resist, he could be hung. Leif was forced to admit defeat. He was now an exiled man. He calmed himself and shook out of the knights' grip. He dreaded what was awaiting him but he could at least face the situation with dignity. The men waited outside so Leif could break the news to his family.

Rachel was working on her embroidery when he entered the house. She looked out the window every few seconds as if expecting someone. A look of suppressed concern was on her face. Leif realized that she was waiting for him. He hadn't returned home the previous night, instead being kept in the dungeons. He gently cleared his throat. Rachel's head popped up and she leaped from her chair, her embroidery falling to the floor. Seeing Leif, she let out a cry of relief. She flung her arms around his neck and he gently returned the embrace.

"Where have you been? What happened? We've been so worried," She stepped back and looked at him. She noticed his head injury first where he had been struck during the riot and knocked out. Leif let her fuss about but he kept his eyes downcast.

"What's wrong?" she asked seeing the look on his face. Rachel had always been good at reading people; it was one of the things he loved so much about her.

At her words the full realization of what happened finally closed in on him. He took several deep breaths, fighting to gain control of his emotions.

He had to be strong, not just for himself but for his family.

When he finished explaining what had happened during the riot, the accusations against him, and the result, exile, he looked into Rachel's eyes. Tears drifted down her face and she held him tight as her whole frame shook. After a minute, she stepped back. Leif watched as her demeanor changed from one of fear and grief to anger.

"How can the duke do this? You've been loyal to him for years and he still won't believe you!" Her hands curled into fists. Rachel was not easily angered. A moment later her expression once again altered, this time to one of concern as she noticed the wound on Leif's arm, courtesy of the men who had ambushed him during the riot.

"Your arm."

Truth be told, he had been so worried about how he was going to break the news of being exiled to his family that he had all but forgotten the wound. Blood-soaked through the rough cloth he had tied around it.

"Oh, it's nothing," he lied.

Now that he had been reminded of the wound it throbbed painfully. He managed to hide his grimace but Rachel gave him a knowing look before disappearing into the back room of the house. She returned holding a small jar with some healing salve and a clean bandage. She gestured to a chair by the table and Leif sat down.

"I'm ashamed I didn't notice sooner," she said, "I saw your head wound, I'll have to keep an eye on that, but

I didn't notice your arm. You're lucky it's not infected after the day you went through."

Rachel worked quickly but gently as she properly bandaged his arm. Leif smiled softly as he watched her.

She bit her lip in concentration and her eyes were half-hidden by her eyelashes as she focused on her task.

As Leif let Rachel take a moment to patch him up, he started to feel the exhaustion and pain from the last few days creep up on him. Even though each of her movements was gentle, they still sent pain arching through his arm. His back and shoulder were sore from sleeping in the dungeon and the stress of the last few days started to overwhelm him. Sunlight streaked through the window landing on Rachel's face and Leif was mesmerized watching her.

He nearly fell asleep by the time Rachel finished. She took a half step back to examine her handiwork and gave a small nod when she was satisfied. Leif managed to jerk himself out of his stupor.

"Now," Rachel said, dusting her hands on her skirt, "We have other pressing matters to attend to."

Leif, who had been inspecting the bandage over his arm, looked up. She was right. They couldn't delay the inevitable much longer.

"Come," Rachel told him holding out her hands, "We should prepare as much as possible."

Rachel never ceased to amaze him. She took control of the situation and accepted their fate in stride. As long as Leif had known her, she had always been content wherever she was.

She had grown up very poor but always maintained a positive attitude. She could look at anything or anyone and see the good. Leif admired her for that, and he sometimes wished he could be so strong and optimistic.

She trusted completely in God and His plan. Now she was doing it again, putting on a brave face and trying to make the best out of a bad situation.

She had kept up that attitude throughout their exile. He knew taking care of the sick and dying was painful and difficult for her. She was a very caring person by nature and seeing people suffer put a weight on her heart. Still, she spent endless hours bandaging wounds and caring for the ill. He grasped her hand. Rachel looked up, meeting his eyes.

"This death makes the seventh one," she muttered, "We have to do something. We just don't have the supplies. All we've been able to do is wait for them to die. There's no medicine, not enough blankets, we can't go on like this."

Leif nodded. With the cold had come illness, a terrible illness that had quickly spread among the inhabitants of the camp. A few people had recovered, but those who were weaker were less fortunate. The elders had already met numerous times on the issue; they had yet to come up with a solution.

"The elders are trying to make a decision," Leif reminded her.

This was not the first time he and Rachel had this conversation. Leif was only one man on a council of eleven. He could make suggestions, or raise a complaint, but every issue had to be decided on by the majority.

Rachel sighed and reached for her cloak. Leif furrowed his brow in confusion. It was late, and Rachel usually came home for the night as soon as the sun went down.

One of the other women usually made the rounds at

night.

"Maggie caught the illness," Rachel said in explanation, "I'll have to make the rounds for her tonight."

"Rachel," Leif said, worried that she would be out at night alone.

"Don't worry," Rachel gave him a weak smile, "I'll have the new trainee with me. She shows great promise for someone so young. I'm certain she would have had a wonderful future as a healer if not for the exile."

Leif knew that to be true for many of the young outcasts. They could have all had bright futures. Now their future looked grim and burdensome.

Rachel shared a smile with Leif. He knew she was beyond frustrated at the lack of supplies and all the people who were suffering because of it. Still, she tried to put on a brave face.

Suddenly the door was pushed open.

"Are you sure you're all right Reid, that cough doesn't sound good," Brier remarked as she and Reid strolled through the door.

"I'm fine. Why do you even care?" Reid muttered. His shoulders were hunched and his arms were wrapped tightly around himself to ward off the cold.

Judging by the bows in their hands, Leif guessed that Brier and Reid had been out practicing.

"What cough?" Rachel asked, a hint of concern rising in her voice.

"It's nothing," Reid claimed before dissolving into a fit of dry rasping coughs.

"See, I told you it sounds bad," Brier said. Reid glared at her.

"How long have you been feeling poorly?" Rachel

asked. She walked toward Reid, moving to place her hand against his forehead.

"I'm fine," Reid insisted, jerking away.

"Reid," Leif warned.

Reid stilled and Rachel tested his temperature. After a moment, she turned to look at Leif, a worried expression on her face.

"Reid, go lie down and rest," Rachel instructed. Reid didn't bother to argue, simply left his bow by the door and walked to his room. Brier looked between her father and mother, confused and starting to grow worried.

"This is why you shouldn't be practicing in this weather," Rachel turned on Brier.

"But mom," Brier started to say. Leif held up a hand to silence her.

"Why don't you go outside and unstring yours and Reid's bows," Leif suggested.

Brier scrunched her face but grabbed Reid's bow and left.

Leif turned to Rachel.

"He has a fever," she said, tears starting to gather in her eyes.

Leif looked at the little corner where Reid slept. He could hear Reid's coughing past the curtain. Enough was enough. He would call a meeting of the elders; they needed to find a solution *now*.

CHAPTER 9

Leif marched through the snow toward the small supply hut.

The wind whipped his cloak exposing him to the cold. He didn't care. There had been another death last night. That made eight. When he checked on Reid that morning, the boy had been sweating under his thin blanket, his face pale. When he opened his eyes to look at Leif, there was pain in them.

Leif threw open the tarp that was still being used as a door for the hut. Once winter hit, construction on the supply hut had been halted, replaced with the completion of the other huts. A lot of things had been put on hold lately. The other elders were already gathered. They looked up upon his entrance.

A small table had been built for them to use and several pieces of parchment covered its surface. Leif knew these papers to be lists. One with only a fourth of the page written on listed the supplies the outcasts had on hand. Another paper, filled from end to end, listed the supplies needed. A small list accounted for all those who had fallen ill, eight lines crossed out eight names on the list.

"Leif," Warren said in greeting.

Leif nodded at his friend but did not reply. After

everything that had happened, needless to say, he was not in a good mood.

The council of elders consisted of eleven members. Nine men, Warren, Leif, Liam, David, James, Henry, Gregory, Timothy, and William.

And two women, Warren's wife, Rhea, and one of the healers, Bess.

"We all know why we're gathered here today," David began as Leif found a place to lean against the wall.

"Obviously, we're gathered to discuss the illness and the other problems. But why, if we can't find a solution?" Gregory asked.

"We will get to that, I assure you," David replied, "But first, I'm sure we're all aware that the death last night made eight fatalities due to this illness."

The elders nodded somberly.

"It's obvious we need to come up with a solution, which is why Leif called for this meeting immediately."

Timothy stood up from his place sitting on a crate. "I understand that this is a problem but I think we should be more concerned with the shortage of food. Besides, Leif didn't seem to show this much concern until that boy, Reid, caught the fever."

Leif bristled and Warren held out an arm to stop him from making any rash movements.

"I agree with Timothy," Gregory said, "It is a shame that so many people are falling ill and that some are even dying, but the good of the whole must be considered. We will do whatever we can to help the ill, but the food issue should be dealt with first. As for Reid, he is young and healthy; he will likely survive, and even if he didn't, Leif would have still fulfilled his duty to his friend by taking him in. The boy is not his son after all."

Leif pushed away Warren's restraining arm and leaped at Gregory. This morning seeing Reid so sick, just like all the others, had made Leif truly realize what a problem this illness was.

Seeing Reid so miserable had struck something inside him. Of course, he was responsible for the boy now that Rowan was dead but after the months of watching Reid as he trained and grieved and proved himself again and again, Leif no longer thought of him only as his friend's son.

"How could you not care about the ill? How can you sit back and watch them die? As for Reid, he may not be my son by blood, but I care for him as well as any father would!" Leif shouted.

"Enough!" David yelled as Warren pulled Leif back and Gregory looked sheepishly away. "Wouldn't it be better to discuss the issue and search for a solution, rather than start arguments?"

"I, for one, agree on that point," Liam spoke up.

"There are plenty of issues to discuss," James added, "We shouldn't waste any time."

Leif winced. James's voice shook him out of his anger. If anyone had a reason to want an end to this it would be him. James had already lost his wife to the illness. Leif regretted speaking so inconsiderately. He was on edge from the events of the past few months. He prayed that God would give him patience and that he wouldn't speak so rashly again.

"Yes, my point exactly," David agreed, "Bess, perhaps you would give a report on the situation and what can be done about it."

Bess nodded and stepped forward to retrieve the list of names from the table.

"There are currently twelve cases excluding those who have died. Out of our total of forty-six people, this number is far too high. There have been eight deaths thus far.

I've seen this illness back in the village and it can easily be treated with the proper medicine and care. The fever is the most dangerous aspect so it is important for constant treatment to be provided and for the sick person to be kept warm. The fact is, if the proper supplies can be obtained, I am confident that the fatality rate will decrease significantly and maybe even completely disappear."

"At least that is some good news," Rhea said, resting her hand softly on Warren's arm.

"What medicine and supplies would be needed, Bess?" William asked.

"Blankets of course," she, responded, "some materials to make broth to warm the sick people up, and herbs to make the proper medicine. I'm sure if a few more deer could be hunted, we could use the bones and some meat to make the broth, and perhaps even the hides could be made into blankets. As for the medicine, I'm afraid it can't be gathered in the forest."

"So, we'll work hard to bring in some more deer, which will also help with the food shortage. We'll have to make do without the medicine," Timothy suggested.

"Would it be possible to go without the medicine?" David asked.

Bess shook her head, "I'm certain that the broth and blankets will help some, but I fear it will not be enough. Especially if there is another cold snap."

Leif thought of Reid's shivering form.

Reid was strong and resilient, but what about the

others who were sick. If Reid was suffering so much, Leif feared that the others would not last long.

He stepped forward. Timothy shrunk back, perhaps expecting Leif to attack him next, but Leif calmly strode toward the table.

He turned so everyone could see him and then spoke.

"What if we went to a village for the supplies?"

Immediately there were cries of surprise, vehement protests, and even a hysterical laugh from Liam.

"That would never work," William calmly stated

"Besides, how would we purchase any of the goods? We don't have money," Gregory added.

"The idea does seem a little far-fetched," Warren said quietly.

Leif glared at his friend. He wouldn't have suggested something like this if he hadn't already had a solution to the issue of money.

"We've already decided we'll have to hunt more deer," Leif said waiting until he had everyone's full attention, "If we started to hunt rabbits also, we could use the meat and take the furs, which are small and not useful to us, to the village to sell. Rabbit furs are expensive and we would make a large enough profit to purchase the medicine and perhaps some other supplies."

"That could work," David admitted, "But remember, Leif, we are exiled, we cannot go into a village."

"The village doesn't need to know we're exiles," Warren put in, warming to the idea.

"We could bring in the furs, sell them, get the supplies we need, and be out of town before anyone knew where we came from. We could send a single man to do the work so we don't attract attention and we would go to a small village instead of a large one like Mac'tire."

Liam nodded in agreement, "Sounds like a solution to me, as long as I'm not the one you're planning on sending."

David looked at Leif. "Let's put it to a vote then. If you agree with Leif's plan then say aye."

There was a chorus of ayes from Warren, Rhea, Bess, Leif, Liam, David, James, and William.

"The majority votes rule," David said. "William, I nominate you to go to the village. We'll still need to decide where you'll go but I think we can be prepared to leave by tomorrow."

William nodded in acceptance.

"Very well, meeting adjourned."

Leif let out a breath of relief.

After all the talking and endless arguments, it was good to finally come to an agreement. It had already been a long winter and the stress was getting on everyone's nerves but now they had something to sustain them that they hadn't before, hope.

CHAPTER 10

Brier wished she were back home.

She longed to sit in front of the warm fire in the hut. She longed to be in dry clothes and eat a hot meal. Instead, she was in the rain struggling to keep warm under her cloak and ankle-deep in soft mud. It had been a trying winter but now it was spring, and forester training had resumed in all its glory. It was a rainy day but Leif had insisted they train regardless. They needed to make up for the lost time. He said it would be perfect weather to learn a new skill, tracking.

Brier didn't see anything perfect about the weather but she was looking forward to learning how to track an animal. If only it weren't so wet and cold.

"When it's muddy," Leif told them, "tracks are easier to distinguish. You can tell what tracks are new because the rain will have washed the old ones away. It'll take practice to find the less recent tracks but we'll focus on identifying the new tracks today."

The way he said 'today' made Brier dread that she had more of these wet, miserable tracking days in her near future.

Leif explained the basic characteristics of most of the tracks they would encounter, as they were walking. He told them where the best places to look for tracks would be, the side trails and near the bushes.

"Spring is when most of the animals are moving around. We should find plenty of evidence of that," Leif excitedly stated.

So far, they had seen nothing. No tracks, and definitely no animals. The only progress they had made was getting wet and becoming miserable.

Brier wondered if the animals, which so often roamed around, had all gone into hiding the minute the foresters in training were forced to look for signs of them. Or maybe, unlike them, the animals had wisely chosen to find shelter from the rain.

Brier's one consolation was that at least she wouldn't have to explain her muddy appearance to her mother. This had been Leif's idea. He would have to do the explaining.

However, their day was not destined to be completely fruitless.

The first track they found belonged to a rabbit. Reid pointed it out showing as much excitement as he ever did, a slightly higher than normal voice and a two-syllable response. Although Brier was less than thrilled to be training alongside him, she was still relieved when he made a full recovery from the illness which had ravaged the little camp. She had partially blamed herself for his being sick. She had, after all, insisted they train despite the freezing weather.

Leif stooped to inspect the rabbit track and motioned for Brier and Reid to do the same. It didn't look like much; in fact, Brier may have overlooked it altogether. There were small round markings and longer oval indents.

"The rabbit can be identified first by the shape of the

tracks and secondly by their placement, which implies a hopping motion," Leif explained.

Brier tried to stay focused but the wind had started to pick up and it was blowing the rain directly into her face, stinging her.

Eventually, they moved on, finding other evidence of animal presence but nothing as interesting as the first track.

Brier was so cold she wasn't even upset that Reid had made the discovery. She was thinking about how wonderful the stew she had seen her mother beginning to prepare before they left would taste. Suddenly, Leif held up his hand for them to stop. He turned around and smiled.

"One of you tell me what this track is," he pointed to an indent in the mud. Brier and Reid stepped forward at the same time to study the track. Brier felt the mud seep through her pants as she knelt and once again was glad she wouldn't have to explain the mess to her mother. Brier tried to ignore Reid's presence beside her as she examined the mud. At least she would get the chance to identify a track. She could prove to her father that she was just as good at this as Reid.

The imprint was a little smaller than the palm of her hand. It was padded like a dog's and at first, Brier froze, thinking it belonged to a wolf. Then she noticed the telltale sign of a wolf track wasn't there. There were no claw marks. It must belong to some kind of large cat that could retract its claws.

"It's some kind of cat," Brier remarked looking at her father for confirmation.

Leif nodded, "Yes, but what kind of cat?"

Brier inspected the track closer.

The depressions weren't deep enough to belong to a very heavy animal and they were not as defined as she would have expected, there were no sharp lines just an indent in the mud.

There was a significant gap between the pad and the toes. Brier tried to piece all this information together to form a conclusion.

Eventually, she shook her head in defeat, "I don't know."

Leif put a hand on her shoulder. "It's alright Brier. It can be quite difficult to tell. It just takes practice."

He looked over at Reid to see if the boy wanted to try but Reid was looking off into the trees. Leif shrugged and started to point out the differences between different large cat species.

"These are lynx tracks," he explained. "They can easily be mistaken for Cougar tracks because of their size. However, lynx tracks are not as defined because of the fur around the lynx's paws."

Brier nodded; glad she had at least not voiced her first concern of the tracks belonging to a wolf. She mentally scored this as a point for her since Reid hadn't even attempted a guess and she had at least identified it as belonging to a cat.

A quick movement to Brier's left caught her attention and she jerked her head quickly to look. Reid was staring in the same direction, an arrow on his bowstring. Brier and Leif pushed themselves to their feet and followed his lead. The rustling stopped and Brier relaxed, loosening the tension on her bow. However, she had hardly done so when a large shape flew out of a bush right at her.

She heard a thud as Reid's arrow took it in the side

and it staggered. She saw now what the shape was. It was the very lynx that had left the print.

It was at least two feet high and must have weighed nearly forty pounds. The lynx made a sound almost like yelling.

It turned its head to look at the arrow in its side then bounded towards Reid.

It all happened so fast. The lynx moved in a blur, not seeming to be affected at all by the mud and rain or even the arrow piercing its side.

Brier realized with a shock that the animal must have been watching them all along. Maybe that's why Reid had been looking into the trees.

Reid backed up hurriedly, trying as he went to grab another arrow from his quiver. Brier watched as his trembling hand set the arrow to the string but his foot caught on a tree root and he fell into the mud. Reid continued to back away but now there was a tree in his path and he was trapped.

Brier tried to move, to do anything but her body was frozen. She couldn't pull back her bowstring and she couldn't help Reid. Her heart hammered in her chest.

The lynx jumped onto Reid, standing above him and snarling in rage. Reid closed his eyes; he couldn't even bring up his hands to protect himself since he was encumbered by his bow. Brier started to look away, unable to watch as the lynx raised a paw, claws out, and ready to strike. Then an arrow hit it in the neck. Another arrow followed at blinding speed, landing right next to the first. The Lynx staggered and Reid barely managed to throw himself out of the way as it crashed down where he had just been.

Reid was covered in mud from his head to his boots

and he was shivering uncontrollably. Brier wasn't sure if it was from the cold or his close call with the lynx. She felt herself shivering a bit also. The lynx's teeth had looked so sharp next to Reid's head and its claws could have easily torn into him.

Brier wondered if she should move toward Reid to make sure he was all right. She tried to take a step forward but her limbs felt frozen.

Reid collapsed next to the creature, seemingly in shock, and stared at the arrow protruding from its side. He was breathing heavily and his eyes were wide and unfocused.

Leif made his way over to Reid and knelt beside him with a hand on his shoulder. Brier could hear her father murmuring prayers of thanks and Brier found herself agreeing. Reid looked at Leif in disbelief and panic. Leif pulled him into a hug but Reid was too shocked to return it. He sat there, eyes staring over Leif's shoulder at the lynx. His body shaking like a leaf.

Brier tried to process all that had happened. They had been looking at a track one moment then the next a large animal was coming at her. Then it was pouncing on Reid. She realized that she could be dead. Reid could be dead. He had distracted the lynx, saving her. She didn't know what to think of that.

This simple day detecting animal tracks in the mud had taught them a far more important lesson. Shooting at a wild animal was much different than shooting at a stationary, wooden target.

"I think, it's time to go home," Leif remarked, his voice shaking almost as much as Reid.

Leif pulled Reid to his feet and there was a bit of a fuss checking him for any injuries. Leif made certain that the lynx was dead then slung it over his shoulder to bring back to the camp. Despite their shock and unease, they wouldn't waste such a valuable resource. Leif allowed them a quick moment to catch their breaths then they started back to their little hut.

Reid walked stiffly beside Brier, eyes straight-ahead and distant. His hand absently stroked the scar on his cheek. Brier couldn't think of anything to say so she stayed silent.

As they were walking, Brier wondered how Leif was going to explain Reid's muddied state to Rachel. She hoped she would be able to see that conversation.

CHAPTER 11

For the first time in weeks, Brier was truly enjoying herself.

She and Reid had been given the day off from their training and although Brier still wanted to practice, she was grateful for the break. What with the rigorous training under Leif's guidance and her own training after dark, she was exhausted and sore. She hadn't been planning on taking the break until Flint informed her that he also had the day off from his training. She had only seen him in passing since her training had resumed. It would be nice to spend time with her best friend.

The weather was pleasant, a little cold perhaps but the sun was shining. Any remnants of snow had vanished and the forest was beautifully green. The trees had started to grow back all their leaves and to Brier, all was well in the world.

She struggled to keep up with Flint's long strides as they walked around the camp. For a fourteen-year-old, he was remarkably tall and since Brier had yet to have her growth spurt, she was a good head shorter than him.

Walking beside him she could tell that not only was he taller but his training with the sword had also broadened his shoulders. Flint seemed more serious too.

After the exile, Flint had made it his civic duty to cheer her and everyone else up. Brier had been angry and upset after the exile. The duke had wronged them greatly and Brier found it difficult to trust that this was God's plan for them.

However, she had also felt a sense of relief at being out of the constraints of Mac'tire.

She was filled with confusion which only made her more uncertain. Flint was friendly from the start, not bothered by the fact that she was a girl. He always included her and cheered her up and before long they became inseparable. Throughout it all, Flint had been there. Now he walked with a sense of purpose she hadn't seen before.

It was strange to suddenly notice how different he was. He was still, in many ways, the same Flint though. He had a smile on his face and a spring in his step.

His change of attitude was probably a side effect of the time he spent practicing all day. Using a weapon as powerful as a sword was quite the responsibility and she assumed Flint's father, Warren had drilled that into him hundreds of times. Her father had given many lectures on the seriousness of using a bow.

"Why so quiet, Brier? Feeling prickly?" Flint joked.

"Very funny sparky," she responded, happy to see that his bad jokes about her less than common name were intact. Flint feigned a look of hurt at her attempted joke.

"Seriously though," he said stopping, "is something wrong? It seems like something's on your mind."

"I don't know what you're talking about. I'm fine,"

Brier insisted. She felt a hint of annoyance that Flint was steering the conversation away from comedy and back towards the seriousness of life.

She had wanted to meet with him as an escape from the real world, much as they had after the exile. She didn't want to talk about any feelings. Besides, she really was fine.

Flint slowed his pace and scratched nervously at the back of his neck.

"I just... I heard about what happened when you went tracking the other day. Are you upset over what happened with Reid? It's understandable. After all, he could have died."

"Reid?" Brier asked incredulously.

She couldn't care less about Reid, at least not in the way Flint was thinking. Besides, he hadn't come that close to dying. That's what she kept telling herself.

"I'm fine, Flint. Just drop it. Okay?"

Flint lapsed into silence for a moment before speaking again, "Just, if something is bothering you, you know you can talk to me, right? We're friends after all."

Brier contemplated for a moment. Something was bothering her a little. She considered voicing the concern but she didn't want to ruin her outing with Flint.

She sighed, "Just tired, I guess. I know you just stand around waving a stick in the air for hours but some of us actually have to work hard during the day."

"Wave a stick in the air?" Flint asked incredulously.

Brier gave a wry smile. They often had these verbal sparring matches. Brier supposed it was another example of the comfort they felt around each other.

"You pain me, Brier," Flint teased, "You have no idea how many new combinations of strikes my father has been teaching me. I've never been so tired in my life."

Flint yawned in emphasis, "It will all be worth it though when I become the most revered knight in history."

Brier rolled her eyes. She was tempted to bring up the fact that they were in exile but Flint was in such a good mood she didn't want to ruin it by instigating what was sure to lead to an argument.

Besides, this was one subject that they didn't discuss. While Flint was still hopeful of returning to Mac'tire and being knighted, Brier had no such optimism. She wouldn't even want to return if given the opportunity.

The two friends walked on before stopping under a tree. It wasn't Brier's favorite tree; the path leading to it was still too muddy from the last rain to attempt the trek. The tree they sat under was tall with sweeping branches and they could see the younger children running around playing tag. Brier wondered if they understood that they were in exile. They likely wouldn't remember their time in the shadow of Castle Mac'tire when they were older. They would only know life as outcasts. A little boy no older than eight tackled a girl who was perhaps nine. They laughed and got up running off again. Sometimes Brier wished she could be that carefree. She smiled remembering her first days in exile like they were yesterday. Even though she had been twelve and Flint thirteen, they had spent hours running around the forest near the tents.

They had climbed trees and walked barefoot in creeks. Brier didn't think she had ever had so much fun.

They had both grown up fast in the past months. Especially after that wolf had wandered into the camp. Brier shivered at the memory. She still had nightmares from that day. She shook the thought from her mind, refusing to let it ruin her good mood.

"Hey, Brier?" Flint said softly.

"Hm."

"I want to know what's bothering you."

Brier sighed. She had been hoping Flint wouldn't even notice her distraction. She had been hoping that she could forget her thoughts for a day, but her concerns would not go away so easily.

She didn't want to tell Flint. She didn't want him to think she was silly but, in the end, she couldn't help herself. She needed someone to talk to and she knew Flint would listen.

"It's Reid," she finally said.

Flint looked at her quizzically. "Reid? I thought you said you weren't worried about him."

Brier could understand his confusion. She couldn't believe she was talking about this with him. She didn't like to talk about Reid and when she did, it was usually in a complaint.

"I'm not worried about him in the way you're thinking," Brier responded, "I just wish he wasn't so great at everything."

Flint raised an eyebrow.

"Every time we're practicing, I feel inferior. He's so much better than me. I keep training hard and I feel like I'm not getting any better."

Brier stopped to take a breath. Now that she had started talking, she couldn't stop. "It's obvious my father favors him. He always wanted a son. Now that he's finally got one, what am I supposed to do?"

Brier angrily wiped at her watering eyes. She wouldn't cry, not about something as silly as this.

"Brier?"

"Yeah," she said slowly looking at her friend.

"It's nothing to be ashamed of. I can understand why you're upset but can I give you some advice?"

Brier looked at him expectantly.

"You should stop worrying about how Reid is doing. You might find that you're not as far behind him as you think. I've seen you shoot and your accuracy is amazing. I don't think I could ever do anything like that. As for your father, he's probably just looking out for Reid. I know when he got sick it kind of scared everybody. Reid could never replace you."

Brier smiled. Flint always knew just what to say.

"Thank you, Flint."

"Sure thing, Prickly."

CHAPTER 12

Reid wished he could disappear.

Honestly, for how hard he tried, he figured he at least deserved to be ignored.

Leif had started to give them one day every week off and Reid was enjoying the chance to be alone. He could tell that it was driving Brier crazy just to take one day away from training but Reid enjoyed the chance to escape. He closed his eyes and sighed in pleasure. He was reclined at the base of a tall tree. The sun felt warm against his skin and the birds were chirping in the distance. At times like these, he felt sorry for people who talked all the time. They missed so much. They were always in a hurry, not stopping to take notice of the simple things like the birds singing their song.

Perhaps he had been like those people once. Always talking excitedly about various unimportant things. Now, he appreciated the quietness of being alone. It wasn't that he didn't like people, although many of the people he knew he wasn't particularly fond of. It was more that he didn't like being forced into conversation. Talking only caused trouble. Friendships only led to betrayals. Being alone provided him the perfect opportunity to control his thoughts and feelings and to try to hear God's voice. He wanted badly to have the same peace that Leif seemed to feel. When he was around others it became overwhelming, almost suffocating, but alone he had gained a measure of control.

The command he held over himself was the only thing he could count on.

Perhaps that's why archery came so easily to him. When he was loosing an arrow, he could control his every movement and reflex.

His thoughts were focused solely on the act of drawing and loosing. It was an escape and a welcome one at that.

Alone, lying under the tree with the sun shining down on him and the birds gently chirping, Reid started to feel a sense of peace. He was beginning to doze off when a loud noise shocked him awake. He reluctantly pried open an eyelid and groaned.

Strutting towards Reid, followed by several of his friends, was Flint.

Reid hoped the loud and boisterous boy wouldn't see him and just keep walking. Of course, he was not so fortunate.

"Hey, Reid," Flint greeted, skidding to a stop in front of him.

Reid closed his eyes and willed himself to disappear but after a few moments, he realized Flint was waiting for a response.

Reid opened his eyes and gave a strained smile. He had been told by Brier that his smile was enough to scare anyone away. He thought she might be right; his scar looked ugly when he smiled. Still, he hoped the poor excuse of a smile would be enough to satisfy Flint's overly friendly nature or at the very least scare him off.

Flint always tried to be nice to him, probably because he was Brier's friend or maybe it was just in his personality.

Reid mostly wished he would leave him alone. It wasn't like Brier cared if Flint befriended him.

Reid closed his eyes again and hoped that Flint would leave.

He waited a moment then cracked his eye open again. The annoying copper-haired boy was still in front of him. When Flint opened his mouth to talk, Reid knew his quiet afternoon was done for.

"Mind if we practice here?" Flint asked and Reid noticed for the first time the swords that he and the other boys carried.

He wondered briefly where they had gotten real swords and if they were supposed to be practicing with them but he cast the thought aside. It was none of his business. If they wanted to practice with real metal swords then he wouldn't stop them. He shrugged, not wanting to continue the conversation and not seeing any harm in letting them practice by his tree. The sound from the swords would be loud but he didn't want to move from his comfortable spot and he didn't want an argument. It had taken him a considerable amount of time to find the ideal tree, far from the camp and people. Maybe he should have gone a little farther.

Flint smiled and called for his friends to start practicing. Reid watched as the boys got into their positions then he closed his eyes again.

He regretted his decision almost immediately when the ringing of the swords started. Reid thought he had made bounds in progress over the last months. He thought he had finally pulled himself together but as the swords clashed, memories from Mac'tire flashed before him.

He saw the day of the riot. Images bombarded him that, although he wouldn't admit it to anyone, had kept him up late into the night on more than one occasion.

He saw swords clashing together and colliding with flesh. He saw castle guards racing through the streets.

Each yell of excitement from the boys fighting in front of him turned into cries of anguish and hatred from rioters and knights.

Reid threw his eyes open. Suddenly he was back in the forest, surrounded by boys not much older than himself, safe. He took several calming breaths hoping to still his racing heart. The riot was over. He was safe.

He had finally started to calm down when he caught the glint of sunlight off of Flint's sword as Flint jabbed at his opponent.

The glint of moonlight reflected off a sword.

The sickening crunch as it was thrust into a body.

The dripping of blood onto the floor as the sword was pulled away.

Then the crash as a body fell to the ground and the distant scream of a boy who had just lost everything.

"Stop!" Reid shouted, jumping up from his spot under the tree.

The boys stopped fighting and looked at him quizzically. Reid wished he could fade into the tree and be forgotten. He wished he could take back his outburst but most of all he wished he could get the horrific image of his father's death out of his mind. Reid stood still, trying to fight back the tears that threatened to spill over, and stared at the blade in Flint's hands.

Flint started to move toward him to ask what was

wrong. Reid felt like he was going to be sick.

Before any of the boys could come any closer, he raced off into the trees wishing he could disappear.

CHAPTER 13

Brier stared at the weapon in her father's hand with a sense of foreboding.

She had just started getting used to the bow. Now Leif wanted to introduce an entirely new weapon to their repertoire. Reid looked more than happy, maybe even eager, to learn how to use a knife. Brier felt only dread.

The blade was little more than a hunting knife, the kind used to skin animals. It wasn't very long but it was thick with an end that tapered to a sharp point. She wondered what the use of this lesson was. She had learned how to skin an animal a long time ago.

"Today I will begin to teach you how to fight with a knife," Leif explained, handing the weapon he was holding to Reid. He reached into a case at his feet and pulled out two more knives that looked identical. He handed one to Brier and kept the other in his hand. Brier was surprised at the weight of the knife. It was well balanced. She hadn't noticed when she was skinning a deer but now, she could tell the knife was made of good quality metal.

"You might be wondering why you need to use a knife since you can already shoot the bow," Leif continued. "You use the knife when you don't have the time or distance to use the bow. I hope it never comes to that but it's best to be prepared."

Brier looked down at her weapon and grew slightly more interested.

"Also," Leif stated, his voice taking on a serious tone, "If you're in a fight with a person, the knife might be your best option to defend yourself."

Brier and Reid listened to Leif with rapt attention.

"A person is agile and intelligent. They also make for a slim target. If they see you preparing to shoot an arrow at them, they might dodge it. If they are coming at you with a weapon, you may not have time to ready your bow and if they have a shield your arrows would be ineffective. Knowing how to properly wield a knife may be the difference between life or death in one of these situations."

Leif waited for Brier and Reid to nod in understanding.

"First, you'll need to know how to hold the knife correctly," Leif, explained when he was satisfied that they understood what they were getting into, "If you don't grip the handle the right way you could hurt yourself. The worst thing that can happen in a knife fight is if your opponent manages to disarm you or gain control of your knife."

Leif demonstrated how to hold the weapon. "You want your grip to be tight but your wrist loose for easy movement."

Brier tried the grip and found that although it felt a little awkward, she could probably get used to it. Reid who was left-handed had greater difficulty. He struggled to copy Leif's right-handed grip.

Leif gave them a short lecture on the dangers of a

knife and warned them to use extra caution. Then he demonstrated some basic slices and jabs.

Brier watched with a sense of awe as he went through combinations not all that different from what she had seen Flint do with the sword.

They were different in some ways though; there were no flourishing movements as with the sword, and each strike was brutal and effective.

"You'll learn how to defend yourself against animals and humans," Leif explained, "Though, I expect you won't have to deal with the latter, I intend to give you the full training of a forester. You'll learn to fight against knife and sword."

"Sword?" Reid murmured nervously.

Leif continued, "You'll start out learning the basic strikes and parries. You can take turns practicing on this tree while I watch."

Brier and Reid took turns striking the tree with Leif adjusting their form and making small comments on how they could improve. It was tough work and numerous times Brier was told to stop and adjust her grip. For once Reid was struggling more than her. He even dropped his knife once, narrowly missing his foot, and earning a sharp reprimand from Leif. Reid only grew more determined.

Brier's wrist ached and her hand was cramping from gripping the knife. Every time the blade embedded itself in the dense tree bark, she would have to yank it free, careful at the same time to maintain a firm grip so it didn't go flying. She was soon drenched in sweat and panting heavily. When Leif called for a break Reid was also sweating and there was a look of discouragement on his face.

At least, Brier was finally better than him at something. Or, she thought so until Leif announced they would switch to using their left hands. Brier had just started to enjoy her edge against Reid so she wasn't particularly happy about having to do twice the work and with her non-dominant hand.

"Just because Reid's left-handed why do I have to learn to use my left hand?"

"I'm not just making you do this because of Reid," Leif told her, "There have been several times when I've been forced to fight using my left hand because my right was injured. Being clumsy with your left hand, or right in Reid's case can be the cause of life or death in a fight."

Brier didn't object further. She still remembered the day after the riot when her father had come home with a bloodied right arm. Leif rubbed that arm as if remembering the same thing.

Brier was sloppy with her left hand, which was only more obvious next to Reid who quickly picked things up and even seemed to be enjoying himself. Brier didn't know why he felt that way. Her hand and wrist were sore and she could barely hold the knife let alone execute a strike with it. She much preferred archery.

She discovered by the end of the lesson that she was mediocre with both hands while Reid could only use his left effectively. His skills right-handed were atrocious. She counted a point to herself in their ongoing competition of skills.

After another short break, Leif threw Brier and Reid two pieces of wood.

"What's this?" Brier asked. She was reclining in the cool grass still trying to catch her breath. The pieces of wood were smooth and shaped with a curve.

"It's a practice knife," Leif explained, "You don't think I would have you two practice with real knives right away, do you?"

"Isn't that what we were just doing?" Brier asked.

"Yes, but this time you'll be practicing against each other."

Reid looked at Brier with a sense of foreboding. Brier gave him a sinister smile. She liked the way that sounded. Leif motioned for them to stand. Reid looked hesitant while Brier obeyed eagerly. She was looking forward to this.

"First, right-handed," Leif, instructed. "The goal of this exercise is to deflect any of your opponent's strikes, whoever lands the first strike or manages to disarm the other wins."

Brier fell into an easy stance ready to strike first. Reid took up a defensive position.

"Go," Leif said.

Brier surged forward; practice knife held in a jab. Reid's eyes went wide as he scurried backward. At the last moment, he stepped to the side and blocked Brier's strike. He sighed in relief but Brier wasn't finished yet. She switched her attack to a backward slash. She smiled as the wooden blade hit Reid's neck. He choked rubbing at his throat.

"Point to Brier," Leif said, sounding disappointed in Reid's performance. "Go again."

Brier and Reid returned to their starting positions. Brier moved first again but this time Reid was ready.

He had felt the wooden blade hit him and he knew that though it stung it wouldn't injure him. He wouldn't be hit again. Brier struck with an overhead strike, which Reid clumsily deflected by blocking with his practice blade tilted so Brier's knife would slide off. Brier felt her heart pumping with adrenalin. She had finally found something she was better at. She was determined not to lose.

Brier tried a few more attacks all of which Reid managed to block or sidestep.

It would be easy enough to keep striking but she knew she would wear herself out if she kept this up. And just like that, an idea came to her.

Brier stepped back and took on a defensive position, inviting Reid to attack instead. Reid swallowed hard as Brier stood at the ready but eventually, he fell for the bait. He could hardly block with the knife in his right hand but he was far worse at attacking. All she had to do was wait.

Reid clumsily adjusted his grip and then went in with a hesitant forward thrust. Instead of avoiding the attack or deflecting it, Brier stepped forward, trapping Reid's arm. Surprised, he tried to twist out of her hold but Brier dislodged the knife from his grip, sending it flying.

"Point Brier," Leif said again.

Brier smiled in a self-satisfied way and smugly reached down to pick up Reid's knife and return it to him. He took it, embarrassed.

"Switch hands," Leif announced, and Brier immediately felt her smug smile disappear.

Reid's shoulders squared as the knife was switched to his left hand. Brier fell into a defensive position this time. The knife felt awkward in her hand.

"Go."

Reid didn't dart in as Brier had in her confidence. Instead, he circled her, calculating. Then he made his strike, aiming for her stomach. Brier barely had time to sidestep the thrust and block the blade.

She had scarcely done so when Reid swiveled around and struck again. Brier managed to block the weapon but just barely.

Reid started to fall into a graceful rhythm and his strikes grew sure and quick. Brier was forced to retreat and she felt her face grow hot in anger.

She wouldn't lose to Reid. In her frustration, Brier blocked Reid's strike and returned it with one of her own. Just as Reid had been sloppy with his right hand, so was she with her left. The strike was ill-aimed and although caught slightly off guard, Reid's reflexes were quick. He reached forward with his right hand, grabbing Brier's wrist. Then bracing his left arm, he pressed his knife against her throat and used his left leg to sweep her feet out from under her.

Brier felt the ground coming up fast but at the last moment, Reid grabbed her collar stopping her fall. She was frozen in midair as Reid kept hold of her. He seemed just as surprised as she was. However, Brier's surprise quickly faded, replaced with anger.

She regained her feet and shoved Reid's arm away.

"Point Reid," Leif said, making Brier even more upset.

Leif must have sensed her rising anger because he stepped forward then. "All right, that's enough for today. I'll show you how to take care of your knives then we'll call it a night."

Brier glared at Reid as Leif instructed them how to clean and care for their weapons. They were each presented with a sharpening stone and sheath.

"Remember to sharpen them after every practice. It

would do no good to get caught in a fight with a dull blade," Leif instructed.

Then he showed them how to attach the knife sheath to their belts.

"From now on, you'll take these knives everywhere with you," Leif explained, "Good job today but remember to keep practicing with the wooden knives. You'll continue with your normal archery schedule. This will be another addition."

Leif didn't have to tell either participant to practice. They were both more determined than he could know. Brier would not fail again; she would not let Reid beat her. Reid was determined to not allow his right hand to be a hindrance to him any longer. He would prove that he wasn't a burden and that he could learn and master whatever a forester was expected to know.

Brier and Reid walked back to the hut with a sense of purpose. Their minds were filled with very different thoughts but their resolution was the same, to master the art of the knife, and to make Leif proud.

CHAPTER 14

Flint didn't see it coming.

He and Brier had chosen to go for a walk on one of their days off. It had become somewhat of a tradition between them. The forest had many places to explore and by the time they were able to see each other they often had much to discuss. When he met up with her, however, she wasn't alone. Reid was standing beside her looking as awkward and uncomfortable as usual. Brier was very annoyed by this. She wouldn't even look at her companion and her arms were across her chest in irritation. Flint was shocked to see them together. Brier and Reid didn't exactly get along. Although the conflict was mostly on Brier's side, Reid was cold and avoided everyone as much as possible.

"My father insisted that Reid come along," Brier said in explanation.

"Fine with me."

Flint relaxed. He, like everyone else, thought Reid was strange but he didn't dislike him and he didn't mind if he tagged along. He even held out the hope that he and Reid could be friends someday. Flint didn't want to consider that anyone might not like him. He believed that it was God's will for him to befriend everyone he could. Flint eyed Reid warily nonetheless. The last time he had talked to him Reid had run full-pelt into the woods. Flint still wasn't sure what had happened and why Reid had acted so oddly. Maybe today he would have the opportunity to find out.

Reid looked just as unhappy as Brier about having to come along. He focused on the ground and remained completely silent as they started off.

He didn't say a word to Flint in greeting. Brier, Flint could tell, was trying her best to forget Reid was there and resorted to making small talk.

Flint had always been intrigued by the relationship between Brier and Reid. There was obvious tension between them and sometimes Flint wondered if they hated each other. Brier's strong dislike was obvious and Flint wondered how Reid felt. It was impossible to know. Reid's feelings about everything were guarded by a thick, stone wall that could very well be impenetrable. It was difficult to believe that they hated each other though. He suspected that Brier was mostly jealous of the attention her father gave Reid and Reid was likely being defensive because of her obvious dislike for him. Flint had prayed on more than one occasion that someday they might all be friends. But that day seemed far off.

Flint followed Brier's lead and started to talk about training. Soon any sense of unease due to Reid's presence started to vanish. Flint glanced at Reid occasionally but Reid never met his gaze. He was always focused on the ground or on the sword that hung from Flint's belt.

Flint had just earned the privilege of wearing the sword after a long argument with his father. He had only won the argument by bringing up the wolf attack and convincing his father that he needed a way to protect himself and his friends.

Finally, Warren had consented to him carrying the sword under the condition that he didn't participate in any more practice bouts with the other boys using it.

Flint winced, remembering the lecture he had received after that particular incident.

The sword was one his father had commissioned to be made for him right before the exile. Warren had planned to present it to Flint with the news that he would start training but after the riot, his plans had been interrupted. The sword was the weapon of a warrior, not for show. It was plain, with few embellishments but it was heavy and made of good metal. It was the sword of a knight. Flint was proud to carry the weapon at his side. He wondered why Reid seemed so interested in it.

"And then the lynx jumped at Reid," Brier continued her story. Flint had asked Brier to share the complete tale of her encounter with the animal. He had only heard second-hand accounts and rumors. In a small camp like theirs, stories traveled fast. Flint had wanted to hear what happened directly from her and he thought now would be the time to ask. Reid was present so it was a way of including him in the conversation too. Flint looked over at Reid who appeared very uncomfortable remembering the event.

"Then what happened?" Flint asked.

Brier smiled, "Then my father shot it through the neck twice. It almost fell on top of Reid but he managed to roll out of the way. We made sure it was dead then brought it back to camp."

Flint couldn't imagine coming that close to death.

It was incredible that Reid hadn't been injured by the event.

Flint always thought training to be a knight was more difficult than training as a forester. At least as a knight, he didn't have to wander around in the forest with wild animals ready to attack.

The most dangerous animal he would ever have to deal with was man.

As Brier's story came to an end, they stopped under a tall, shady tree to sit. Reid found a spot some distance away.

"Well?" Brier asked, "aren't you going to show off your new sword?"

Flint grinned; she knew him too well. He had been waiting ever since he got the sword to show her. Brier must have sensed his eagerness. Flint stood up and unsheathed the blade letting the light that filtered through the trees reflect off of it. Brier oohed and awed sarcastically as he spun it around. He made a few stabbing and slicing motions with it before turning to face her.

"Very nice," she said with a laugh. He smiled widely and continued to swing the sword around. He heard an audible groan from where Reid was sitting and turned to face him.

"What's wrong?" he asked.

There was a pause from Reid. He looked pale and sickly but maybe it was just the lighting. It took a moment but Reid composed himself.

"Nothing's wrong, just waiting for you to stop waving that stick around like you're trying to swat a fly," Reid said shocking Flint.

Was that a joke? No, it couldn't have been. Reid

didn't joke.

Flint wasn't expecting a response. Normally Reid would have only shrugged. He was notoriously quiet, unnervingly so. Flint hadn't known Reid was even capable of joking.

Flint tried to hide his surprise and responded with a joke of his own.

"Well, at least I don't stand around all day looking like a statue. It's a wonder the birds don't land on you."

He heard Brier trying and failing to stifle her laughter beside him.

That's when Reid did something Flint wasn't expecting, he stood up and opened his mouth to speak again. This time Reid was more serious.

"I expect your father wouldn't trust you with that blade if he knew you were swinging it around like a child with a rattle."

Flint looked at him in shock. Reid never spoke this much, much less voluntarily. He looked Reid in the eye and saw nervousness. His whole stance was like he was waiting to be attacked. Flint knew he shouldn't respond any further, Reid was obviously uncomfortable, but he just couldn't pass up such a good opportunity.

"Well, I expect your father would be less than impressed by your poor shooting. I suspect you couldn't hit a deer if it were a foot in front of you."

Flint had never witnessed Reid's archery, and he doubted his assessment of his skills was true, but it was the best he could come up with and he was never one to lose in a verbal battle.

Reid stiffened. Flint slashed the sword through the air a few times with a smile on his face. He glanced at Reid again and saw him shaking.

"Something wrong?" Flint asked, wondering at Reid's stranger-than-usual behavior.

Reid opened his mouth then scowled, "You're childish and careless but what was I expecting from a clumsy, useless knight?"

Flint froze and looked at Reid with shock, "What did you say?" his voice lowered as he felt a spark of anger.

Reid swallowed hard and took a deep breath. When he spoke, there was a waver in his voice, "Knights are all the same. They follow orders no matter how terrible they may be. They slaughter and kill and ruin people's lives. They don't care what disaster they leave in their wake. You're just like them. I guess it's not all your fault. You only know what you've been taught after all."

"That's enough," Brier urged them.

Flint's hands clenched into fists but he tried to keep his cool. Something was off with Reid. It was almost like he was looking for a fight. Flint had no idea why. He should have just ignored him but the last remark was too much.

"Was that a dig at my father?" he asked, barely keeping his tone neutral.

Reid didn't respond.

That was answer enough for Flint.

"You know," he said casually, "I could say all foresters are the same too but I've seen Brier practice and I've seen Leif in action so I know that's not true. You're the only one who's a sad excuse for a forester. Like I said, your father wouldn't be impressed."

Reid had taken things a step too far and if he wanted a battle of words then Flint was determined to have the last attack.

He couldn't resist one final comment. One final

chance to get back at Reid. He didn't think before he said it and he instantly regretted the words as soon as they had left his mouth.

"Of course, your father was probably just as bad a forester as you. If he were here, we could test that theory but of course, he's not."

Flint had barely gotten the last word out when the unexpected happened. Calm, composed Reid lashed out at him. Reid let loose a feral snarl and lunged at Flint. He grabbed Flint by the shirt and with surprising strength pushed him into a tree. Brier scrambled back, surprised and Flint gasped as the air rushed out of his lungs. He barely had time to register what had just happened when Reid's arm lifted and came back to punch him square in the nose. Flint heard a sickening crack and a wave of pain shot through his skull. His eyes watered but he was too shocked to do anything.

Reid had always been the quiet one. He had never fit in with the other boys and Flint had always suspected that he didn't want to. Reid had never gotten into a fight before. He had never caused any trouble. Flint was caught completely off guard.

He ducked to the side as another punch came his way and tried to twist out of Reid's reach. Reid grasped him by the collar and Flint lost his balance on a tree root, falling to the ground and dragging Reid with him.

Reid was shocked but quickly regained his composure. Before long he was fighting again. Flint tried to roll away but Reid came with him and then they were both rolling across the forest floor, each trying to gain the upper hand.

Brier shouted at them to stop but they didn't listen. Flint didn't want to fight but he had to defend himself.

He fought back, hitting Reid in the face bruising his eye, and splitting open his lip. Then there was blood everywhere, but neither boy noticed.

Reid yelled incoherently and Flint was only able to make out a couple of words. "Don't...dare...speak...father...again."

They wrestled on the ground, trying to gain an advantage over the other. They threw wild punches, which didn't do much damage but managed to tire them out. Flint was exhilarated. The thrill of battle came over him and he didn't feel any of Reid's glancing blows. He was focused, and the noises around him started to fade away. This was his first real fight.

Suddenly he wasn't just fighting in defense, he was fighting to win. Every punch that connected with Reid's body sent a surge of excitement through Flint. He felt an unexplainable urge to laugh. Reid was a good fighter, a worthy opponent. Flint had never experienced anything quite like this before.

He might have taken things too far had Brier's yelling not snapped him out of his trance. She was trying to get close to them to break things up but they kept rolling out of her reach. She yelled their names and Flint suddenly remembered what was happening and who he was fighting. He remembered that he didn't want to fight and his punches slowed. Brier's shouts affected Reid too and finally, he stopped, breathing heavily and shaking with adrenalin. Flint quickly rolled out of Reid's reach and got to his feet running over to where Brier stood, hands on her hips looking incredibly angry.

"Reid!" she shouted.

Reid didn't bother waiting around. He quickly stood

up and without so much as a backward glance stalked away into the trees. Flint had no idea what just happened but suddenly he felt anger rising inside him. Hadn't Reid understood it was just a joke?

He was the one to start all of this. He was the one who had taken things too far.

Flint didn't even know what it was that had upset the usually calm Reid to the point of throwing punches.

He fingered his sore nose, feeling a trickle of blood flowing down it. He hoped it wasn't broken. He dreaded the lecture he was sure to get from his father for this. Flint tried to ignore the shaking figure disappearing into the trees. Reid must be feeling the same adrenalin rush that was still wearing out of his system. Flint had never understood Reid, but fighting a person often opened up a whole new window of understanding. Reid still didn't make sense to Flint but he had felt the unrestrained fury in every punch Reid had thrown. The boy may seem calm and quiet on the outside but there was a storm brewing just beneath the surface. Flint still wasn't sure what had happened but he did know one thing.

Reid sure could throw a punch.

CHAPTER 15

Flint slammed the door behind him as he entered his hut.

One hand held his face trying to stem the bleeding from his nose, and the other curled into a fist at his side.

"Stupid, unpredictable forester," Flint grumbled under his breath as he sulked inside.

He felt dizzy and there was an awful throbbing pain coming from his nose. It must be broken. He still wasn't sure what had happened. He had been talking one moment and the next Reid had charged him, throwing him into a tree and pummeling him with punches. What had he said? Why had Reid suddenly lost it?

Flint's mother and father would be getting home from an elder's meeting soon. He wondered if he could patch himself up before then. He would get in trouble if they found out he had been in a fight, even if he hadn't been the one to start it.

His question was answered for him when the front door creaked open. Flint muttered a curse under his breath. Things happened unnaturally slow as his mother and father entered the house. Flint stood frozen in the middle of the room waiting for their anger. He must look so foolish with blood dripping down his face and unease in his eyes.

He covered his face hoping they wouldn't ask any questions and he could put this all off as a nosebleed.

Unfortunately, it would be hard to explain the cut above his eyebrow and the swelling around his nose and eye.

He knew he couldn't escape their notice though. He could only hope that Reid would get in just as much if not more trouble when he talked with Leif.

"Flint!" his mother gasped when she finally noticed him.

His father wasn't far behind, "What happened?"

Flint looked away, "Nothing," he lied.

"That's a likely story," Warren's tone grew annoyed. "Let's hear the truth, shall we?"

Flint grumbled.

"Sit down at the table," Flint's mother, Rhea ordered, taking his arm and forcing him to sit.

She gently pried his hands away from his face and hissed when she saw the extent of his injuries, "It looks like you were in a fight," she said offhandedly. Then, "*Flint*, were you in a fight?"

Flint didn't answer, but that was enough to prove his mother's guess correct.

"Flint!" Warren berated.

"It's not like I started it," Flint muttered.

His mother went off to get bandages and water to clean his wounds. When she returned, she sat in front of him with an annoyed expression on her face. She dabbed a cloth in the water and started to wipe away the blood around his nose and on his forehead. Flint hissed in pain and shoved her hand away.

"The nose looks broken," she said sympathetically.

Flint grimaced. Warren was more concerned with

what had happened to cause such an injury.

"Well, if you didn't start the fight then who did?" Warren asked.

Flint picked at a loose thread on his shirt.

"I'm waiting."

"Reid, started it," Flint murmured.

Warren stared at him for a moment before letting out a short bark of laughter. "Reid?"

"Yes, Reid, I don't know why, I was talking, and then suddenly he jumped at me. I didn't want to fight back but he kept punching me and I had to defend myself."

Warren paced the room with a look of disbelief on his face. "What could you have possibly said to make stoic Reid attack you?"

Flint yelped as his mother touched his nose.

"Sorry," she said, "But I'll have to try and set it so it heals properly."

Flint drew his hands into fists and closed his eyes tight against the pain.

"Here," his father said offering Flint his hand.

Flint grasped the hand gratefully as his mother quickly worked to reposition his broken nose. He whimpered in pain but before too long it was over.

"It will probably always be crooked," she warned him as she stood to wash her hands, "Maybe that will be a reminder for you to stay out of trouble."

Flint touched his nose and winced at the throbbing pain.

"I swear I didn't mean to get in the fight, I don't even know what I did to make him so mad."

"Well, what did you say?" Warren asked.

Flint thought for a moment. He had been showing off his sword to Brier, doing some simple strikes and parries.

Then Reid had made a mocking comment and Flint had countered with his own playful insult. They had gone back and forth a few times and then Reid had attacked him.

"I was showing Brier my new sword and Reid started to mock me," Flint explained.

"I made my rebuttal and we went back and forth like that for a while. Reid was acting strange. I don't think I've ever seen him talk so much. Then he insulted you and all other knights. He said some... he said some nasty stuff about us. I wanted to have the final word so I responded with another insult, though not as serious as the ones he was making. Then suddenly he attacked me. Maybe I said something that angered him too much. I'm not sure."

Warren sighed and paced back and forth across the room. "I can't condone fighting, but if you didn't start the fight then I won't punish you either. I would suggest you apologize to Reid though. It wouldn't do to have hard feelings between you two."

"But Reid's the one who started it," Flint argued not liking the idea of apologizing for something he wasn't at fault for.

"I won't force you to apologize; you're old enough to make your own decisions. Just know that it's never wise to hold a grudge. Remember that the Bible says in 1st Peter, *Do not repay evil with evil or insult with insult. On the contrary, repay evil with blessing, because to this you were called so that you may inherit a blessing.*"

Flint nodded, ashamed that he had to be scolded.

"I do wonder who won though," Warren remarked offhandedly.

Flint grimaced, "I don't know actually. I think we both got a little carried away. If Brier hadn't yelled and snapped us out of it, we might have ended up hurt a lot worse. Reid ran off as soon as the fight was over. I don't know where he went but he sure can throw a punch. Kind of surprising for a forester."

Warren laughed, "If I can give you one piece of advice it would be, never underestimate a forester."

CHAPTER 16

If only the day would end.

It was difficult to focus on training when all Brier could think about was the fight. Reid practiced beside her without a care in the world. It was as if he didn't even remember his fight with Flint. It had only been a day. Brier had not forgotten. How could he have attacked Flint? And for what, a joke? Maybe they had both taken things a little too far but Reid's behavior was inexcusable.

Brier wouldn't even look at him. She moved as far away as possible and refused to acknowledge his presence. Reid, likewise, ignored her, which was normal of course, but now he did it with a sense of coldness.

Why had he spoken at all yesterday? He usually wasn't one to rise to the bait of a verbal duel. Why had he gotten so upset after Flint teased him? He had instigated the fight with his insults. There had never been hostility between the two boys before.

Whatever the cause for Reid's behavior, Brier was pleased to see that he had earned an ugly bruise around his eye and a cut on his lip. He looked truly frightening with his new injuries alongside his scar. Flint had managed to land a few good punches during the fight, although when she had seen him earlier that morning, he looked considerably worse than Reid.

Brier and Reid studiously ignored each other, occasionally sneaking glares when the other wasn't looking.

Brier's accuracy as she practiced suffered from the distraction but Reid's suffered more.

When his arrows repeatedly missed the target, even Brier wondered if something was seriously wrong.

A half-hour into the practice Leif told them to stop. He usually didn't call for a break until they had practiced for a full hour.

"Come here," Leif gestured. Brier and Reid exchanged a nervous glance.

"What's going on? You two have been completely ignoring each other all morning and Reid, your eye is swollen and black. What happened?"

Brier couldn't resist a smile. Reid hardly ever got in trouble. He wouldn't get out of this one though.

Reid hung his head. Brier thought she caught a hint of defiance in his eyes. She eagerly stepped forward to tell Leif what had happened.

"Reid got into a fight," Brier said smugly.

"I can see that," Leif said, "You look fine though, no bruises that I can see, so I assume the fight wasn't with you."

Brier narrowed her eyes, upset that he would suspect her, but not so upset that she didn't see why.

"Reid attacked Flint," she retorted.

"He what!" Leif looked wide-eyed at Reid.

"Flint made a joke and Reid threw him into a tree. Before long they were rolling around in the grass exchanging punches."

Leif dragged a hand down his face and sighed. "Is

this true, Reid?"

Reid gave a curt nod.

"How did this fight start?"

Brier could taste the sweet victory. Finally, Reid was going to get in trouble for something.

"Flint was practicing with his sword, showing me the moves his father taught him. Reid decided to insult him. He called Flint childish and said horrible things about knights. When Flint retaliated with an insult of his own, Reid lost it and before I knew it, they were fighting."

"That's not why I attacked him," Reid protested, "I don't care that he insulted me. I'm used to that."

"So, why did you attack him, Reid?" Leif asked more gently.

"He insulted my father, that's why," Reid's voice was so quiet that Brier strained to hear.

Reid grabbed his bow and stormed off into the trees. Leif watched him go.

"Aren't you going to go after him?" Brier asked, annoyed at Reid's lack of punishment.

Leif shook his head. "I'll talk to him later when he's had time to cool off."

CHAPTER 17

Leif missed Mac'tire.

He missed the imposing castle, and his little cottage; he even missed the noise of the town. But most of all, he missed being a forester.

Maybe he was even more of one now that he lived in the forest. Still, it didn't feel the same. This forest was his home but he wasn't protecting it. He was just trying to survive. What had once been his passion was now a necessity. He trusted that God had a plan for his life and the lives of his family but he couldn't help missing the place that had once been his home.

If only he could return to Mac'tire, make things right, and undo any damage Corvus had caused in the nearly two years since the exile. He felt that it was his fault that they were all in this mess. He had grown a lot over the last few years and he had been given plenty of time to think things over. He shouldn't have let his pride interfere with his work. He shouldn't have been more persistent in his attempts to report to the duke. What he had discovered was dire and urgent news yet he had faltered in his duty. He wanted things to go back to the way they were. It felt wrong to train Brier and Reid as foresters even though they would never hold the position. Because of his actions, they had been sent into exile. He wanted a future for them, not the fate that awaited them now.

News of Mac'tire was not common. There was no way to find out what was going on in the town. Occasionally they heard bits and pieces on their trips to nearby villages for supplies. But Leif still worried about the dukedom in his absence.

When he was called for an elders' meeting late one evening in the fall, he was eager to hear the news.

It was raining, hard. The trees did little to block the downpour. Leif shielded his head with an arm as he jogged to the half-finished hut the elders used as a base of operations. It had become an ongoing joke that the hut would never be finished. There was always something more important to do. The elders didn't mind, they just needed a place to gather.

Mud coated Leif's legs from his knees down and the rain stung as it hit him. His cloak did little to keep him dry. The wind howled. It sounded almost wolf-like. Leif wasn't sure if it was the cold or the sound that sent a shiver down his spine. There was no moon, meaning Leif had to find his way through the darkness. He stumbled through the night, almost tripping on a tree root once and sinking deep into the mud on another occasion. His boots were caked in grime and his clothes clung wetly to him. He kept pushing onward until finally, he reached his destination.

Tarps covered the sides of the building where the walls were still incomplete and the wind whipped against them. Leif pushed back the canvas serving as a door and entered. One of the camp's few precious oil lamps illuminated the room and it took a moment for Leif's eyes to adjust to the sudden brightness. Gathered around the table were the eleven elders.

"Finally, you're here," Warren greeted, "Liam has some news which you'll be glad to hear."

Liam was a rather plain man with pale blond hair and watery blue eyes. He had been a butcher at Mac'tire and would often prepare the meat from the animals that Leif, Brier, and Reid hunted.

Leif removed his wet cloak, laying it on a stool in the corner of the room. Judging by the serious atmosphere in the room, this could prove to be a long meeting. Hopefully, his cloak would dry by the end of it.

After the first winter, the outcasts continued to send men to neighboring towns for supplies. They sold meat and furs from different animals and in exchange, gathered much-needed equipment. The trips were scheduled every four months. The elders took every precaution. If they were caught, they would be dealt with harshly. Outcasts would never be welcome in some places.

Different men were sent on each of the excursions and a different village was visited whenever possible. Unfortunately, all towns were a three-day journey away. They were forced to settle far from civilization so they wouldn't be considered poaching when they hunted.

Some of the elders were still against these trips but the benefits outweighed the risks. They gained vegetables and grains to be planted and harvested and were able to obtain any medicine needed for those who were sick.

Liam had just returned from one of these trips and called for a meeting. Leif hoped whatever news Liam had was worth trudging through the rain for.

"I heard news of Mac'tire," Liam announced.

He was serious. Liam was rarely serious. He was always telling jokes to lighten the mood during a dull and dreary meeting.

If Liam was serious, this must be important. They hadn't heard much about Mac'tire since the exile.

"What kind of news?" David asked, "Start from the beginning. Where did you hear it?"

"Well, um," Liam cleared his throat, "I stopped in at the tavern to have a drink."

Gregory laughed, "Of course you did. That's the only reason you volunteered to go, wasn't it?"

Liam's cheeks reddened, Leif wondered if it was from the insult, the cold, or perhaps a residual side effect from his time in the tavern.

"Isn't that why we all volunteer?" he protested, "Besides, I didn't let it interfere with me doing my job. If I hadn't gone, I wouldn't have heard the information about Mac'tire."

"Yes," Warren cut in, getting impatient, "And what exactly was this information you gathered?"

"When I entered the tavern, a man was talking. He was loud and I couldn't help but overhear. Mind you, this bar was a bit of a shady place. I was about to leave when I heard him mention Mac'tire."

"Yes, yes, go on," Rhea urged.

"Well, the man had obviously had a few too many drinks because he announced to his drinking buddies that he was a mercenary, in a rather loud voice I might add. He was talking about a job in Mac'tire. Some nobleman had paid a bunch of mercenaries to take the castle."

Leif leaned forward.

"Did he mention the name of the nobleman?" Leif asked, trying to keep calm.

If a nobleman had been involved that would be proof that it hadn't been an unorganized riot but an assault on the castle.

It would also explain what Leif had found the day before the riot.

It might even throw off some of his traitorous suspicions of who was behind the chaos.

Leif had been trying to reason to himself that the man he believed to be at least partially guilty couldn't possibly be.

Liam shook his head, "He was so drunk I doubt he remembered who hired him. His friends didn't believe him so he pulled a letter from his jacket and placed it on the table. I couldn't make out much but I saw the seal."

"What was it?" Warren asked, the excitement obvious in his voice.

"It was some kind of dog."

"A wolf," Leif muttered under his breath.

Thoughts were racing through his head. A memory pushed itself to the forefront of his mind.

Leif was so horrified by what he found that he stepped on a twig.

Snap!

He froze.

In the quiet of the forest, the sound reverberated. If someone had heard him, he had no chance of escaping.

There was a sound coming from behind him. It was a low growl, almost undetectable. Leif's sharp ears, hyperaware after the snapping twig, heard it. Staying still and listening as hard as he could, Leif realized that whatever the sound was, it was getting closer. He was trained to detect the different sounds of animals and he was sure that this growl was coming from a wolf.

Leif forced himself to remain calm although every instinct told him to run. Any sudden movements might cause the creature to attack. There was still a slight chance the beast hadn't heard him. He sent up a silent petition to God for safety. He just wanted to get home to his family again. Leif slowly turned.

Standing roughly ten yards away was a gigantic, completely black wolf. Its eerie yellow eyes bored into Leif. It took all his restraint to not throw caution to the wind and run. Despite the balmy fall weather, he shivered. He had come across wolves before but something was different about this one. Intelligence gleamed in its eyes. The wolf stood completely still, staring at him.

The smallest movement might cause the creature to attack. Leif had his bow, but putting an arrow to the string would take precious seconds. Seconds he didn't have. Drawing the bow would take another second. He wouldn't have time to aim. The wolf would start to move at the same time he did. Leif could only hope his instincts and years of practice would fire the arrow true. He would have to be ready in case the first arrow didn't kill the wolf. There wouldn't be time for a second shot. He would have to reach for his knife instead.

The wolf took a step forward, growling softly as it surveyed its prey. Surveyed Leif. Its head was inclined to the side and it foamed at the mouth. Leif stood stock still. If only he could disappear into the background of the trees. His breath came in ragged gasps. When his life should have been flashing before his eyes, Leif could only think that if he died, at least, he wouldn't have to answer to the duke about what he had found. He quickly pushed the thought aside. Although he did not fear what awaited him after death, he knew he could not die now. Not only was it his duty to own to his mistake and warn the duke, but he also had a wife and daughter to provide for. Time slowed as the wolf crouched down. Leif waited, arm twitching, for it to pounce. He would make his shot while the wolf was in the air. Its chest would be vulnerable while it jumped. The wolf's muscles bunched. Leif drew in a shaky breath.

Then the wolf froze.

Leif stood in wide-eyed disbelief. He dared not move. Dared not even breathe. The wolf cocked its head to the side. Its ears pricked as if listening to something. Leif strained his ears trying to detect the sound that had caught the wolf's attention.

Nothing.

It felt like hours that Leif stood there waiting for certain death but the wolf did not move.

Then, with one last growl, the wolf turned and vanished into the forest.

Leif stood for a moment more before collapsing to his knees in the semi-damp leaves. He stared into the trees where the wolf disappeared. Had it even been there at all?

Leif pressed his fingers to his temples and groaned softly. He hated wolves.

"Is everything alright, Leif?" Warren questioned.

Leif nodded, "Fine, fine, just get on with the story."

"The mercenary told his friends that the nobleman had called him back to try to take the castle again. The last time a riot broke out and ruined everything."

There were gasps throughout the room.

"You're sure he mentioned a riot?" Timothy asked.

Liam nodded enthusiastically, "Let me finish my story. The mercenary said he wasn't going back. He said he'd had enough of that cursed castle."

"So, whoever this nobleman is he's the one who started the first riot and he's going to try to take the castle again," Warren thought out loud.

Liam nodded. Silence stretched thin.

"What are we going to do about it?" William asked.

"We're going back to warn Duke Orion of course!" Warren exclaimed.

"Wait just one second. Even if we got through the front gates of the town, why would the duke believe a bunch of outcasts?" Gregory reminded them.

"It's too dangerous," Bess agreed.

"Why should we go back?" Henry stepped forward, "The duke betrayed us by exiling us without a trial. He just assumed us commoners were guilty and treated it as a mercy to not have us killed instead."

"He's right," James said softly, "My family were just merchants, we didn't even take part in the riot. We were respectable people; never did anything wrong. The duke wouldn't even give us a chance to explain."

Some of the elders lowered their heads in remembrance of the suffering they had faced as a result of the duke's decision. There was no question that the man had made a mistake. But Leif knew that's all it had been.

The duke was only human, and humans were destined for failure if they trusted only their understanding.

Leif remained silent though and did not voice his thoughts on the matter. He had no place to speak. As a forester, he had been given a trial, biased as it may have been.

"No!" Warren protested, slamming his hand on the table. Rhea reached for him but he pushed her away.

"This is not the duke's fault. We were exiled due to a terrible misunderstanding. If we return to the dukedom and warn him about the attack that is coming, if we tell him everything, he will believe us. He's a just man and he will judge us fairly. It is our duty to warn him about this nobleman and his plans."

Warren had never voiced any hope of returning to Mac'tire. Now Leif saw hope in Warren's every feature. Still, the elders were not convinced.

"Any duty we might have held to the duke disappeared the moment he exiled us," James argued.

"There's another reason we should return," Leif explained, "We may have been treated unfairly before. I will never forget that the duke did not believe my word. However, if we stay in this forest, there will be constant danger. We have to return and restore our good names. When we are no longer outcasts, then you can all do as you please. You can leave Mac'tire and never return. If we stay here, we have no future. Our children have no future."

The elders exchanged looks.

"Shall we put it to a vote?" David asked.

It was unanimous.

They would return to Mac'tire.

"That's great and all," Timothy remarked, "But how exactly are we going to prove that we're telling the truth? Why would the duke believe a ridiculous story told by outcasts?"

"Because we have this," Liam said, reaching into his

sack and producing a letter. The letter with the wolf seal. "Why didn't you tell us you had that in the first place?" Warren asked smacking Liam across the head.

CHAPTER 18

It was two years to the day since the exile.

Despite that fact, Brier's good mood would not be shaken. It was a lovely fall afternoon and for once, she was alone in her practice. Leif had insisted that Reid stay away from the practice field. He was too distracted and it was dangerous to handle a bow when your thoughts were elsewhere. Brier couldn't help but agree. Reid had hidden away the past week. The few times Brier had seen him he was like a ghost, pale and traveling aimlessly from one spot to the next. When she asked if he was all right, he didn't respond. It was like he was in a trance. She hadn't realized why until she asked her father.

"What's wrong with Reid?"

"People mourn differently," was Leif's response, "Remember, the exile meant a lot of changes for everyone. It marked the day we lost our home, but it also marks the day Reid lost his father."

Brier avoided Reid altogether after that realization.

When Leif barred Reid from practicing, it was the one thing to trigger a spark of life in him. "You can't," Reid protested, "You can't take it away from me. You can't stop me from practicing!"

However, Leif insisted that in his current mental

state Reid would probably shoot someone in the foot. Reid seemed more worried about losing his edge than any damage he might inflict on himself or others.

He even tried to sneak away to practice once. When Leif caught him, all further attempts were halted.

With Reid absent, Brier was focused. She released another volley of five arrows, satisfied to see four had landed in the middle of the target with less than three centimeters of space between them. The last impacted the second ring from the center. It was a great set of arrows.

She should be mourning the date they had been forced to leave their home, but Brier couldn't be happier. She loved it in the forest and never wanted to go back.

She went to retrieve her arrows with a spring to her step. As she pulled the last of them from the target, she felt a hand on her shoulder. She jumped in surprise before realizing that it was only Leif.

"How about we take a break?" he suggested.

Brier nodded. In truth, she had been hoping he would call a break for lunch She was starting to get hungry.

Leif gestured toward a path that led to a small clearing. The two of them walked in comfortable silence. It was a beautiful day. The sun was shining and a light breeze blew through the trees. Leaves cast tiny flickering shadows across their path. When they reached the clearing at the end of the trail, Brier was surprised to see a blanket and wicker basket laid out on the grass.

"I thought we might have a picnic," Leif suggested.

Brier smiled. It had been a long time since they spent time together. Usually, Reid tagged along. Brier missed the days in Mac'tire when it had just been her and her parents.

She remembered the times when Leif would tell stories by the light of their fireplace.

He would tell her about the great heroes of the Bible, David, and Samson, and even women like Mary, Deborah, and Jael. That had been a long time ago. Brier had been small enough to sit on Leif's knee. Now she was almost fifteen.

Leif led her to the blanket and they sat down. Birds were chirping and a small creek below them gurgled softly. She remembered fishing here once with Flint. They hadn't caught anything but it was a fond memory nonetheless. Leif opened the basket and produced two loaves of bread, some apples, cheese, and meat. Brier's stomach growled at the smell of the freshly baked bread. The apples were a luxury that had come from a recent excursion to a nearby village. It was a rare treat for fresh fruit to find its way to the camp. One of those trips had brought back the goats whose milk was used to make the cheese. Brier could still remember the excitement that had caused. The mischief those creatures constantly found themselves in, chasing small children around and ramming their thick skulls into trees brought a grin to Brier's face.

Her father prayed over the food and they both dug in. Soon a wandering conversation started and Brier found that she was enjoying herself.

Her father talked about her progress in training and memories of Mac'tire; the goats were even brought into the conversation at one point, leading to much laughter.

Brier realized that this might have been the first alone time she had with her father since before the exile.

Between Reid and training and Leif's duties as an elder, there had never been time for the two of them to bond.

She wondered if this was his way of extending an olive branch to her.

After a while, Leif shifted and Brier could sense the conversation was about to change to a more serious note.

"I'm proud of you, Brier," he began and Brier smiled at the praise, "You've been working very hard and there's an obvious improvement in your abilities. I also think you should know I'm aware of your late-night training sessions."

Brier couldn't tell if her father was proud or upset. Why hadn't he brought this up sooner? The night-time sessions had become few and far between, now more a way to relieve stress than anything else.

"I just wanted more practice," Brier said in defense.

"I understand," Leif, assured her, "I've always appreciated your drive to be better. If you were in trouble, I would have told you so a long time ago."

Brier looked away, embarrassed. She thought her late-night training had been a secret.

"I'm convinced that you're more than capable of defending yourself," Leif continued.

Again, Brier smiled at the praise.

"Which, is why I can go back to Mac'tire with the other elders to sort things out."

Brier knew that today had been too good to be true. "What?" she asked.

"The elders have decided to send representatives to Mac'tire to restore our names and return from exile."

"Why would you want to return when we can stay here?" Brier argued, scooting away.

Leif sighed, "It's not safe here. This is only temporary. It always has been. We always wanted to return and prove our innocence."

Brier glared at him. "Why now? After all this time why are you going back?"

Leif swiped a hand through his hair. "We have a letter that could prove we weren't behind the riot."

"How?" Brier asked, growing frustrated.

"There were events leading up to the riot that may have been orchestrated behind the scenes. If we show the duke the letter, the real culprits could be tracked down."

"The duke didn't listen to you last time, what makes you think a letter will make him believe you?"

"It's already been decided, the elders are returning to Mac'tire and I'm going with them."

Brier sighed. She didn't bother pointing out his lack of an answer. He could see the flaws in the elders' plan. Either that, or he wasn't telling her everything. She sensed there was no stopping him from going back though. The elders had probably already planned the whole trip.

She knew this was too good to be true. She was at peace with her new life; she loved living in the forest, but she wasn't an elder. She didn't argue further with her father. She didn't have a say in the matter and she didn't want to sour the nice lunch they had shared by arguing. However, she wasn't about to let him go without her.

"If you have to go, let me come with you."

"No, absolutely not. You have to stay here."

"You said yourself that I've proven myself capable."

"You may be capable but there are dangers that you're not yet ready to face. You've trained against animals and wooden targets. There's a chance we'll face more than that on this journey. I'm sorry, but you have to stay. Besides, we'll be back before too long."

Brier studied the grass.

Leif laid a hand on her shoulder. "There's no reason to worry. I'll be back before you know it."

Brier met her father's eyes. He was telling the truth. Still...

"When do you leave?" Brier asked.

"Soon. If all goes well, the trip to Mac'tire and back should only take a month. Then we'll all be able to go home."

"It'll be dangerous," Brier insisted.

"I know. I'll be careful," Leif patted Brier's head in a way he hadn't done since she was young.

"Promise?"

"Promise."

CHAPTER 19

"You're both leaving?" Flint's voice shook.

His father said that the key to bravery was not letting the fear show. There was no doubting that Flint was afraid. There was a throbbing in his chest and he felt short of breath. His mind struggled to comprehend what he was hearing. As one of the duke's guards, Warren had never faced the possibility of going to battle. As far as the duties of a knight went, it was a relatively low-risk occupation. Flint had never worried that his father might leave and never return. Now, not only was his father leaving but his mother also.

Flint had always had his parents by his side. He knew they loved him and cared for him deeply. He never doubted that. They might be strict at times but he realized that only further proved that they worried for his wellbeing. Now, they were leaving. Leaving him behind.

"I don't understand. Why are you both going?"

Warren placed a firm hand on his son's shoulder, "I'm one of the elders, and I was one of the duke's most trusted guards. I have to go. Leif and I are the only people the duke might listen to. Your mother is going both as an elder and to represent the women and children that have suffered because of this exile. This might be our only chance to be accepted back. I must tell the duke about the letter we found. It's my duty to warn him that there might be trouble."

Flint had heard plenty of talk about duty and sacrifice in his lifetime.

His entire life, the values of chivalry were drilled into his head. He knew his father had to do this but that didn't make it any easier to see him go.

Flint feared for his father. He feared for himself. He didn't want to be left alone. He had enough experience with the sword to defend himself but he had never needed to before. His father had always been there to protect and guide him. He knew that if he ever ran into trouble, he could rely on his father's help. For once he wished that something else could come before duty and honor. It was a selfish wish.

"What about me?"

Flint's mother pulled him into a tight hug. Flint was taller than her now, but the hug brought back memories of when he was a small child.

"You have to stay and protect the others," she said gently, "God will protect you and guide you and we'll be back before you know it."

Flint saw tears starting to form in her warm, brown eyes, so much like his own. He sniffled and blinked to clear his vision lifting a hand to wipe his eyes. He had to be brave. *Bravery is not letting the fear show.* He rested a hand on the sword at his belt. *I can do this.*

His mother and father might be leaving but they would return. When they did, they would be able to go back to Mac'tire. He would fulfill his dream of becoming a knight and his father's honor would finally be restored. They would finally be safe.

Flint stepped away from his mother's embrace and stood a little straighter. He studied his parents' faces and nodded.

"I'll make you proud dad," Flint grasped his father's hand.

Warren smiled warmly, "You already have."

CHAPTER 20

The days leading up to the departure were stressful but exciting.

Leif hadn't looked forward to something so much since he was waiting for Brier to be born. He was finally being given the opportunity he had prayed for to make things right. And he knew everything would work together for their benefit in the end as long as they listened to God's plan for them. It would be a rough journey, without a doubt and they would surely face many dangers but Leif wasn't worried. He trusted that God would guide them. Telling his family the news of his upcoming departure had been the most difficult part of the preparations. Brier had taken it poorly, not wanting him to leave. Her arguments and pleading to go with him didn't make things easier. In contrast, Reid stayed silent while Leif told him the news. He retreated into the dark corner of his mind that Leif knew him to inhabit when he was unsure or scared.

Leif didn't want to leave them, but he had to return to Mac'tire. It wasn't just for the good of the people who were exiled. It was to ensure that Duke Orion knew of the threat of a coup. The previous riot happened because of Leif's past negligence. Now he would finally have the chance to make things right. He prayed that the duke would listen.

Despite his excitement, Leif felt a strange sense of foreboding at what lay ahead.

So, when Warren suggested a walk to discuss a few things, Leif readily obliged.

It was cold. The oncoming fall weather was just another thing to worry about. If it snowed, Leif dreaded the obstacles they would face during their travels. He also worried about leaving the camp to fend for itself during the brutal winter months. They could wait till spring, of course, but they all felt a sense of urgency to return. And for now, the sky was clear. Leif knew that God would provide adequate weather for their journey.

As the date of departure drew near, Leif spent more and more time in prayer. He felt that they were meant to return to Mac'tire but the sense of wrongness that hovered over him refused to dissipate. Warren looked just as nervous as Leif felt.

They walked in silence for a long time. Neither man was sure what to say, despite Warren having suggested they talk. Leif tried not to think about everything concerning him. He wanted to enjoy the brief respite of a walk with his friend.

"It's odd to think that we're going back?" Warren finally broke the silence.

Leif grunted in response. He looked forward to arriving in Mac'tire, returning to his home, perhaps even working as a forester once again. Still, it was difficult to imagine leaving this little camp behind. It would be hard to reacclimate to life in Mac'tire. He had gotten used to the freedom of the camp. He was no longer under the judging scrutiny of Corvus. He was free to do as he pleased.

"Do you think he'll even listen to us?" Warren asked and then Leif knew why he had wanted to talk.

Warren didn't need to explain who the "he" being referred to was. Duke Orion's possible response was heavy on everyone's minds as of late.

"I hope the letter will be sufficient proof to convince him," Leif answered, "Though if Corvus has any say in the matter, we'll be hung for stepping foot in the dukedom."

Warren sighed, "I've been thinking more about that lately, Leif."

"And?"

"And I don't think Corvus is the enemy here. I was mistaken in my assumptions back at the castle. I was in the wrong attacking him. If the duke trusts him then I must not question it."

Leif clenched his fists. Warren often voiced doubts about his actions before the riot. Unlike Leif, Warren hadn't taken part in the riot itself. He had been in the castle dungeon before the event even took place. Warren's crime was following his instincts and potentially saving the duke's life. Of course, many wouldn't see threatening the duke's advisor in the same fashion. Try as he might to reassure his friend that his actions were just, Leif could not convince Warren.

"No," Leif tried to keep his voice calm, "Your duty was to protect the duke and you did that. If your suspicion was correct then you saved the duke's life. Corvus has done nothing but arouse suspicion. I will never trust him."

Warren shook his head, "I'm afraid we'll never quite agree on matters that involve Corvus. So, let's not talk about that now. How did Brier and Reid react when you told them you were leaving?"

Leif groaned and Warren laughed at his friend's reaction.

"I take it that means they didn't handle the news well."

Leif ran a hand through his hair in frustration, "Brier was more upset than I thought she would be. She doesn't want to return to Mac'tire but when I told her it was already decided, she begged to come with."

"That's about how Flint reacted. It's going to be difficult for him since Rhea and I are both going but he's strong. He'll step up while we're gone," Warren smiled fondly, "What about Reid, how did he take the news?"

"Honestly, I have no idea. He kind of shut down, retreating into his mind as he sometimes does. It worries me but I don't know what to do about it. Reid's unpredictable, I never know what he's thinking."

"Who would have guessed he would start a fight with Flint?" Warren remarked.

Leif grimaced, "Sorry about that by the way. I talked with him and apparently, Flint said something about his father that upset him. Reid still hasn't overcome his grief. I've been in constant prayer over the situation and I hoped he would have made more progress by now. I think that he is under great spiritual attack. I trust that God will deliver him."

"Hm… I'll keep the situation in my prayers as well. I had been wondering what Flint might have said to make Reid so angry."

Warren was the first-person Leif talked to after the exile. He had explained the death of his good friend Rowan and his new responsibility to Reid.

They had prayed together for wisdom for Leif to

handle the situation and peace for both him and Reid.

Warren had been supportive of Leif's decision to bring Reid into exile with him and it had been a great reassurance as Leif himself had doubted his judgment.

"A boy needs a father figure," Warren said, "he trusts you. It will be difficult for him, but it would be far more so if you left him in Mac'tire."

Leif knew that helping Reid through his grief would be a challenge but he hadn't anticipated how great of a challenge. Witnessing his father's death in such a cruel fashion had traumatized Reid. Leif thought he was starting to move past his grief but the fight with Flint had reopened old wounds. Or perhaps, Leif had been mistaken in thinking Reid was healing at all. Rowan's son had inherited several traits from his father, one of them being hiding the pain in his life so he would not burden others.

Rowan had acted much the same after the death of his wife. Leif remembered thinking how well Rowan was handling the tragedy before finding him one day, crying in the forest overcome with grief.

"Did Flint ever apologize to Reid?" Warren asked, pulling Leif from his thoughts.

"Not that I know of, though I've learned quickly that Reid doesn't share everything with me."

Warren sighed, "I hoped Flint would make an effort to patch things up. I don't want hard feelings to dwell between the boys. Flint is partially responsible after all. Sometimes his mouth moves before his brain can catch up."

Leif waved off Warren's words, "I understand that problem better than most, I'm afraid. I couldn't name all the times I've found trouble because I didn't think before I spoke. Flint is a good kid and he will be a good man.

"You've raised him well and taught him the importance of a relationship with God. He'll learn to be careful with his words one day."

When Warren didn't look convinced, Leif added, "Besides, as I understand it, he wasn't the only one saying hurtful things. Brier claimed that Reid was the first to insult Flint and that his words were scathing, to say the least."

Warren nodded, "Flint was upset by something Reid said about knights. He's a little protective of me after the exile. He's sensitive on the topic of honor and titles."

"I suppose it's to be expected that boys will get into fights. Though, I am a little concerned that Reid lost his temper so easily. I'm worried about what will happen while I'm gone. Reid and Brier don't get along and their relationship seems to be deteriorating as time goes by."

"Oh? How so?"

"Reid is withdrawn and moody and Brier is headstrong and proud. Then there's the competition between them. They're constantly trying to best each other in training."

"What they need is a common experience," Warren remarked.

"What do you mean?"

"Well, they already train as foresters and live under the same roof. As you've noted, there's a bit of a rivalry between them and probably some vying for your attention. If they had an experience that brought them together, like having to work towards a common goal, it would force them to set aside their differences. They would probably discover they have more in common than they thought."

Leif nodded. "I'll have to think of something for when we get back from Mac'tire. Maybe I'll send them on a hunting trip together or," Leif laughed softly, "or I could come up with some ridiculous task they have to do to finish their training as foresters."

Warren smiled, "Either way, I understand your concern. Reid's been through a lot. He's troubled in a way no one his age should be but he's in good hands while in your care. I'm sure the problems between him and Brier will be sorted out before too long."

"Once we get back to Mac'tire, things will be better," Leif said, though he doubted it would be that simple.

As he and Warren walked towards their homes, Leif kept repeating that thought in his head. *Things will be better.*

CHAPTER 21

Brier pulled the hood of her cloak lower over her face and shrunk further into the shadows.

It was essential that she not be seen. Her plan was risky and foolish. But as she saw it, necessary. If she was spotted, she would be sent back to the outcasts' camp immediately. All of her hard work would be for nothing. Despite what she told her father, Brier was determined to go with him and the other elders to Mac'tire. She wouldn't let him leave without her. She hadn't had much time to plan so there were a few flaws to the overall idea. She didn't plan on staying hidden indefinitely, just until they were far enough from the camp that she wouldn't risk being sent back. That could mean a few hours or a few days depending on how quickly the group moved.

As the elders stopped to rest, Brier studied the group. Her father hadn't explained in detail who else was going on this expedition. Along with Leif, there were Flint's parents Warren and Rhea. Flint had admitted that he also wanted to go with the group. He would be upset to find out she had gone after the elders without him. She had considered inviting Flint but he would have tried to talk her out of it claiming that they should just follow their parents' wishes.

The other elders present were Gregory, James, and Henry. Brier didn't know them well. She tried to avoid conversation with the elders whenever possible. Anything they said was usually dull and serious.

Gregory opposed her father on many issues during elder meetings and James had two children around her age.

Henry was a blacksmith who made their arrowheads. He hadn't wanted to return to Mac'tire. Brier had always liked Henry.

She was pulled from her thoughts as the group started to move again. She carefully crept forward, trying to keep pace. It was hard work and she prayed that she wouldn't be left behind.

Although her stalking skills were not very good, Brier was sure that she could remain unseen as long as she kept enough distance between herself and the group. The dense trees helped her remain out of sight but they also made the area hard to traverse. She had to stay closer to the group than she would have liked to keep them in view.

Getting past her mother had been easy enough. Rachel was gone for the day collecting medicinal herbs with several other healers. Brier knew that it was wrong to sneak away and she could only imagine how disappointed her parents would be when they found out. She didn't like to make them worry and she understood that she should listen to her father and stay behind. But she felt desperate to follow them.

She was scared. She didn't want her father to return to Mac'tire. The duke had wronged them once before. Nothing was stopping the man from having the outcasts hung when they returned.

Brier had left a note explaining where she was going for when her mother came back. She didn't want a search party being sent after her.

Though her note wasn't likely to ease her mother's worry. She had kept it brief, *Gone with dad, don't worry - Brier.*

Of course, telling a mother not to worry was a surefire way of making them do just that. Rachel wasn't supposed to be back until late into the night anyway. Brier would be too far away by then for anyone to come after her.

It had been easy to get past Reid too. Brier hadn't told him her plan. She didn't want him to tag along. He had left for the training field as soon as Leif said his goodbyes. Brier was relieved that she didn't have to evade him. She had waited several minutes to make sure her father wouldn't see her, then hurriedly followed after him.

Her father was perceptive so it was difficult to avoid his notice. She had to slow for a moment to watch her footing as she slid down a small hill. When she reached the base, she could no longer see the group ahead of her. She could hear their voices ahead and she rushed to catch up. If she lost sight of them, she might get lost. She wasn't sure she would be able to find her way back to the camp from her current position. She would be stuck in the forest, alone. She had a brief moment of panic. Maybe this had been a bad idea. She should have told someone where she was going. With the cryptic letter she left her mother, it would be assumed that she met up with her father. No one would come looking for her. *Please God, let me catch up to the others,* she prayed. Brier sped up, desperate to reach the others. She had just caught sight of them again when, in her haste, a twig snapped beneath her foot.

Brier froze.

Every muscle in her body urged her to make a run for it but she remained still.

If she ran, she would easily be spotted. Amazingly nobody even turned to look in her direction.

She smirked; her father must be getting rusty. Convinced that she hadn't been detected, Brier kept moving.

The elders were moving at a quick pace and she struggled to keep up while staying undetected. She didn't dare risk trading speed for subtlety though. She couldn't make another mistake. One may be overlooked but if she caused another noise to draw attention she would surely be caught.

How would she explain herself to her father when she did reveal her presence? The conversation would not be a pleasant one. Leif would be furious and he would have every right to be. However, if all went according to plan, he wouldn't have a choice except to let her follow them the rest of the way.

Brier maintained her distance and quick pace all day. She only had one more close call when the group stopped for lunch and her stomach started to growl. She hadn't thought to bring any food along with her. The elders stopped, confused and concerned at the noise but after a few moments, they seemed to put it off as a small animal of some sort. They maintained a guard throughout the meal and Brier had to be cautious not to make any other sounds. Once they started moving again, things went back to the relaxed state of before.

A little after midday, Brier started to feel an odd

sensation as if someone were watching her.

It was an eerie feeling and the longer she walked, the worse the feeling became. She could practically feel someone's eyes on her and her skin crawled.

She walked a few more paces then swung around quickly. Nothing. She tried to reason with herself that it was only her imagination.

Still, she couldn't shake the uneasy feeling. She tried a technique her father had taught her and faltered a step, hoping to catch anyone who might be following off guard. As much as she wanted to believe that no one was behind her, she was a little concerned when her trick didn't work. It would have been easier to discover someone or something because there was no other explanation for the strange feeling that had settled in her gut.

Brier tried to ignore the feeling and move on. There was nothing she could do about it and she needed to stay focused. However, after several more minutes, she was still on edge. Her mouth was dry and she was taut with tension. The group sat down to take another break and Brier happily followed their example. Between the emotional strain of feeling like she was being followed and the physical exertions of staying hidden while keeping up with the group, she was completely drained. Her muscles were tight and she wanted nothing more than to stop where she was and make camp but she couldn't stop until the others did. Besides, it would be better to get as far away from the outcasts' camp as possible so she could make her presence known when they stopped for the night.

Brier sighed as she settled behind a bush. She could use it for cover while still keeping an eye on the others.

She stretched.

The sun was still high in the sky. They would probably keep traveling for several more hours. She needed to rest now to keep up.

Behind her, there was a slight noise. Brier turned to see what it was and felt a hand on her arm. She opened her mouth to scream but before she could get any noise out another hand closed over her mouth.

She turned, expecting to find a bandit or criminal but it was worse. Reid.

Brier wasn't sure if she was relieved or disappointed. She struggled to keep herself from yelling at him and giving away her position. She settled for glaring instead. Reid's hand slowly moved away from her mouth and he released her arm. They sat in silence for a moment, staring at each other.

"What are you doing here?" Brier whispered angrily. She wanted to grab her knife and pin it to his throat for scaring her like that.

"I could ask you the same thing," Reid replied in a much softer tone.

Brier glared at him. "You followed me."

"You mean like how you're following them?" Reid's dark grey eyes bored through her.

A glint of amusement flashed in his usually emotionless gaze. Brier barely withheld a frustrated growl. She hated Reid's uncanny ability to turn an argument on her in seconds.

"That's different," she retorted.

"Is it?"

Brier wanted nothing more than to slap him. She restrained herself, barely.

"You should work on your observation skills," Reid

pointed out.

"If I had been a bandit, you would be dead."

Brier expected to see a look of amusement on his face but he was dead serious. Reid would make a good bandit. He even had a big, ugly scar running down his face. She wondered if he had been following her or the elders.

"I didn't intend to let Leif leave me behind either," he said, answering her unspoken question.

As much as Brier hated the idea of working with Reid, they had the same goal and he wouldn't turn her in. She'd have to put up with him for the time being.

"Come on, they're moving again," Reid told her.

Brier looked over the bush and saw that Reid was right. Of course, *he* had stolen the only break she would get.

The pair got up and, staying in the shadows, continued to follow the others. It was different with Reid at her side. The feeling of being watched hadn't completely gone away but now that she knew Reid had been the cause, she was relieved. He was so silent that she forgot he was there at times but his presence was still reassuring. Although she disliked his company, it was nice to have someone watching her back.

Reid stopped and she followed suit. She looked ahead and saw what had caught his attention. Her father bent down to examine a track in the dirt. The rest of the group was gathered around waiting for Leif. They mumbled about something but Brier couldn't hear the words. Then Leif stood up and the group started to move again. He looked wary; his hand rested on the knife at his belt.

That's when Brier heard it, a low rumbling sound. At

first, she thought she was imagining things but Reid's pale face proved that he had heard it too.

The sound wasn't loud but it seemed to echo through the trees. Brier recognized the noise immediately. It was the growl of a wolf. The deep, throaty sound sent a shiver down her spine. The sound had haunted her nightmares since the attack on the camp.

The elders didn't seem to hear the sound.

They continued walking, unaware of the encroaching danger.

Brier tried to yell for them to watch out but her voice disappeared in the midst of her fear. *God, please. Please, let them hear it,* she pleaded.

Reid clutched his dagger and Brier reached for hers as well. She wasn't very skilled with the weapon but she couldn't fire a shot from her bow through the thick foliage. The growl sounded again. This time much closer. Brier's hand froze. She reached for her bow instead. She would take the risk to have a more familiar weapon in hand.

The group stopped, finally hearing the noise, and glanced hurriedly around.

"What was that?" James hissed.

"I don't know," Henry said.

"Leif?" Warren asked.

Leif's eyes widened. He reached for the bow slung over his shoulder but the wolf chose that moment to attack. The creature had a sleek black coat and cold yellow eyes. It foamed at the mouth in rage. Its bared teeth were as long as Brier's finger and it stood nearly four feet tall at the shoulder.

It moved so fast. Everything happened in a blur.

Before Brier knew it, her whole world began to crumble before her very eyes.

The wolf leaped out of the bushes on the edge of the path and landed on Gregory, biting his exposed neck and killing him instantly. There was no struggle and there was no time for anyone to process what had happened. Before any of them could react, the wolf had taken down Henry. Henry tried desperately to get away, clawing at the creature with his hands, but the wolf was too powerful.

Henry thrashed back and forth and then laid still.

Then the monster leaped onto James. James had his knife at the ready. When the wolf attacked, he managed to deliver a sharp cut across its eye. The wolf staggered back, swiping at its face with a paw but then its head lifted, tilting to the side. It shook its head as if nothing had happened and brought its razor-sharp teeth down before James could get out of the way.

The wolf pivoted neatly around and pounced on Warren. Warren hadn't managed to work his sword out of its scabbard. He struggled desperately, tugging at the sword that was now trapped beneath him. The wolf snarled and Brier and Reid tried to react but they were frozen in fear. Warren's wife, Rhea was screaming and Leif was yelling, trying to grab an arrow from his quiver, but the sickening crunch of the wolf biting Warren's neck could still be heard over the noise.

Brier stood frozen, not quite processing what was happening. The wolf was too fast; it was all happening too fast. She could only watch as blood coated the ground and the wolf moved forward.

Rhea was the next victim; she had started toward Warren in desperation and despite Leif's attempts, he couldn't reach her before the wolf.

Rhea collapsed, her hand still reaching towards Warren's. The world seemed frozen for a brief moment as her fingers fell inches from Warren's outstretched hand.

There was a momentary break in the bloodshed. Leif had finally worked an arrow free from his quiver but his hands were shaking too badly to place it on his bowstring. Brier caught sight of her father's face and saw the absolute anguish written in his every feature. He was the only one left. Leif threw the arrow aside.

He drew his knife instead and stood, hands shaking, knees quivering, ready to face the wolf. Brier's heart hammered wildly and she placed an arrow on her bowstring, aiming at the creature. She hated how her arm shook but she couldn't stop it, she was struggling just to stay on her feet.

All she could see were the bodies and the wolf slowly approaching her father.

The creature moved closer and closer to Leif. Brier panicked. She couldn't pull back the arrow. Her entire body was frozen in fear. She felt the sweat dripping from her forehead into her eyes. She couldn't draw in a full breath. She couldn't do it. She tried to pray for help but her mind couldn't form a coherent idea. She was in too great of a shock to do anything but watch. Then the wolf was too close to Leif and her opportunity to help was gone. With her arm shaking, she was afraid she would hit her father instead of the beast.

Reid trembled beside her like a tree in a storm. His eyes were unfocused as if he was seeing something other than the horror unfolding before them. Reid was still in a position to throw his knife at the wolf and he didn't hesitate once a good shot was available.

Brier suddenly wasn't so upset that he was better at using the knife than her. She just hoped he would hit his target. Leif had shown them how to throw the knives. He said that throwing a knife accurately could be a matter of life or death someday. Today was that day. Brier watched as Reid flicked his wrist and sent the knife on its way. The knife spun in the air, flipping end over end. The sun glinted off of the blade and blinded Brier for a brief moment. The world stood still in anticipation. It was a beautiful throw. It was a perfect throw.

The knife missed.

Everything stopped as the reality of the situation sunk in.

Brier reached for her knife but it was already too late.

There was no stopping the wolf.

Blood dripped down its face from the cut James had given it and its shoulders bunched as it prepared to leap. Brier watched in horror as it sprung unto her father clawing at him mercilessly.

Tears clouded Brier's vision. She wanted to scream but she couldn't make a sound. Reid's hand rested on her shoulder. Tears fell from his eyes but there was also hardness and finality in his gaze that broke her heart. It was hopeless, there was nothing they could do but watch. *Please, God, no,* she was finally able to pray. It seemed she was too late.

Finally, the wolf dragged Leif, its last victim into the bushes and out of sight. Brier's heart was torn from her chest as she watched him disappear, gone forever. The clearing stood in stark silence. The chaos from before disappeared and was replaced by an eerie quiet.

Brier and Reid collapsed to the ground, their legs giving out in tandem. For a long time, they could do nothing except stare at the spot where the bodies were strewn. Brier shook with sobs and Reid's face was blank and lifeless as he stared at the spot where the wolf had appeared from the bushes. They were unable to move, unable to think, unable to accept what had happened. *Why?* She asked. It was the only word that came to her mind. Why did this have to happen to them? They had already lost so much. Their homes, their freedom, their dignity. Now, this.

Brier would have stayed there forever in her grief if Reid hadn't squeezed her shoulder gently.

"We have to get back to camp and tell the others," His voice was thick with emotion.

Brier reluctantly stood up wiping at her eyes. There was nothing they could do. This was all her fault. She hadn't been able to warn them, she'd been so frozen in fear she hadn't done anything except watch. She couldn't just leave now.

Despite the way her stomach churned at the mere thought, she knew they had to examine the bodies. They had to make sure they were dead. Brier swallowed hard, thinking about Flint and wishing desperately that she didn't have to tell him his parents were gone. She wished this was just some twisted nightmare.

She started toward the bodies and Reid followed wordlessly behind her. When they reached the elders, Brier was immediately sick at the gruesome sight. Reid averted his gaze.

The bodies were relatively normal looking from the shoulders down but the necks and faces where the wolf had dealt its killing blows were gruesome. Perhaps it was a blessing that she didn't have to look at her father's lifeless form.

She and Reid couldn't give the bodies a proper burial, there wasn't time and they didn't have any tools to dig a hole with. They settled for covering the bodies with a loose layer of the fall leaves, which were strewn all around. It was an insufficient job but it was the best they could do.

Brier forced herself to approach Warren. A fresh set of sobs escaped her. Warren's once friendly, smile-lined face was now streaked red with blood.

His eyes stared blankly ahead. She didn't look beyond his face; she couldn't bring herself to. She reached blindly for his hand and checked for a pulse. Her heart shattered a bit more when she found nothing.

Reid had checked the other bodies and followed the same procedure. He must have found the same results because he returned to her side quickly. They couldn't carry the bodies back to camp but Brier couldn't just leave them here. Not Warren. Warren had been her father's best friend. He was Flint's father. Her gaze fell to the scabbard that he had so desperately tried to free his sword from in his final moments. It was covered in blood. So was she.

Brier swallowed hard and as gently as she could unraveled the strap attaching the scabbard to Warren's belt. She freed it and held it close to her. Brier hoped maybe the blade would give Flint a modicum of comfort when he heard the news.

Reid came forward then and shut Warren's eyes, a task Brier couldn't bring herself to watch. She looked away and tried to hold back her sobs. The little action seemed to make everything so final. As Reid's fingers hovered over Warren's face, Brier heard him mutter a few words. She couldn't hear what he said but she understood what he was doing. Fresh tears rose to the surface as Reid said a final prayer over Warren's still, lifeless body.

Reid spread the leaves over Warren and Brier kept her eyes closed tight. When she finally forced them open, Warren had disappeared under a blanket of leaves.

Five elders, five bodies buried under leaves and branches.

Brier rose unsteadily to her feet and turned her attention to the trees where the wolf had disappeared.

The sun was setting but she couldn't leave without searching for her father. Reid silently followed behind her. They spent what must have been at least an hour searching through the dense forest for Leif. There was no body. There was no wolf. Only a few drops of blood led off into the darkness.

Brier wanted to follow the trail until they found him but it was getting dark and cold and Reid eventually pulled her away.

With a loud sniff, Brier took Reid's offered hand and they started towards the camp. All the way, Brier was flooded with what-ifs. If she hadn't hesitated in her shot, the wolf would be dead and her father would still be alive, everyone would be. Leif had always told her to trust herself and not hesitate.

Now he was dead because of her actions. Brier stared at the sword in her hand. Flint would be grateful for the possession but it would do nothing to alleviate the pain of losing his parents.

Brier wanted to see her father. She didn't care how horribly the wolf might have mauled him. She just wanted to say goodbye, to take his bow, and have something to remember him by. She would always have the memories but she wanted something physical that she could touch and hold. She wanted to trace her fingers across the curved wooden surface, feel the nicks left behind by arrows, and remember her father's touch, firm but gentle.

Brier and Reid spent the entire night stumbling back to the camp. The distance between them had faded. After what they had seen, there was no sense in holding a grudge or worrying about a rivalry. They were no longer competitors. They were just two kids horrified by what they had seen.

They used less caution than they should have and took no breaks to rest themselves. They moved at a quick pace though neither had their minds on the task. They had not eaten since morning. Weak, and tired, their minds were still back in the clearing with the wolf. Occasionally she could hear Reid muttering to himself but then the words would be snatched away by the wind.

When it got cold, they walked closer together hoping to share some body heat. When Brier didn't think she could carry on, Reid offered her his arm in support. Brier clung gratefully to it, glad that she at least wasn't alone.

Eventually, they stumbled into the camp. It was still dark and the wind had started to pick up.

They were bone-weary and still in shock over everything that had happened but they managed to head in the direction of their hut. Brier dreaded to tell her mother the news but she wanted nothing more than to be held in her mother's arms and reassured that everything would be all right. She knew it would be a lie. Nothing was all right. It would never be alright again.

When they opened the door to the hut, she and Reid were reminded that Rachel was gathering herbs with the other healers. Her mother had warned them that she might be out until late in the night or even early the next morning. They had no idea when she would be back but they couldn't wait. Brier and Reid headed for the elders' hut.

They were so tired and distracted that neither considered how late it was and that the elders would be in their homes sleeping. By the time they arrived in the little supply hut and found it empty, they didn't have the energy or willpower to search any further for help.

Instead, they found a stray blanket and curled up against the wall, trying to warm themselves. Brier didn't think of her dislike of Reid at that moment. Reid did not think of how poorly Brier had treated him.

They sat with each other, wrapped in the blanket, shaking from the cold and everything that had happened. Reid started praying and Brier listened to his words. He sounded unsure as he murmured requests for peace and comfort for themselves and the other outcasts. The words sounded rehearsed as if he was repeating something someone else had told him. Reid didn't appear to take any comfort from the prayers but Brier listened attentively.

Before long, the words faded away and soon after that, they were both fast asleep.

The next morning one of the elders, Bess, came to the supply hut. She found the two teenagers sleeping in the corner and roused them from their slumber. It took a moment for Brier and Reid to remember the events of the night before but once they did, Brier managed to give a tearful explanation.

Bess rushed to gather the other elders for a meeting. Brier and Reid waited silently for their return. The only thought on Brier's mind was of how she would tell her mother the news. She thought of Flint who would have no mother or father to mourn with. Warren's sword still laid at her side and Brier's finger idly traced over it.

For most of the meeting with the elders, Brier was in a daze. Reid did all of the talking while she stood in the corner trying to hold in her tears. They wanted to know everything and Reid somehow managed to explain it all. When the meeting was over, they were dismissed. There was only one place to go and they both dreaded what they must do when they arrived.

They walked through the camp at a slow pace. Brier's eyes fought to stay open and her shoulders were weighed with exhaustion and grief. The day had just begun. The sky was grey reflecting their moods and they both walked sluggishly forward. When the camp awoke, they would be met with the news that six of their elders were dead.

When they finally arrived at the hut, Brier and Reid braced themselves to tell Rachel the news.

It went worse than expected.

Brier's mother was torn apart. She sunk to the floor with shaking sobs that rattled her entire body. Brier knew that her parents had been deeply in love. A kind of love Brier could scarcely comprehend at her age. She still found boys annoying and a waste of time but her parents' love made her feel happy and warm. That warmth was lost in an instant.

Brier could tell that Reid was uncomfortable. This wasn't his real family; they had been dead for a long time now. He stood off to the side, not sure what to do but Brier knew at that moment that he felt the loss just as keenly.

A few hours later, as Brier tried to preserve a small part of her mother's shattered heart, she heard Reid outside. She heard the sound of choking sobs and a single scream equal parts frustrated and heartbroken that shattered the silence of the morning and made her blood run cold.

CHAPTER 22

Later that day the bodies were retrieved.

There were cries from the families of the victims as the motionless figures were carried into the camp on stretchers. The grief was palpable in the air. Brier's chest ached and her eyes burned. She almost hadn't shown up. She dreaded seeing the bodies again. She dreaded seeing the marks of the wolf.

The short and restless nap in the elders' tent was the only sleep she had gotten. She had tried to rest when she and Reid returned to their hut but every time she closed her eyes, the memories of the attack resurfaced. She fought between her exhaustion and the fear of seeing the wolf again.

Then there was the worry over her mother. Rachel was nearly unresponsive after hearing the news about Leif. She had refused to eat or drink. The only thing she would do was stare blankly into the distance.

Brier and Reid hadn't known what to do so they called for Bess the healer. Bess's diagnosis had not eased their worry. She said that Rachel's reaction was due to grief. Nothing could be done. They could only wait and hope that she would overcome the shock and despair and return to her old self. Rachel had always been so strong so it was all the more difficult to see her like this. Rachel had suffered much in her life and Leif's death was simply the final thread that snapped her composure.

Brier hadn't wanted to leave her mother alone in her current state. Reid had elected to stay with Rachel while Brier came to see the bodies buried.

The only reason she came was for Flint. After all, Leif's body had never been found. The men told her that they had searched as far into the forest as they dared while a wolf was on the loose. The only signs left were blood and cloth torn from his clothes. The body was lost for good. They marked a burial for him anyway.

Brier had feared that the bodies would be gone, taken away by wild animals. She was almost grateful to see the still forms. She wasn't sure whether to feel sad or relieved that only five stretchers were brought back. As much as she would have liked a chance to say goodbye to her father, she wasn't sure she could bear seeing him in such a lifeless state.

She held Flint's shaking hand as the stretchers were carried in. He squeezed her fingers so hard she lost feeling in them. In the end, one of the elders had broken the news to Flint, saving Brier from even more heartache. She hadn't been able to bring herself to see him until the burial. Flint managed to maintain his composure until the bodies of his parents were brought close enough that he could see the wolf's handiwork. Flint let out a massive sob when he saw his father's face and if it hadn't been for Brier supporting him, he would have sunk to his knees. Brier closed her eyes. She couldn't handle seeing Warren's face again.

The burial was a quiet one and Brier spent the majority of it trying to keep Flint upright. She didn't want to release any tears alongside him. She didn't have the right.

If it hadn't been for her indecision, she could have warned the elders what was coming and none of this would have happened.

She hadn't told Flint anything yet. She was afraid he would hate her when he found out how cowardly she had been.

After the bodies were buried, Brier led Flint back to her hut to fix him some tea. She didn't want to leave him alone after everything that had happened. As soon as they entered, Flint crumbled into a chair and buried his face in his hands. Brier peeked past the curtain of her mother's room and saw that she was sleeping. Reid was sitting on a chair beside her. The chairs were a new addition to the huts. Everyone had started to think their lives here would go on forever. How wrong they had been.

Reid looked up at Brier and she noticed the dark circles under his eyes. He stood and followed her into the main room. When he noticed Flint, sitting hunched at the table, Reid left to get more firewood. Brier didn't see a reason to draw attention to the logs already stacked high in the corner of the hut.

Brier returned to Flint with two hot cups of tea and settled into a chair next to him. She rested a hand on his knee and he looked up at her. She had to hold back her tears when she saw the hopeless expression on his face. Brier reached forward to embrace him. Flint laid his head on her shoulder and cried into her tunic. His sobs were anguished and heartbroken. Each new sound felt like an arrow piercing through Brier's chest.

Flint had always been the happy one, even after

being exiled. He had always been the first to offer a smile or try to cheer someone up.

Now it felt like the Flint she knew was gone. Eventually, the tears slowed then passed and Flint managed to pull himself together.

"Sorry," he muttered.

Brier tilted her head, "Why?"

"I… I'm being inconsiderate. You lost someone too and here I am acting like I'm the only one who's in pain."

Brier looked at her hands, the hands that had been unable to release the arrow, the hands that had been covered with the blood of her mistakes.

"I didn't even get to bury him," she murmured. Flint wrapped his arms around her, letting her lean on him now. Brier finally let the tears fall.

"I just let it happen, I couldn't even stop it."

"It's not your fault," Flint murmured in between his sobs.

Brier nodded against him but she knew that it was a lie. It was her fault, all of it was.

They cried together for a long time before breaking apart. Flint reached for his tea, hands shaking.

"I'm sorry you had to watch it," he said slowly.

Brier stared into the cup in her hands watching the tea slosh around in little greenish waves. Images of the wolf flashed in her mind, the wolf and the bodies. She could feel Flint watching her carefully.

"I'll manage," she said, "It'll take time, but we all will."

Suddenly she remembered the sword. She stood up so fast that a few drops of tea spilled over the rim of her cup. Flint looked at her like she'd lost her mind.

"What're you…"

Brier was already racing off to where she'd left the sword. She found the blood-covered scabbard and wondered for a moment how Flint would react. She grabbed it anyway. It belonged to him.

If she had been given the opportunity to retrieve her father's bow or knife, she would have taken it.

She walked back to her friend and held the weapon out to him. Flint sat up quickly, setting his tea aside. Tears started to gather in his eyes. Maybe it had been a mistake to show this to him. Perhaps she should have waited and given it to him later, instead of immediately after the burial.

Flint reached for the scabbard then paused. He stretched his fingers like he wanted to grab it but couldn't. Brier waited until he finally ventured to curl his fingers around it. He held it in his hands and Brier resumed her seat across from him.

"Where? How?" Flint asked, running his fingers along the leather scabbard.

"I pulled it from the…from the body," Brier said, her voice cracking on the last word.

Flint held the sword close like a lifeline and tears streamed down his face. He took a few deep breaths to calm himself. Brier wondered if he was mad. Maybe she shouldn't have retrieved the sword at all. Maybe Flint would have rather had it buried with his father. He pulled the blade a little from the scabbard and looked at his reflection in the metal. Despite everything that had happened the sword still gleamed brightly.

Brier watched as Flint's reflection morphed from sadness to resolution to acceptance. He swallowed hard then sheathed the sword and stood up.

He removed his scabbard from his waist and tied his

fathers onto his belt.
Brier wondered how such a little action could cause so much change. Flint looked like a different person. He stood taller, his eyes were harder, and his face was determined. He looked like his father.
"Thank you," Flint said as he sat back down and reached for Brier's hand, "Thank you, Brier."

CHAPTER 23

Reid couldn't take it anymore.

Every second he spent in that hut he was assaulted by memories. He had become too comfortable, too complacent. It had started to feel too much like home. Now he regretted thinking that he could ever have a normal life.

He should have known better. After all, this wasn't the first time this had happened to him. He had started to be at ease a few months after his mother's death. He had grown accustomed to the quiet life shared with his father, then that too had been taken from him. He knew better than most how easily something as simple as happiness could be pulled out from beneath your feet.

Despite knowing what might happen, he let himself relax. He let down his guard. He felt at peace. He would never forget his father and mother and there would never be a day that went by where he didn't wish things could go back to the way they had been. But Leif and Rachel had treated him like family and Reid had started to think of them in the same way.

Just like before, the ones he loved had been torn away.

Leif had taken Reid in when he had nowhere to go. He had continued to train him as a forester when his father could not. He had talked to him and comforted him and been there for him after his whole world had fallen apart. He made Reid feel at ease. Maybe it was the prayers that Leif said over them every night.

Reid's father had prayed a lot too but not as much as Leif. Reid admired Leif's relationship with God. It seemed so personal and trusting.

He didn't just pray, he talked to God. It seemed natural for him and Reid strived to have the same attitude. Maybe Leif's behavior put him too at ease. He almost forgot that tragedy could strike at any moment. And strike it did. Reid had begun to see Leif as more than a mentor. Now Leif was gone, dragged away by the wolf. His body lost somewhere in the dense forest.

Even Rachel, who had welcomed Reid and treated him like her own child, was gone now. She was still there physically, but mentally she was somewhere far away. Her mental instability affected even her health. She was laid up in bed all day, pale and lifeless as she stared blankly ahead. It was disconcerting to see someone so strong reduced to such a pitiable state. Brier claimed that her mother had suffered much in her life and this must be the occurrence that pushed her over the edge. Reid just wished she would go back to the way she had been. He had tried to talk to her on the day of the burial. Brier was gone and, overcome with thoughts and doubts Reid had needed someone to listen to him. It had all been so fresh, so painful.

Rachel had always listened before. She was so much like his own mother. His mother, Lyra, had been kind and gentle. She had rarely spoken of herself, and looking back Reid realized that he knew very little about her. He did not know the things she liked or the places she had been. She always listened when Reid or Rowan came to her with a problem.

Oftentimes, she could not offer a solution but the simple act of listening was comforting nonetheless. Looking back, Reid wished he had listened to her.

Reid didn't talk to Rachel often. There was an invisible boundary between them, one he was certain he created.

He accepted Leif as a mentor because that was what his father had wanted but the only role Rachel could fill, Reid was not ready to replace. Reid did not want another maternal figure. He still grieved his mother. If he accepted Rachel, it felt like he would be harming the memory of everything his mother had done for him. So, he hadn't approached Rachel. However, her steady presence and patience towards him were appreciated more than she could ever know.

With Brier gone and the events from the previous night pounding away at every fiber of his being, he had gone to Rachel. Whether it was out of desperation to talk to someone or just the need to be near a comforting presence, he finally approached her. She did not respond.

It was like she was no longer the same person. Rachel had waited for him, letting him take the time he needed to approach her. Yet, when Reid had finally worked up the courage or perhaps the desperation, she was changed. The woman before him was not the same; she was only a lifeless shell.

Reid couldn't bear to be around her any longer. Every moment he was in the hut sitting at her bedside he relived a similar, unbearable situation from not so long ago. His mother Lyra's illness had come on slowly.

There had been times when it was thought she would recover even though she had been mostly confined to her bed. Reid had sat by her bedside when she was sick.

Lyra would talk to him on the good days but on the days when she was especially weak, there would be silence like there was now.

The sadness of seeing her in such a weak state had deeply wounded Reid's young mind but worse yet was the agony of waiting. There would be times of hope when Reid and his father expected her to recover, only for that feeling to be snatched away. Reid had spent many hours waiting and praying for his mother to be healed and watching as her condition continued to deteriorate. He recognized the signs of a hopeless case when he saw it.

He hated to sit by and do nothing but he knew there was nothing he could do. If he hadn't missed when he threw his knife, then Leif would still be here and Rachel wouldn't be so distraught. Reid angrily swept his hand across his eyes. There was no use crying. He had learned that lesson long ago.

Tears were useless, they didn't change anything. When his mother died, he had cried for weeks even though he knew it wouldn't bring her back. He had done the same for his father, crying himself to sleep at night. He learned something then. No one liked to see you cry. They might pretend to care and be concerned but the only thing they really cared about was silencing you.

After the exile, everyone had been miserable. They hadn't wanted another crying child.

They didn't understand the pain Reid felt, only the unpleasant consequence. He was a burden to Leif and

Rachel, and Brier detested his presence. He didn't have control over many things in his life but there was one thing he could, for the most part, control, his outward emotions.

There were still days when the pain was overwhelming and Reid was swept away by the loneliness and hopelessness but he found there were better outlets than tears.

He built walls around himself to keep his emotions in check and he gained some semblance of control. He stayed away from the other children and closed himself off from the curious adults. He didn't mind if they all thought him strange or crazy.

He threw himself into his training as a distraction and he managed all right. Until now that is. Now his emotions were stirring dangerously and Reid feared he couldn't control them much longer. Treacherous thoughts filled his head, distracting him. Thoughts he had hidden away started to resurface.

Despite the early hour, Rachel was asleep. Brier wasn't home and it was his job to stay at Rachel's side, watching over her. Reid stared blankly ahead finding it painful to look at Rachel. He couldn't take it any longer. He stood up, reaching for his bow and quiver. He slung the weapon over his shoulder, fastened his cloak around his neck, and made sure his knife was safely secured in the sheath at his belt.

He might have failed to save Leif and he might not be able to help Rachel but there was one thing he could do. He could kill that wolf and make it pay for what it had taken from him, from everyone.

Reid glanced behind him, making sure Rachel was still asleep. She looked peaceful with her eyes closed.

The furrow between her brows disappeared. It was a rare occurrence for her to be at peace. He shouldn't leave her, he knew that, but he also knew that in her current state she wouldn't be going anywhere.

It did no good to sit around watching her all day. Reid opened the door to the hut and stepped outside. Brier would be furious if she found out that he left Rachel alone. But he couldn't sit still and watch her fade any longer. He couldn't sit around while his thoughts haunted him.

Reid made for the forest. He followed the same trail he had taken several days ago when he had followed Leif. It was funny, how Brier had the same idea. Maybe their minds weren't as different as he had once believed. Neither of them wanted Leif to leave and neither of them were willing to let him go without them. Reid hadn't even realized Brier was ahead of him until she stepped on that twig. It was a careless move and it had given her away. However, it was the only mistake she made in hours. He still wasn't sure how he hadn't noticed her sooner. They had both been so focused on the group ahead that they hadn't been aware of each other's presence.

As Reid walked the path again, he went at a slower pace. There was no need to hurry, he didn't have to keep up with the elders this time. There was a long distance to cover and Reid would conserve his energy the best he could. Besides, he wasn't eager to return to the spot where Leif had been dragged away. However, he was determined to put an end to the wolf.

He didn't consider what he would do if he found Leif's body. He didn't want to imagine what the wolf might have done to it. The only goal in his mind was to put an arrow through that creature's heart and end it. He wouldn't let it hurt anyone else. He didn't think about what would happen if he failed, he wouldn't fail, not again.

Without realizing he was doing it, Reid picked up his pace until he was jogging, then running. His mind was empty of all thought except keeping himself moving. It was a welcome respite from the darkness that usually plagued him.

At the pace he was making, it didn't take long for him to get far away from the camp. When he realized the distance he had covered, Reid slowed. He grew vigilant now, listening for any noises and looking for any signs of the wolf. He kept his bow in hand with an arrow on the string, ready to fire at a second's notice. He would not be caught off guard again. This time he wouldn't miss. Having the bow in hand made traversing the sometimes-rough terrain all the more difficult but Reid was not willing to sacrifice safety for speed.

A strong breeze blew through the trees and he flinched, mistaking the sound of the wind for a wolf's howl. He looked carefully at every shadow, thinking he saw eyes staring at him from the darkness. At one point, a squirrel scampered across the trail in front of him and Reid fired his arrow on instinct. The squirrel managed to evade the arrow and quickly disappeared into the foliage. Reid laid a new arrow to his bowstring, deciding to leave the other behind; he didn't want to venture into the thick undergrowth in search of it.

He forced himself to take several deep breaths. It would be no good if he found the wolf and was too nervous to fire an arrow straight. The last thing the camp needed was another casualty and Reid hadn't told anyone where he was going. It would take days, maybe weeks for anyone to track his body down if something happened. That is if anyone went looking for him at all.

Reid spent hours walking the path. There was no one to follow this time but Reid knew the direction he needed to go. There was no sign of the wolf. It was as if it had never existed at all. It was strange. Usually, a predator would stay in the area of a kill for some time after.

Then again, nothing about that wolf had been normal. It had killed the elders with quick decisive moves so fast there was no chance of stopping it. The attacks had been brutal, efficient, and calculated. The wolf hadn't even been affected by the knife cutting its eye. A strike like that should have incapacitated the creature long enough for the elders to get their bearings and fight back. Yet the wolf had tilted its head to the side and continued its attack. It hadn't stayed to celebrate its victory either. Once the elders were dead, the wolf hadn't touched them again.

"The strange thing is," Brier had told him after the burial, "covering them with the leaves must have been enough. I thought for sure the wolf or some other wild animal would come back to scavenge but other than the killing strikes, the bodies were untouched."

As much as Reid didn't want to dwell on the sickening thought, the wolf should have returned. It's what a predator would have done. They killed to eat.

There was something strange about the creature. It seemed to possess human-like intelligence. Reid couldn't quite shake the memory of the gleam in its eyes. It was a foolish idea but Reid couldn't help being unnerved by the wolf's strange behavior.

Needless to say, he kept on constant guard.

Finally, he reached the place where the wolf had attacked. He stayed in the bushes, unable to bring himself to step into the clearing.

He didn't want to see the bloodstains on the grass that marked the wolf's handiwork. If the wolf was in the area, this was as good a place as any to stop and have a look around. He had made good time. Being alone and not having to stay hidden or take breaks, he had easily bested the time it had taken the elders to get this far.

Now that he had arrived, Reid wasn't sure what to do. He hadn't anticipated that the wolf might not be waiting there for him. He stood with his bow at the ready and waited. Eventually, when it became obvious that the creature wasn't going to jump out of the bushes and attack, Reid started to wander around.

He walked the perimeter of the clearing. Nothing. No sounds, no tracks, no sign at all of a predator.

Reid spent what felt like hours watching, waiting, and searching for the wolf. The elusive creature was nowhere to be found. He started to grow frustrated. None of this made any sense. The wolf should be here. It should have stayed after its attack to continue hunting. He gripped his bow tighter and continued his fruitless search.

"Come out and fight me already!" Reid yelled when the wolf didn't show.

He breathed heavily, his heart racing, and his hands shaking in anger and anticipation. The wolf didn't listen. Reid sat down, exhausted and discouraged. He leaned against a tree and stared in the direction of the clearing.

He had failed, again. Why wouldn't the wolf come

out? Why couldn't he for once be allowed to do something right? All he wanted was to put an end to the creature that had caused so much pain. All he wanted was to kill the wolf.

As the sun started to sink below the horizon, Reid realized it was over. The wolf was gone. It wasn't coming back. He couldn't avenge Leif and the others. He was useless. He had failed to kill the wolf before and now he would never get a second chance.

Reid buried his face in his hands and took several deep breaths, trying to calm himself. He had to move on. There was nothing he could do. He knew that. So, why was this so hard?

It was growing dark. He should return to the camp but he didn't want to leave. Not until he finished what he had set out to do.

Reid sat there until the sun was barely shining in the sky before he finally stood, defeated. As he walked back to the camp, terrible words floated around his head, *useless, weak, foolish.* What had made him think he could make amends for what had happened? What made him think he was strong enough even if he did run into the wolf? Leif would surely tell him that the words were lies from the enemy but Leif was gone and it was Reid's fault.

When he arrived back at the camp, it was fully dark. Only a few stars lighted his way.

No doubt it was nearing midnight. Reid went straight to the little hut, dreading what awaited him inside.

There was a light shining, bleeding out beneath the door. He had hoped everyone would be asleep when he got back.

He didn't want a confrontation or questions. He hovered outside the door for a moment, staring at it and wondering if it would be better for everyone if he just slept in the forest that night. But it was getting cold and there was still a wolf on the prowl. Reid sighed and pushed open the door.

He found Brier sitting beside Rachel's bed. She was talking to her mother but as Reid entered, she quickly turned to face him. She was mad. He could see it in her eyes.

Brier had always been bad at hiding her emotions. Anger was not uncommon when Reid was around. He recognized the fury etched in her face and the pure, unbridled contempt in her eyes. This time it was stronger and more concentrated than he had ever seen and tinged with... hurt. Her hands were clenched at her sides, shaking. Her eyes were hard as stone. Her lips pulled into a snarl of disgust and her stance suggested that she was ready for a fight. Reid didn't want to talk; he didn't want to argue. He was tired; he just wanted to sleep.

He tried to walk past Brier, thinking that perhaps ignoring her would be the wisest course of action, but she stepped into his path.

"Where have you been!" She yelled.

Reid stood still, bracing himself for her verbal attack.

Reid's silence only angered her more.

"You were supposed to be here, watching mom," Brier continued in the same loud tone. "How could you leave her alone?"

Reid assumed that Brier did not want an answer. She didn't allow him time to give one.

"You're despicable! How could you, Reid? How could you possibly be so selfish after everything that's happened?"

Tears started to form in Brier's eyes and Reid started to panic. Why was she crying? Wasn't she supposed to be mad?

"Where did you go? Answer me, Reid!" she yelled through the tears.

Reid shuffled his feet. He didn't want to answer. He didn't want to tell her how he had failed. Brier was waiting for him to say something.

"I needed out," Reid said, "I couldn't sit here any longer."

Brier was silent. She looked surprised. The anger quickly returned, even stronger than before.

"You needed out?" she asked.

Reid nodded.

"You're so selfish," she continued, "Do you think this is any easier on me? This isn't your mother who's lying here sick. It wasn't your father who was dragged off by wolves who's... who's dead."

Reid took a step back in surprise. His own hands started to shake in anger. Brier continued.

"But why should you care? You've never cared about anything before. I doubt you're even capable of thinking of someone other than yourself. It's obvious that nothing that's happened here means anything to you."

Reid felt something inside him snap.

"You're right," he said and Brier looked surprised, "You're right, they aren't my parents. Leif wasn't my father. My father was already dead!"

Brier stared at him in horror, at last realizing the folly of her words.

"I do care, more than you could ever know!"

Reid threw his bow and quiver aside and pushed past her toward his curtained-off room. Brier stood frozen, staring after him.

Reid pulled the curtain closed behind him and sunk to his bed on the floor. He pulled the knife scabbard from his belt and kicked off his boots angrily sending them flying across the floor.

The anger slowly started to recede but something greater remained.

Brier was right.

Leif wasn't his father. Yet, he had put so much effort into seeking revenge for him. Why hadn't he done the same for his own father? Didn't Rowan deserve justice? Shouldn't the men who killed him pay for what they had done?

Reid could practically hear Leif's words in his head, "I know you're mad, Reid, you may resent the fact that your father was taken from you. But remember that vengeance is the Lord's. You must let go of your anger or it will eat you up from the inside. You have to trust that whoever is responsible for this will face judgment, if not in this life, then in the next. It's not up to you to deliver that punishment. Only God can do that."

The words seemed hollow and meaningless now that Leif was gone. Would he even still think that way after what had happened to him?

Besides, Reid knew of another Biblical concept, an eye for an eye and a tooth for a tooth. Surely, they all deserved recompense for what had been taken from them.

Reid lay awake for some time. He could hear Brier talking quietly to Rachel past the curtain and he could hear great emotion in her voice. She didn't sound angry anymore. Her words were tinged with hurt and sadness and betrayal.

Reid knew that his actions were wrong. He had betrayed her. They had just reached an understanding and he had ruined everything once again. He longed for his mother. She had always known what to do. Reid didn't know what to do.

He was starting to realize that Leif's presence had been an anchor tethering him to the present.

Now that Leif was gone, he once again lost himself to the past.

It had been some time since he thought about his father's death. Now Reid forced himself to relive every gory detail. He was lost and untethered. He didn't know what to do going forward but he was starting to form an idea.

CHAPTER 24

Brier sat beneath her favorite tree overlooking the camp. It was a peaceful morning, or was it nearing afternoon? The outcasts went about their days down below unaware that they were being watched. Even after all of the tragedies which had taken place, life went on.

She remembered the day she had sat in this same spot and witnessed the first attack on the camp. The yellow eyes of a wolf flashed into Brier's mind and she shivered. Luckily for the outcasts, her father had jumped in and stopped the wolf before it could cause too much damage. He had saved everyone that day. That was a long time ago. A lot had changed since then. The outcasts had survived three winters in exile. They had built homes, cleared land and planted crops, even buried their dead.

Yes, a lot had changed since her father's death. Things had been…difficult. Last winter had been a hard one, not due to sickness or hunger or even bitter cold but because of the six deaths, which had preceded it.

With the eleven elders reduced to a meager five, the camp was struggling. They mourned the loss of their leaders, their loved ones, and their protectors. Brier mourned the loss of her father. For as long as she could remember, he had always been there for her. He had protected her, cared for her, and comforted her.

Now he was gone and she was left to fend for herself.

And then there was the responsibility of looking after her mother. Reid couldn't be trusted, he had more than proved that.

Brier sighed and dragged a hand through her hair in frustration. The simple gesture triggered a series of memories. Her father had always run his hand through his hair when he was upset or anxious. Brier let her hand fall back to her lap, wishing every small action wouldn't remind her of him. It was difficult enough carrying on without the constant bombardment of unhelpful memories.

Brier was motionless beneath the tree. She had long believed the hill hosting this great oak boasted the best view of the clearing. She could see the children running carefree, giving chase to the stubborn old goat that had made itself right at home in the forest. She could see the adults and older children at work cutting firewood and preparing venison to be smoked. Her mind cataloged each of these details but did not focus on them. This was how she spent many of her afternoons these days.

The few moments when she was able to get away from the bustle of the camp and the constant chore of watching over her mother, she spent training, or here, on this hill, staring blankly ahead. It was easier not to do anything, letting her mind be quiet. She tried to pray sometimes, but it was difficult to express her feelings in words. Everything seemed so hopeless.

Life had gone on and the outcasts kept on living but nothing was the same. There were times when Brier was still afraid to close her eyes, for fear of what lay waiting in the dark.

However, the nightmares hardly ceased even when she opened her eyes. They were only replaced with different ones.

Instead of seeing her father dragged off, she saw her mother fading before her very eyes.

Rachel's despondency had only worsened and the winter had weakened her physical state. Mentally she was already lost. The healers all said the same thing. Nothing could be done.

Everything in Brier's life was falling to pieces around her. Escaping to this refuge to process her thoughts was the only way she kept going.

It was like a great fog was hanging over her, making everything blurred and unreal. How could it be real? It was too unfair.

If only things could go back to the way they had been.

The sound of a footstep in the grass caused Brier to turn. She hadn't expected anyone to find her here. Not many knew about this spot and its significance to her. Fewer still would make the effort of trekking up the steep and treacherous hill. The difficult terrain served to ward off anyone who might bother her, another aspect of the hill that she appreciated. These footsteps belonged to a welcome visitor.

Flint stood taking in the view. A breeze ruffled his hair. It was getting long and in need of a cut. His mother had always cut it for him. Brier watched him blankly. This wasn't the first time he had joined her on the hill. The routine was embedded in each of them and there were certain steps that they followed at each meeting.

Flint would speak first. He always spoke first.

He sat beside her, leaning back and propping himself up with his hands.

They had drawn strength from each other after the attack.

Flint was a strong, steady force in Brier's otherwise chaotic life and when Flint felt lonely, Brier was there for him as a friend and an ally.

Eventually, she shared her secret spot with him. Meeting on the hill was practically a tradition now. Sometimes they wouldn't talk at all, other times they would share all their troubles and fears. It was their way of checking up on each other.

It was the only time they saw each other anymore. They had both thrown themselves into their training, spending hours honing their abilities. The guilt of not taking action haunted Brier and Flint was determined that he would be ready and present if something like the wolf attack happened again. With Rachel's failing health, the rest of Brier's time was spent at her mother's bedside.

It was impossible to say how Reid was processing things. When he wasn't taking his turn watching over Rachel, they saw little of each other and they never talked. Reid would disappear, not to be seen until he relieved her in the evening. When Brier took the evening shifts, she would hear him coming into the hut late at night.

She never bothered to ask him where he had been. It was obvious he wanted to be left alone. As for the stunt he had pulled a few months ago, leaving Rachel alone, Brier still hadn't forgiven him. She had believed that they could finally be on good terms. She had put aside any ill feelings towards him the night of the attack.

They were supposed to be in things together after that point. Brier thought she could handle whatever came as long as she wasn't alone. Then Reid had left. He had deserted her in the time of her greatest need.

She couldn't even look at him after that. She didn't want to see any more of Reid than necessary.

It wasn't fair the way he cut himself off from everyone. He didn't have the right. They were all struggling in their own ways. That didn't give him an excuse to disappear.

Brier was overwhelmed and stressed and Reid was no help. His disappearance the day he was supposed to be watching her mother was the worst kind of betrayal. There was no point in trying to stop him from wandering off though. He didn't care about helping her. He didn't care about anything. She shouldn't have been surprised. This wasn't his family.

But she *had* been surprised. After what they had been through, watching the wolf attack together, she had started to think that despite everything, despite all that had happened, she could at least count on Reid. She thought he understood what she was experiencing and would be there for her. Apparently, she was wrong.

Sometimes Brier wondered if the only reason she was able to keep going was her daily conversation with Flint. After his breakdown on the day of the burial, Flint stayed strong. He still had bad days when he would meet Brier under the tree with red, swollen eyes and sit in silence.

On the other occasions, he always did his best to cheer her up. It was like when they were younger, right after the exile.

Flint would tell her ridiculous jokes to make her laugh and they would talk about the good times, enjoying each other's company. Months after the failed quest and the death of the elders, things were finally starting to get better.

Flint shifted, informing Brier that today was a day for talking. She glanced over and saw him carefully contemplating his words.

It must be a serious topic. She leaned forward, inviting him to speak.

"The elders want to talk to you," Flint finally said.

The elders had mostly left her and Reid alone after the incident with the wolf. Most people didn't want to bother the kids who had witnessed the attack. It was an uncomfortable topic and one that didn't encourage casual conversation. Brier suspected that many of the outcasts blamed her and Reid for not taking action. If they were there, why hadn't they done anything to stop the attack? They might be young but they were trained as foresters. No one could blame Brier more than she already blamed herself.

"Why would they want to talk to me?" Brier asked.

"Well, not just you actually," Flint rubbed his neck, "They want to talk to all the kids who lost someone."

Brier groaned. So that's what this was about. Ever since the failed quest, the elders had discussed sending another group to Mac'tire. They had argued about the issue for months.

Some still insisted that there was no future for the outcasts. If the duke hadn't believed them before then surely, he wouldn't now. Some pointed out that it was too dangerous to try another expedition.

Others claimed that they *must* return and *make*

the duke understand that they were innocent. Brier tended to side with those who wanted to avoid Mac'tire altogether.

Lately, there had been rumors that the children of the elders who were killed would be sent.

Most of the children who had lost their parents could hardly be called that anymore. They were on the verge of adulthood and would be able to handle themselves under the proper leadership.

They were young and would make quicker time back to Mac'tire with less difficulty. They were also expendable. While their help would be missed around the camp, they could carry on without them. The remaining elders needed to stay behind to lead and most of the other adults had families to take care of. The children of the elders had already lost their families. Since their parents had been the ones exiled, they might stand a better chance of entering Mac'tire without repercussions and speaking with the duke. With the help of the letter, some believed their chances of being accepted back were certain.

Brier thought it was a horrible idea. The wolf had been like an omen, warning them not to return. It was too dangerous, too ill-planned. She didn't care what the elders were hiding away that might prove them innocent; it would do no good if they couldn't even reach the castle.

Even with Brier's distaste for the situation, she had noticed the elders meeting more often and she had heard the rumors that they were coming close to a decision. She hadn't expected one this soon though.

Flint must have seen the look of disappointment and annoyance on her face because there was no humor or teasing in his voice when he spoke, "I know you don't want to leave the camp, but this is important. If you can't do it for the other outcasts, then do it for me."

Brier sighed, not able to meet his eyes, "Look, Flint, I know this means a lot to you but…"

Flint's eyes pleaded with her. This journey might mean more to him than anyone. They both knew that. He still held onto the hope that the outcasts would return to Mac'tire.

He would do almost anything to see the dream that his parents had died for become a reality and to make his dream of becoming a knight like his father come true. He hadn't talked much about that dream lately. Brier knew that he still believed in it. The hours he had dedicated to practicing and bettering his abilities were proof enough of that.

The intensity in Flint's amber eyes was shocking and Brier was taken aback by it. She had never seen such fire in him. When he spoke, his voice was unwavering, "This isn't just about being a knight, Brier. This is about saving everyone. We can't stay here any longer. Too many people have died. My father believed that it was God's will for us to return and I believe that too. If we return to Mac'tire, we can make the duke listen to us."

Brier huffed in annoyance, "You really believe that? I hoped you wouldn't fall for that nonsense that the elders are telling everyone."

"*Brier*," There was a note of warning in Flint's voice.

This wouldn't be the first time they had this argument. There were times when Brier would take Flint's warning and not push the subject any further. This was not one of those times.

"Do you think that if we return to Mac'tire it will

fix everything? What a lie that is! Our parents are gone, Flint. Gone! Whose fault is that? They were innocent. The duke didn't listen to them though. He sent them into the forest to die. He won't believe us; he wouldn't even listen to our parents who served him for years."

She took a deep breath, "Even if he does hear us out, even if we were allowed back, it wouldn't fix anything. It wouldn't bring our parents back! Nothing will."

"You don't know that; he might let us back. We have the letter; it will explain everything. I believe that God will open the duke's eyes and protect us on the journey. And I know our parents are gone. God, I know," Flint's voice cracked and he looked away. Brier felt a pang of regret. She hadn't meant to remind him of what he had lost. She sat awkwardly while he composed himself. After a moment, he let out a shaky sigh and faced her again, "Even if it won't bring our parents back, there are still other people we can save. Please, Brier, just go to the meeting."

Brier didn't respond right away. She didn't want to leave the forest and she certainly didn't want to return to Mac'tire. She enjoyed the freedom she had now. She had more of a future here than she ever would if she returned.

Girls didn't get to fight as knights or catch poachers as foresters. Flint might get to live his dream if he returned but Brier would only be stuck in a nightmare.

She couldn't find it in herself to give up this life, not even for Flint.

Besides, if they somehow got accepted back, Flint's dream was still improbable. No one would trust an outcast, much less fight beside one. And she couldn't live under the duke's rule. Not after everything he had done.

"Whatever the elders want to discuss, they can do it without me," Brier finally said.

She could feel Flint's disappointed gaze brush against her.

"I can't make you do it and I won't beg. But if you would only hear them out. Just because you come to this meeting, doesn't mean you have to go on the journey. At least don't make me go alone."

Brier sighed.

She could argue further, make Flint understand that the last thing she wanted to do was step foot into the elders' hut but there was no point. It would only cause him to be angry with her and she didn't have the energy to fight anymore.

Reluctantly Brier stood and brushed the grass from her legs. As much as she didn't want to do this, as much as she detested the mere thought of it, she knew how much this meant to Flint. She could at least go to the meeting. He would do the same for her.

"Thank you, Brier," Flint said softly as she started the trek downhill. He ran a few strides to catch up with her then they settled into a casual walk. Brier had to take two steps to match every one of Flint's long strides. He was a good six inches taller than her.

Once they had descended the hill, the breeze died down and the heat from the sun became increasingly apparent. As they made their way to the elders' hut, Brier felt a growing sense of dread.

She didn't want to hear them out, she didn't want to listen to their crazed idea that the duke would listen to them. She considered for a moment turning back and letting Flint go on his own. When she turned to tell him that she couldn't do this and saw the hopeful look on his face, she couldn't bring herself to speak.

They walked in silence until the hut was in sight. The building was still under construction even after years of exile. Multi-tasking as a supply hut, it had never been deemed a priority to finish.

With the arguments over whether the outcasts would return to Mac'tire, no one wanted to put the effort into finishing a supply hut if they would only be abandoning it later.

The walls had been built up and there were beams outlining the roof but the roof itself was still a tarp and a real door had yet to replace the canvas hanging in the empty doorframe.

Brier was trying to decide whether or not to enter when Flint chose for her and pulled back the canvas tarp. He gestured for her to go before him. Brier sent a subtle glare his way for dragging her into this. She peered inside the hut and noticed that, instead of all of the elders gathered as she had anticipated, there was only David. Seeing her standing uncertainly in the doorway, he gestured for her to come in.

It took a moment for her eyes to adjust to the darkness of the room. The table in the center of the hut was littered with papers and maps.

Crates were piled high throughout the space. The room was filled with the young adults of the camp.

It wasn't just those who had lost family to the wolf. There were several boys who had trained as blacksmiths under the elder Henry and some girls and boys who lost parents to the illness which had swept through the camp the first winter. There was one thing they all had in common, they had all lost someone they cared about because of the exile.

Brier knew them all by sight and name but she hardly knew anything about them. What were they good at? What did they enjoy? What had their lives been like before the exile? After the first wolf attack, Brier hadn't had much time to socialize with those her age.

She had been busy training, only making time for Flint and forced to spend time with Reid. It had been a long while since she spared a thought for one of the other young adults.

The only people she moderately knew were the children of Gregory, James, and Henry. Gregory had three children, all boys. They had objected to her playing with the boys after the exile. They were all tall with dark hair like their father and tan skin from long days in the sun. They had never been overly friendly to Brier, or Reid for that matter. Brier had made it her purpose to avoid them whenever possible.

Henry had one child, a shy girl by the name of Mira. Mira often helped her father in the smithery and sometimes made arrowheads for Brier, Reid, and in the past Leif.

Other than that, Brier didn't know a lot about her, though the four boys who had apprenticed under Henry tended to follow her around camp with dreamy looks in their eyes. She was admittedly pretty. James had two children, a boy, and a girl, though they could hardly be seen as siblings by anyone who didn't know better.

Gregory's nieces and nephews were also present. Gregory's brother had been exiled after the riot and with how closely-knit the family was, it was no surprise that they would be here for the chance to honor their deceased uncle.

Needless to say, the hut was crowded.

Brier moved to stand in a corner. She wasn't keen to make conversation. She didn't want to be here in the first place. Flint followed though Brier suspected he would rather stand in the center of the room. It was hot, a combination of warm weather and the number of bodies pressed into the small room.

Brier shuffled her feet, already uncomfortable. A low murmur of conversation swept around but it was quickly hushed when David cleared his throat.

Before anything could be said, the canvas opened once more and an unwelcome black-haired boy with a scar entered the room. Reid.

Why was *he* here? It wouldn't be the first time he had wandered off when he was supposed to be watching Rachel but Brier was still surprised. Why would he come here anyway? Shouldn't he be wandering aimlessly through the forest or something? How had he even found out about this meeting?

Reid glanced at her before moving to the opposite corner, wisely keeping his distance from her. He seemed to fade into the shadows and she had to appease her anger by glaring straight ahead instead of at him.

"Now that we're all here," David said, forcing Brier to focus on the matter at hand instead of her anger towards Reid, "We can begin. As you all know, my name is David. I'll be in charge of this meeting. I'm sure many of you have already guessed why you're here."

Nods and murmurs of confirmation answered David.

"The elders have decided to send a group of you to Mac'tire. Your job will be to convince the duke of your parents' innocence and make it possible for all of us to return."

As quiet conversation swept through the group, Brier better surveyed their faces. Everyone was young. The majority seemed to be the same age as her, maybe a few years older. They were in reality still children, the oldest of them barely crossing the threshold of adulthood.

They had grown up too fast and been faced with too many responsibilities. They were all old enough to understand the severity of their situation.

They had all lost someone because of the exile. Yet, they still wanted to return to Mac'tire. Brier couldn't understand that. The duke betrayed them and forced them into exile without cause. Brier had long ago accepted that they would never be able to return. Why was she the only one who seemed to comprehend that?

David looked at each of them, his eyes hesitating for a second when they passed over Brier.

His vision darted around the room, only pleased when he saw Reid hiding in the shadows. Brier tried to ignore the uneasy feeling that came with the look. She was starting to get used to it. The look of pity and distrust was often cast on her and Reid.

They had witnessed the wolf attack and done nothing to stop it. They might be young but they were trained as foresters. They should have done something. The elders had heard the story straight from their lips.

"The elders recognize the dangers of returning but we also recognize the necessity of it. Too many lives have been lost because of this exile. We've spent too long hidden away. We are innocent! We intend to prove it."

Silence. Plenty could be said but no one had the

courage. No doubt many of them wondered how their innocence could be proven or why the duke would suddenly accept them back.

Brier crossed her arms and leaned against the wall. It would be interesting to see David's answer to such questions. Hopefully, he had more solid evidence than a letter.

"Only a select few of you will be chosen for this journey," David continued, "Those who are chosen will face great challenges. First, you must make it to the castle. Several of the elders made a trip to a nearby village last night where they acquired five horses. The horses will shorten the length of the journey. Still, it will take five days to reach Mac'tire. Once you arrive, the real challenge will begin. You must convince the duke of your family's innocence."

"How?" one of Gregory's nephews asked.

"That's a discussion I will have with the five who are chosen," David explained.

Were the contents of the letter being kept a secret now? Perhaps all aspects of the journey were being kept quiet. They were all still hurting from the last failed quest.

The topic of returning to Mac'tire was sensitive and if the details of the letter were exposed to all of the outcasts there would likely be a hot debate about whether it was worth the risk of returning at all.

"Once you convince the duke of your innocence, you'll return to the camp and lead us back to Mac'tire. Keep in mind that the duke may not hear you out. He may have you punished for returning from your exile. This is a serious mission and you should all consider that very carefully. Now, any volunteers."

Everyone took an involuntary half-step back as David posed the question.

Under her breath, Brier was sending a silent plea to Flint. *Please don't volunteer. Please don't volunteer.*

Predictably, Flint was the first to step forward.

"I'll go, sir."

Brier wiped a hand down her face in annoyance. Of course, Flint would volunteer.

She wanted nothing more than to step forward, grab him by the arm and haul him out of the hut. This was ridiculous. It was dangerous and foolish, and Brier had no idea what to do about it. If Flint left, she would be all alone.

Seemingly motivated by Flint, several others stepped out from the crowd. There were timid declarations of "I'll go" and "I volunteer." Flint looked at Brier, his eyes pleading with her.

Brier crossed her arms and looked away. She wouldn't go; she couldn't. After everything that had happened, she absolutely was not going back to Mac'tire. There was no sufficient proof, no reason to return other than the small hope that things might go back to normal. Why couldn't everyone else accept that this was normal now? They could never go back, there was no point in trying.

Brier tried not to look at Flint's crestfallen face but the pained sadness in his eyes was hard to ignore. Flint had always been loyal to her.

She hated that she was even considering the idea. There was no way she could go. She didn't want to go. What did it matter if Flint left? She saw a wolf in her mind's eye stalking Flint through the forest. She closed her eyes, trying to rid the thought from her mind. Flint

could take care of himself. She knew he could. But still...
No! She had to think of her mother. Brier couldn't just leave her. Then again, sitting around wasn't doing her or her mother any good. Maybe if Brier showed that she was carrying on with life, then her mother would begin to recover from her grief. And Bess would be able to care for her mother while she was gone.

Brier couldn't leave. It was against everything she stood for.

Returning to Mac'tire would be like telling the duke that he won. She wouldn't be part of that. She wouldn't let the duke think that she wanted to be accepted back. She would rather live out all her days in the forest where she was free.

But leaving *would* be an excuse to get away from Reid.

Brier took a deep breath and stepped forward.

"I volunteer."

No sooner had she spoken, than she looked over and saw Reid's hand also raised. An overwhelming sense of disappointment flooded her. *So much for escaping from Reid*, she thought bitterly.

Brier opened her mouth to say that she had misspoken and no, she didn't want to go but the sheer joy and relief on Flint's face stopped her. She was glad he was happy, because if she had to go on this journey with Reid in tow, then Flint was going to have to put up with a lot of complaining.

More than Flint's happiness though, there was a small voice in her head that told her she had made the right decision.

David gave a proud smile, "Okay, volunteers please step forward, the rest of you are free to go."

There was a rustle of movement as the people who had not volunteered shuffled out of the room talking amongst themselves. Brier wished she were with them. She watched longingly as the canvas flap closed, leaving her behind.

When the volunteers continued to linger back, David gestured them forward, "Come closer, come closer."

Flint grabbed Brier's arm, dragging her to the center of the room with the other volunteers. She followed him, sad to leave the shadows and safety of her corner.

"First things first. I want each of your names and ages," David instructed them, "I've been asked to record each volunteer for future reference. Then I'll interview you separately to see if you're compatible for this journey."

One of the first volunteers stepped forward.

"My name is Echo," he announced, "I'm eighteen and the son of the elder James."

Brier recognized Echo instantly. He was not the most popular of the young people around camp. He had obtained a reputation for being a bit of a 'stick in the mud'.

His standing with the elders was good and if anyone was likely to be chosen it would be him. He had volunteered to do many different jobs after the exile and was eager to please. Brier had always thought he was bossy and tried to avoid him.

He always found a way to put an end to anything fun. When Brier was younger, she thought his name was strange. She had eventually learned that Echo wasn't his real name. She didn't know what his birth name was. He had gotten his nickname due to his constant following of orders from the elders, much to the annoyance of others.

David wrote Echo's name, age, and father's name on a piece of parchment and then waited for the next person to step forward.

Flint went next. Brier tried not to glare too hard. It was thanks to him she had gotten into this mess.

After Flint, Gregory's three boys stepped forward then a girl who had lost both her parents to the illness. Brier had never been close to them and she didn't pay much attention as they talked. Her mind started to drift. How was she going to get out of this?

Finally, Echo's sister, Erin, stepped forward. Erin was sixteen, Flint's age, and very pretty with long blonde hair and icy blue eyes. For months after the exile, Brier hadn't realized that Erin and Echo were related.

They didn't look alike. Erin was thin and fair while Echo was stockier with dark hair. Their only resemblance was in their light eyes.

Reid went next, stepping forward and muttering the least number of syllables required, "Reid, fifteen."

David waited a moment as if expecting him to say more. He wasn't well acquainted with Reid's oddities. Reid didn't even announce who his father was or that he had trained under Leif. Finally, David could wait no longer and turned to the next volunteer.

Brier waited as long as she could to speak, hoping the group would forget that she was there. She regretted her decision because she was forced to speak last, drawing even more attention to herself.

Flint nudged her in the side and Brier turned her nastiest glare on him. He had the nerve to smile.

Brier gave an almost inaudible groan and stepped

forward, "My name is Brier and I'm fifteen," she announced quickly. She didn't bother to tell them who her father was. They would already know about her. Everyone's eyes were on her, the girl who had witnessed the attack and done nothing. Brier wanted nothing more than to shrink into the shadows in the corner. Her skin was crawling from their stares.

"Now that everyone is accounted for," David broke the awkward silence that had enveloped the room, "time for interviews."

CHAPTER 25

Everyone shuffled outside and Brier was dragged along with them. The interviews would be private. Brier dreaded having to talk with David on her own. She didn't think she would be able to keep up the act of wanting to go on this journey. Echo had eagerly volunteered to take the first interview leaving the rest of the group to step outside to wait. Flint seemed hesitant to release her arm when they stepped out of the makeshift building, perhaps fearing that she would make a run for it. Brier had to admit she was tempted. It would be so easy to run away or even say she had changed her mind. She could still get out of this and never have to leave the forest but that wouldn't fix anything. Flint was still planning on leaving whether she went with him or not. If she didn't join him, he would face all of the dangers and challenges of the journey on his own. If only there was some way she could convince him not to go. Maybe if she put her foot down and refused to leave, he would change his mind. The resolute set to his face convinced her that she wouldn't be able to persuade him to stay. That scared her.

She remembered her father being dragged off and the sightless eyes of the elders. She couldn't let that happen to Flint. She couldn't let him go without her and face that danger alone. *Please God don't let Flint come to the same fate that the last group did.* Brier didn't think she could handle losing anyone else dear to her.

Without Flint to cheer her up and force her to remember the good things in life, she wasn't sure she could carry on.

Brier felt a hand grip hers. It was warm and calloused and reassuring.

"Thank you, Brier," Flint murmured, "You don't know how much this means to me."

She did know how much this meant to him. It was the only reason she hadn't run off. It was the only reason she was putting aside her feelings and standing here with him. This meant more than anything to Flint. He squeezed her hand one more time before releasing it. Brier sighed. If nothing else, she could at least go through with the interview.

In the meantime, she needed to distract herself. She turned her attention to Reid. He was standing away from the main group. As usual, he was awkward at the best of times when it came to social interactions. He emanated stay-away-from-me energy. His cold looks and hunched shoulders seemed to do the trick because no one bothered to approach him. Brier kept looking at him, her annoyance rising. Their eyes met across the crowd and anger flared in Brier's chest.

"Reid," she growled.

She started to push her way toward him, ignoring the looks she was getting from the other people gathered.

"Uh oh," Flint murmured, quickly following after her.

Reid waited for her, making no attempt to escape. Her anger grew. His constant silence was infuriating. It was like he was hiding something or maybe just ignoring her.

Then there was the fact that he had abandoned her when she needed him most. When things had gotten hard, she had hoped she could at least rely on him.

How wrong she had been. Things had been just fine without Reid. She wished they had stayed that way.

"Why are you here!" she yelled, coming to a stop in front of him.

Flint stood by her side uncomfortably.

Reid shrugged, "Same reason as you."

There it was again, Brier thought, *the same sort of vague, dismissive response that Reid so often used.*

"You disappear for hours at a time! No one *ever* knows where you go off to and now you just show up so you can go on this trip? What does it matter to you anyway?"

"I have my reasons," Reid looked away and mumbled, "I could ask the same of you."

"It's none of your business why I'm going!"

Reid raised an eyebrow and glanced at Flint but said nothing. Brier held back a snarl.

"You're supposed to be at the hut," She reminded him in a growl.

"I didn't leave her alone," Reid responded calmly, "Bess informed me of the meeting and offered to stay with her while I came here."

At least Rachel hadn't been left alone. Brier couldn't push aside her anger so easily though. Why? Why did Reid have to volunteer?

"You shouldn't be here," Brier took a step closer to

him, "You've never cared enough to do anything before. Why are you suddenly so interested in acting like a member of this camp?"

Reid met her glare head-on. "I told you, I have my reasons, reasons you don't need to know about."

Brier would have strangled him right then and there if Flint hadn't put a hand on her arm to stop her, "Brier," Flint warned.

His eyes flitted towards the others who had stopped their conversations to watch the argument. Brier took a deep breath to calm herself but just then she caught the look in Reid's eyes. It was the same look he gave her when they were practicing together and her arrow missed the target. It was a look that undeniably said, *is that the best you can do?* Brier curled her hands into fists. Flint might not let her fight Reid but that wouldn't stop her from winning this argument and hopefully stopping him from going on this journey. A small voice in her head told her to leave it be, to walk away right then and there but Brier ignored the voice and charged forward anyway.

"If you go on this trip, everyone will end up dead!"

Reid took a step back in shock but Brier wasn't finished.

"Everyone around you dies in the end. First your parents and now *mine*."

An angry tear trailed down her face. She wasn't sure how long she had been holding in those words but now that she had finally said them, she felt relieved. Reid flinched, a hurt look on his face, but said nothing. The people around them were staring unabashedly. Brier ignored them.

It was Reid's turn to let loose his anger, "You forget,

you were the one who couldn't take the shot. At least I tried to do something!"

Brier's vision went red as she lunged at Reid. Flint grabbed her by the arms, holding her back before she could reach him. Brier didn't care how many people were watching; she'd strangle Reid.

She fought against Flint's grasp but he held tight. Reid didn't even take a step back, only watched her with a bitter look.

Brier had almost broken free of Flint's hold when Echo poked his head through the canvas door of the hut. "Reid, your turn," he announced, then noticing the commotion, "What's going on?"

Reid walked past Brier giving her a sidelong glance, "Nothing," he murmured as he pushed past Echo and into the hut.

Flint waited a moment after Reid was gone before releasing Brier. She stumbled forward and turned her glare on her friend. The other volunteers went back to their conversations, Gregory's sons seeming upset that the argument hadn't turned into a full-fledged fight.

"You shouldn't have held me back. You know he deserves a fight."

Flint scoffed, "Trust me when I say you don't want to brawl with Reid. He throws a nasty punch."

Brier huffed.

"Not to say that you can't fend for yourself in a fight," Flint hastily added, "Just you shouldn't fight. Leif wouldn't want that."

Brier sighed, knowing he was right. That didn't mean she had to like it though. She would have enjoyed making Reid pay for his words.

"Sometimes I wonder how it is that I'm the redhead

when you have such a ready temper," Flint teased her.

"I know I'm not exactly docile when tested but Reid always seems to find a way to spark your anger."

Brier knew Flint was right but she wasn't about to admit that. Reid was in the wrong. He shouldn't be going, not when he had shown such an obvious lack of care before.

Flint looked like he wanted to say something but couldn't find the words. He opened and closed his mouth like some kind of fish.

Finally, Brier couldn't take it anymore, "If there's something you want to say, Flint, then just spit it out."

Flint rubbed the back of his neck, "I was just thinking... I know you and Reid don't exactly get along..."

Brier huffed, "That's an understatement."

Flint laughed softly, "Okay, I know you two *really* don't get along, but maybe if you both went on this trip it would be good for you."

Brier gave him a skeptical look.

Flint sighed, "I just think that you two should try to work things out and make amends."

"You forget, Flint. I've already tried that and Reid just turned around and stabbed me in the back all over again. Maybe I was petty before but now I'm justified in my anger. He deserted me and my mother when we needed him. It's not so easy to work that out."

They waited in silence. Brier could feel the eyes of the other volunteers on her. It made her skin feel prickly but she tried her best to ignore their attention. After all, it was her fault for arguing with Reid in front of such a large audience.

Flint shuffled his feet and glanced towards the hut.

His nerves were starting to annoy Brier.

What did he have to be nervous about? He was the one who had insisted to come to the meeting. Perhaps she should say something to put him at ease but she was still mad at him for dragging her into this.

After a few minutes, Reid reemerged from the hut and gestured to one of Gregory's sons who excitedly entered.

Brier was slightly shocked when Reid left immediately after his interview. She smiled; he must have been rejected.

"You think they've told him no, don't you?" Flint asked, noticing her smile.

Brier nodded.

"You know, I've never really understood the problem between you two. It seems like there's always been this animosity even before the elders were attacked."

"My *problem* is that Reid was always treated like he was better than me," Brier retorted, "My father was always so proud of him. I admit that maybe I took our rivalry too far back then. But now it's more than a rivalry. After everything fell apart all Reid did was hide and leave us to fend for ourselves."

Flint sighed, "I'm not saying what he did was right but people handle grief in different ways. I know there were times when all I wanted to do was hide."

"Why should Reid grieve? It wasn't his father that got killed. It's not his mother who's sick."

"Maybe not," Flint said softly, "But after already losing his parents, maybe Reid started to think of your parents as his family."

Brier huffed. She couldn't imagine that. If Reid thought that way, then he wouldn't have disappeared.

She would have been willing to put their differences aside after the wolf attack if only Reid had stayed around. She would have forgiven him and started over. Reid had made his choice when he left.

"Maybe he has a reason for wanting to go on this trip, just like I do," Flint suggested.

"Like what? I highly doubt he wants to be a knight."

"That's not the only reason I want to go. I want to finish what my parents started. Maybe Reid wants to do the same."

Brier crossed her arms, "Why are you taking his side anyway? Are you forgetting that time he broke your nose?"

Flint laughed, "I'm not taking his side. I just think that your hatred for him is eating away at you. I don't like seeing you upset, Brier. God tells us that we are supposed to forgive others as He forgives us. You should forgive Reid. I have."

Brier opened her mouth to argue further but before she had the chance to speak, Flint was called inside. He offered her a small, nervous smile before disappearing into the hut. Brier was left alone. She grimaced and tried to forget the conversation with Flint. She knew that she should forgive Reid but she couldn't. She had forgiven him once before and he had disappointed her again. She couldn't trust him and she couldn't forget what he had done.

She considered introducing herself to someone else and striking up a conversation to pass the time. It would take her mind off things and allow her to find out more about the others who had volunteered.

Looking around at all the people she hadn't talked to in months, she quickly dismissed the idea. What would she say anyway?

Why are you here? I was dragged unwillingly by Flint. Or better yet, Hi, remember me? I'm the girl you wouldn't let play with you several years ago because I couldn't play rough. I bet you wouldn't call me weak now.

It felt like hours before Flint returned with a huge smile lighting up his face. Brier's heart sank. It seemed that he had been accepted on the quest.

"I'm in," he said happily, confirming her fears, "Your turn Brier."

Brier swallowed past the lump in her throat. She should say something. Congratulate him or beg him to change his mind. But she couldn't find it in herself to say a thing to wipe that silly smile off his face.

Instead, with a sense of foreboding, she pushed open the canvas flap and with one last pleading look in Flint's direction, stepped inside. Everything felt like it was in slow motion. David looked up and smiled at her. The look was maybe a little forced. David had been greeting others all day and was no doubt tired of the constant smiling. Dust floated in the air illuminated by the small string of light that bled through the gap between tarp and wall. Brier breathed deeply, trying to compose herself.

"Hello," David greeted, "Mind if I ask you a few questions?"

He gestured for her to come closer and Brier, unable to form an excuse otherwise, was forced to approach him. She shifted her weight and readied herself for his first question.

"Relax, Brier, I won't ask anything too personal. This will only take a few minutes."

His words didn't have much effect. Brier was too

high-strung to relax and she wasn't worried about personal questions as much as how she was going to get out of this or if she even should.

"So, why is it that you want to go on this trip? What is your motivation?"

Brier couldn't make her mouth move to speak.

"Perhaps you wish to restore your father's name in honor of his sacrifice?" David suggested.

Brier looked away.

She didn't like it when people talked about her father's death. He had been popular among the outcasts and plenty of people missed him. However, it always seemed like they were mocking her when they told her how sorry they were.

If it hadn't been for the ridiculous idea of returning to Mac'tire, her father would still be here. Brier hadn't wanted him to go on that trip, she had tried to talk him out of it. Deep down she had known something would go wrong. She didn't like being reminded of what had happened.

David waited for her answer.

Brier cleared her throat, "Honestly sir, I don't even want to go on this quest. Flint wants to return so desperately and I don't want him to go alone. I would like nothing more than to stay here. I don't even agree with the idea of returning to Mac'tire. I think we should all stay in the forest. First, my father wanted to return and now my friend does and as much as I'd like to stay here, I'm not about to let him go on his own."

Brier was out of breath when she finished but she felt a huge weight lift from her shoulders just by telling David how she felt.

Now that she had said her piece, it would be

completely up to him whether she went or stayed.

After a moment David blinked and cleared his throat, overcoming his surprise at her words, "Are you sure there's no ulterior motive; no hidden reason for your wanting to go on this journey? Perhaps you wish to get recompense for what happened with the exile? Or maybe you want to finish the task your father set out to do?"

Brier considered. She thought of her anger towards the duke, it definitely didn't fuel a desire to return.

It only made her want to never set foot in Mac'tire again. She didn't care about recompense. She wanted to stay in the forest with the ones she cared about and be left alone. She had no desire to finish what her father had started; she had never agreed with the plan to return.

Brier shook her head, "I don't want to go, sir. I only volunteered because of Flint. Maybe it would be better for you to turn me away."

Brier wasn't sure why she said such things. Now that Reid wasn't going, if she left the forest, she would be free of him. She had already decided that Bess would care for her mother while she was gone. And she still felt queasy at the idea of Flint going without her. Yet, as she stood before David, she wanted nothing more than to forget this quest and stay in the forest. Something deep within her argued against that thought and urged her to go anyway.

David glanced at a piece of parchment lying on the table in front of him. He stared at the paper as if he were reading notes but his eyes weren't moving.

Eventually, he lifted his gaze and looked at her long and hard. Brier felt like he wasn't just looking at her but in her. He kept his eyes focused on her for at least a minute before he blinked, seemingly satisfied.

He cleared his throat again and when he spoke, his voice was nonchalant, "Well, given your father's past position as a forester, you would be a valuable asset to the team. Not to mention, you are an adept tracker and hunter. There's a place for you if you wish to go. Do you... wish to go?"

Brier hesitated.

Everything inside her screamed *no*. She had practically accepted the fact that she wouldn't be going.

She loved her life in the forest; she didn't want to leave it behind. But... then she thought about Flint. He had been a loyal friend to her ever since the exile. He had been by her side through thick and thin.

She thought about the joy in his eyes when she had volunteered. Leif had truly believed that it was essential that they return to Mac'tire. He had staked his life on that belief. When had her father ever been wrong? He had always done what he believed was best. Could she argue with that?

Brier pushed all those thoughts aside. No, she wouldn't go. She couldn't.

She opened her mouth to say so but her lips formed different, traitorous words, "Yes, sir, I will go."

David smiled as if he had known what she would say. Brier could only stand there in shock. When David spoke, she finally realized just what she had done.

"Well then, you better start packing Brier, you'll be leaving soon."

CHAPTER 26

Reid let out a breath of relief.

He was returning to Mac'tire.

The anticipation that had been building in his chest since he heard the rumors of the trip had reached its peak. The steady thrill of dread was also at an all-time high.

He shouldn't be excited about this. Not with what he was planning to do once he arrived. He should feel nervous, sick even. Yet, the excitement remained, tingling in his spine and making his hands shake. He finally had the chance to make things right.

He didn't share Brier's reservations about returning. He agreed that they had no future in Mac'tire. He certainly wouldn't. However, he didn't mind tagging along on this little "quest" to return. He needed a way to get back to Mac'tire and this was the perfect opportunity. He wouldn't be alone either; he would have people to watch his back. He wouldn't have to sneak away from the camp; he would be going with the elders' blessing. Once he reached Mac'tire, he would have to break away from the rest of the group. It would be easy enough, no one paid much attention to him anyway. The only difficulty would be getting away from Brier's notice if she went along as well. Reid was tired of milling around doing nothing. For too long, he'd let his life fall apart around him as he sat powerless to stop it.

He'd done a lot of thinking since Leif's death. He finally had direction, a purpose.

His heart and mind fought against him every step of the way but he didn't see any other solution to his problems.

He tried to convince himself that this plan was necessary to stop anyone else from getting hurt and to make amends for the wrongs of the past. The only thing left was finding a way to enact his plan. Luckily, the elders had solved that problem for him.

His interview with David had been short and concise. The elder had been uncomfortable, to say the least. Discussing the wolf attack with one of the two who had witnessed it firsthand was never a pleasant conversation. He seemed to think it was necessary though, asking how Reid was faring as some kind of conversation starter. Reid hadn't bothered to respond. He wasn't so weak that he'd crumble at the mere mention of the attack but he had no intention of talking about it for conversation. He'd gotten good at controlling his memories of the event. He knew the triggers that would send him back there and how to avoid them. One of his main triggers, though, was the hardest to avoid. Brier.

Every time he saw her, he saw the accusation in her eyes. He tried to avoid it, avoid her, any chance he got. It was enough trouble dealing with his mind telling him what a failure he was without adding her voice to the mix.

Any thought that reminded him of what happened to Leif was a dangerous one, bringing back unpleasant memories of everyone else he'd lost.

It was better to not think about it at all. When others talked about it, Reid ignored them. When he couldn't sleep at night, he went for a walk instead. When he wasn't watching Rachel, he stayed as far away from the hut as he could manage.

Unfortunately, he couldn't avoid the camp altogether. The sideways looks thrown his way were becoming the norm. They had never thought much of him before. He was the odd, silent, left-handed boy who stayed with Leif but wasn't his son. Reid had always been an outcast among outcasts. He was grateful for everything Leif had done for him but he would never belong. He didn't mind. People couldn't be trusted, especially those who claimed to be close to you. After the wolf attack, his anonymity disappeared. Concerned and accusatory looks were directed his way whenever he so much as stepped outside. *Reid was there. Why didn't he do anything?* the looks would say.

He had done something though. He had thrown his knife and missed. After all his practice, he still hadn't been good enough. He'd been forced to watch as his knife spiraled through the air, too far from its target to do any good. Had Leif seen it in his last moments? He would have surely recognized who it belonged to, who had thrown it. He would have been disappointed. The thoughts of, *if only it had been a little more to the right* or *if I had only focused more on my target,* swirled constantly through Reid's head. He would have rather been frozen in fear like Brier.

He had trained hard after that, harder than ever before. When he escaped to the forest, he would take his knife and throw it repeatedly.

After the wolf attack, he made a pact with himself to train until he never missed again. His archery skills probably suffered because of his focus on the knife but he had never been as comfortable with the bow.

It was odd how the mere sight of a sword sent him into a state of panic but the knife in his hand felt natural and right. It was a way to protect himself without the inconveniences that came with using a bow. If only he had a knife that night years ago, things might have ended differently.

He kept pushing himself harder and harder, angry at his incompetence. It was never good enough. There were still times when he missed, no matter how hard he practiced. All it would take was one miss. That's all it had taken for the wolf to win. So, he practiced until he could hit the target without a second thought. Drawing the knife and releasing became instinctual.

Brier was right. Everyone around him ended up dead, first his mother, then his father, now Leif. Reid wouldn't let anyone else die, not because of him.

He needed to do something right for once. When he returned to Mac'tire he finally would. He'd practiced long and hard for that reason and thought even harder about what he would do. His resolve to return had been strong for over a month now. When rumors had spread of another group being sent, he told himself he would be part of that group. He didn't care what Brier or anyone else thought. He had to do this to set things right. *Will it make things right?* A voice in his head often questioned. Reid had grown used to ignoring that voice over the last month.

It was easy enough to convince David to let him go. His training as a forester made him the perfect candidate for tracker and hunter. His father's status would automatically gain him favor in the eyes of the duke. Favor that Reid was more than happy to abuse.

Furthermore, Leif had been well respected among the outcasts.

That earned Reid a certain amount of trust also.

"Leif trusted you," David stated, "He would be pleased with the idea of you finishing what he started. He was always talking about the progress you and Brier were making. He was very proud of you two."

The words surprised Reid. It seemed like a long time had passed since Leif's death. Reid hadn't given himself much time to grieve. He had a mission to complete. Perhaps, after that, he would find time to think about everything.

Hearing that Leif had been proud of him caught him off guard. Pressure started to build behind his eyes and a lump lodged in his throat. He had to turn away to compose himself. Leif had always told him that his father, Rowan, would have been proud of him and those words had meant a lot. But hearing that Leif had been proud meant something else entirely. He would never be Leif's son and Leif could never be his father. Training alongside Brier had been painful at times. She was Leif's daughter and their relationship and training together were a constant reminder of what Reid had once had. Hearing that Leif had talked about him a great deal, trusted him, and was proud of him made Reid miss Leif even more.

He pushed aside the feelings. He didn't have time for sentiment. Later, he would ponder what he had meant to Leif. The interview still wasn't over and Reid was determined to keep his composure.

It was when David started asking Reid why he wanted to go on the journey that things became truly uncomfortable.

Reid couldn't very well tell him his reason; he had hoped listing his qualifications would be sufficient.

He gave David a half-truth.

"I want to make things right and ensure that my father and Leif didn't die for nothing," he forced the words out.

Reid's true reason was one he couldn't tell David and one that his father and Leif would surely not see as right.

Luckily David needed no further explanation. He readily believed Reid's words and even appeared moved by them.

"A noble reason," he announced, his voice thick with emotion, "I don't need to hear anymore. You're accepted. Prepare yourself for the dangerous journey ahead."

Reid left the hut thinking one thought. If only what came next was as easy as packing a bag.

CHAPTER 27

The days before the journey were difficult for Brier.

Her mother had taken a turn for the worse and despite the healers' best efforts, it became apparent that Rachel would not recover. The grief that had consumed her since Leif's death had only grown and when winter came, her physical state was weakened also. Her health continued to deteriorate over the following months.

Brier spent every free moment by her mother's bedside caring for her and keeping her company. There was little she could do to help, but sitting beside her mother gave her the sense of doing something worthwhile. She spent much of the time in prayer. She had given up praying for her mother to recover, now all she could do was ask that Rachel would not be in pain. Reid also took his turn at Rachel's side, though he seemed hesitant to do so. Brier supposed he would rather be wandering through the forest, shirking responsibility as usual. Sometimes she was tempted to confront him. If he wanted so desperately to be somewhere else then he should just leave. The faraway look in his eyes and pained expression on his face always stopped her. There was no use starting a fight with him anyway. Brier was too exhausted to argue and she suspected that Reid felt the same.

She could understand Reid's unease. There were times when she too felt the need to escape from it all.

She still couldn't forgive him for leaving especially when he made it clear that he didn't regret his past actions.

He would still disappear when he wasn't taking his turn at Rachel's bedside. When Brier saw him retreating into the trees, her anger would be rekindled.

Flint's words were often in the forefront of her mind. She tried to let go of her anger towards Reid, she really did. But she couldn't. She couldn't forgive him for the lack of care he had shown on so many occasions.

However, even she could see that Reid wasn't disappearing as often. Sometimes when he did leave, she saw him standing just inside the line of trees, close enough to keep an eye on the hut. She was grateful when he took over the vigil at her mother's bedside. Brier enjoyed the chance to go outside and remind herself that the world wasn't confined to their stuffy hut.

Often, Flint would be waiting outside for her. Their time meeting under the tree had come to an end. Brier was unwilling to leave her mother for any length of time and she couldn't bear the thought of being far away if something were to happen. Sometimes she and Flint would go for a short walk with Flint attempting to comfort her by recounting funny stories and jokes. It was reassuring to remember such carefree times.

One day, when Flint had noticed Brier's near distraught state, he'd insisted they take a long walk. It had been one of Rachel's bad days and Brier had almost rejected Flint's offer outright. Reid had overheard their conversation.

"Go ahead," he'd told her, "I won't leave her side until you're back. I'll send someone for you if anything changes."

Brier was surprised at Reid's offer. It seemed so unlike him to sacrifice his own time to allow Brier to get a break.

Perhaps even Reid had noticed her state of hopelessness and exhaustion. Either way, Brier was grateful for the respite and accepted Flint's proposition.

As they started walking, Brier realized they weren't going in any of their normal directions. They were heading towards the clearing where Brier and Reid practiced archery.

"Where are we going?" Brier asked.

Flint smiled mischievously, "You'll see."

Brier wondered if she should be nervous.

When they arrived at their mysterious destination, Brier felt the pinprick of tears in her eyes. Whether the tears were from joy or just surprise, she couldn't say. Flint had brought her to *the* creek, the same creek her father had taken her to for a picnic months ago. It was the last good memory she had of him. He had given her his undivided attention for the first time since the exile. He had talked with her and listened to her and not been concerned with training or Reid or anything else. It had been wonderful.

Brier missed him so much.

"It's the place where we went fishing once," Flint broke the silence, reminding Brier that there was another fond memory attached to this beautiful place.

"I know we didn't catch anything but I figured we could try again. I know you need the break and honestly, with everything going on, I thought it would be nice to do something fun."

Brier laughed wetly, unable to restrain the tears flowing down her face. She pulled Flint into a hug. He was always trying to cheer her up but Brier thought this might have been his best attempt. She noticed two wooden fishing poles lying by the creek and released Flint to pick one up.

The water was shallow and so clear that Brier could see there weren't any fish nearby. She didn't mind. She and Flint stood side by side, their shoulders barely brushing against each other. They threw their fishing lines into the water and watched the fishhooks floating just beneath the surface. Flint joked every few minutes about the giant fish he was sure to catch and how Brier would no doubt catch one even bigger just to show him up. They stayed at the creek for hours and by some bit of luck, Brier managed to catch a little minnow. Flint declared that she had won and Brier released the pathetic little fish back into the creek.

In a time when everything felt like it was falling apart, Flint was there for her. When she returned to her hut that night, she realized he had even managed to make her feel a little better. She would need that little bit of sunshine in the coming days.

They kept up their outings and when Brier insisted on staying closer to the hut, Flint readily obliged. He came to check on her every day. They didn't always take walks. One day he stood by and watched her practice archery instead. She worried she was getting rusty after the days of missed practice.

Flint understood without question and only asked if he could come along to watch and keep her company. Even when she was busy, he would pop by to check up on her and make sure she was still coping with everything.

As Rachel's condition continued to worsen, Reid's disappearances lessoned until they stopped completely. Brier would wake up and expect him to be gone but instead find him sitting by her mother's side.

There were times when he would even encourage her to spend time with Flint instead of hanging around the hut.

She'd always remember the surprise she felt when one day she returned after a walk with Flint and found Reid sobbing by Rachel's side. He was muttering incoherently and Rachel was awake for the first time in days.

Brier stood in shocked silence as her mother murmured something to Reid and he broke down further. It was surprising that Reid, who so often seemed cold and aloof, could show such unrestrained emotion. He seemed so weak and vulnerable at that moment. She always pictured Reid as silent and brooding. She couldn't help thinking that she was seeing a hidden side of him. Brier wondered what her mother had said to evoke such emotion.

Some of the time Brier was away from her mother's side was spent preparing for the dreaded trip. As time went on, she found it more and more difficult to prepare to leave. She wasn't even sure she would leave anymore. Yet, she continued with the preparations as if nothing were wrong.

Meetings were held in the little supply hut in preparation. Five people had been chosen to return to Mac'tire. The others were not much older than Brier. At the first of these meetings, Brier was disappointed to learn that Reid had been chosen. He hadn't bothered to tell her beforehand.

Unlike Brier, Reid seemed to have no reservations about returning to Mac'tire. His determination to go despite Rachel's worsening condition never wavered. His every thought seemed focused on the quest and he spent every spare moment preparing.

At least, Flint was there to restrain her from attacking Reid during the meetings. He also served to remind her why she had agreed to this in the first place.

Brier tried not to let any of Flint's excitement rub off on her. She knew that Flint was as aware of the risks as any of them. Both his parents had died on the last quest to Mac'tire. He'd trained for this moment, readied his mind and body to finish what his parents had started. He was prepared for the danger and the rewards. He might be excited but Brier knew he wouldn't take this quest lightly.

The leader of the group was Echo. The elders had chosen him because of the responsibility and initiative he'd shown around the camp. Echo was the oldest of the group and by far the most serious. He always wore a stern expression on his face and he stood so tense Brier wondered if he would be able to walk without loosening up.

The last member of the group was Erin. She was an attractive girl and Brier noticed that Flint's eyes were often focused on her throughout the meetings.

Brier took on the responsibility of nudging her friend in the side to keep him focused and remind him not to stare. Another side of her found an infinite supply of material to tease Flint about later. Flint hadn't shown signs of liking any girls before and Brier felt that it was her duty as his best friend to tease him about his obvious interest in Erin as much as she could.

Erin was nice enough but Brier wondered how she would fare on such a rough trip. She looked fragile and she certainly hadn't endured the rigorous training that Brier had.

Erin had been given the occupation of healer for the group. She had started training in the medicinal arts soon after the exile and her skills would surely be helpful. Brier suspected that the main reason Erin had been chosen was that Echo was going.

Having her brother leading the group had probably given her an advantage. Brier just hoped having Erin tag along wasn't going to cause them to lose focus on their objective.

The meetings were used as a chance to discuss the trip and come up with a plan for when they reached Mac'tire. As far as Brier knew, the only plan at the moment was *don't die*.

Tents were prepared and dried food was rationed out for each member of the group. Everyone would carry certain supplies, some pots, and pans, others extra blankets and kits for mending clothes and tents. Lastly, they studied maps of the forest and the different routes leading to Mac'tire. Echo seemed particularly fond of this last activity. He eagerly surveyed the maps and commented on how skilled the mapmaker had been.

Brier, having never been one to trust maps over her sense of direction and tracking skills, found this behavior annoying.

As soon as the meetings were concluded, Brier would return to her mother's side. She always felt guilty for leaving. She trusted Bess to keep an eye on things, but she couldn't stop worrying that something would happen while she was gone.

She wondered if she should even be considering this trip. Part of her wanted to drop the matter altogether and tell Flint he would have to go without her. She had every excuse to stay behind. With her mother's failing health, she could easily back out of her obligation.

One afternoon as Brier was nodding off to sleep at her mother's side, she felt a gentle pressure on her hand. She looked down to see her mother's eyes fixed on her.

Rachel had been asleep the entirety of the previous day and Brier was surprised at the life in her mother's eyes.

"Brier," her mother whispered.

"Yes?" Brier responded, leaning closer to better hear her mother's soft words.

Rachel's eyes traced over Brier's face for a long moment, studying her. Brier remained still. Rachel looked so weak, so unlike the strong, resilient woman Brier had always known. She had lost a lot of weight throughout her long sickness and her face was pale and strained.

"Brier, please," Rachel struggled for a moment, "do something for me before I go."

"What are you talking about? Brier asked.

"We both know that I don't have much time left. I'm not going to recover Brier; I'm not going to get better."

Brier wanted to argue, to tell her mother that she was wrong. She would recover. Things would go back to the way they had been. But Brier knew better, had known better for the last month.

"Don't say that," Brier pleaded anyway, her voice strained as she fought back the tears threatening to overflow.

Brier swallowed hard and took a deep breath, trying to quell her emotions.

"Go on the trip, Brier."

Brier jerked her head up in surprise.

"You have to make things right. Your father," Rachel choked on the word, her eyes filling with tears, "Your father would still be alive if we could have stayed in Mac'tire. Others will die too if you don't return and clear everyone's names."

Brier knew her mother spoke the truth, she knew they had to return, but still. Brier didn't want to go back.

"I know you love it here," Rachel stopped and took a deep breath, "but you *can* have a future in Mac'tire. I see such a wonderful future for you. Be strong when I'm gone. Stay with your friends. They'll look out for you. They'll keep you safe, and help you move forward. Reid too. I know you've never been close, but... look out for each other. Keep each other safe. And remember that God will comfort you. You'll never be alone. Return to Mac'tire."

Brier couldn't bring herself to respond.

She couldn't go back, not with everything that was happening. She couldn't leave. Brier felt her hand being squeezed once more.

"Brier, promise me."

"Okay," Brier said as tears started to slide down her face, "I promise."

Rachel smiled weakly. Her hand reached for something lying on the bed beside her.

Brier couldn't see what it was until her mother placed the item in her hand. It was a little piece of cloth. Confused, Brier held it up to see it better. It was a handkerchief with a little scene of a forest embroidered onto it. She recognized her mother's handiwork.

"I brought it with me the day we were exiled," Rachel murmured in explanation, "I had almost finished it and I was so proud. Take it with you, perhaps it will remind you of this forest and all the adventures you've had here. Or perhaps it will remind you of me."

Brier looked from the little handkerchief to her mother.

Seemingly exhausted by the effort of speaking, Rachel closed her eyes. Brier sat there for a long time. Tears streamed down her face and she did nothing to stop them. She cried over everything she had lost and everything she was about to lose. The little handkerchief lay in her hands, ready to wipe away the tears.

The next day Rachel died.

Brier and Reid were both present when she breathed her last. The preparations were made and they attended her burial the following day.

Brier couldn't watch as her mother's body was lowered into the ground. She hadn't been able to bury her father but she decided this was much worse. Reid stood at her side, cold and distant, his expression as hard as stone. Brier remembered her mother's words to look out for him. It would be a difficult promise to keep.

There wasn't time to mourn though.

After the burial, they started to prepare for the quest in earnest.

Brier no longer doubted that she would go. She couldn't ignore her mother's last request even when it filled her with dread.

She buried herself in preparations, refusing to talk

about how she felt. She was tired, so tired and an uncomfortable numbness had settled over her. More than that, she felt very, very alone.

Flint still kept her company, refusing to let her retreat in on herself completely. Brier was grateful that he didn't try to force conversation. She didn't want to talk; she wasn't ready to. Even with Flint, an empty feeling had lodged itself into her chest, and refused to leave.

She prayed for peace over the situation but she couldn't help thinking that this was just another thing the exile and the duke had taken away from her.

While Brier prepared for the trip, Reid altogether disappeared for three days. She didn't know where he went but she imagined he was somewhere deep in the forest. He didn't return to the hut at night, which served to make Brier feel even more lonely. She had to admit to herself that she missed Reid's presence.

Even though he was selfish and horrible, the hut felt empty without him. Brier spent many sleepless nights trying not to think about how eerie the quiet was.

It was obvious that he was upset, but so was she. She added his leaving her the day after her mother died to the growing list of things she could never forgive him for. When Reid returned, there was only one day left until the start of the trip. Brier tried to tell herself that she wasn't mad and she refused to show any relief when he returned.

Several more meetings were held in preparation and Brier remained distant during all of them. She knew she should pay attention. After all, she and Reid had been chosen to navigate the way to the castle. But after everything that had happened, she couldn't bring herself to care.

Every member of the group had a job. Echo was the leader, Erin the healer, Brier and Reid the navigators, and Flint, who had become adept with a sword was to provide any defense needed.

They were a small group, especially for such an important journey. The elders weren't willing to risk any more lives than necessary and they had only been able to acquire five horses.

The day before they left, Brier packed up her few belongings. She hadn't brought much with her out of exile and she hadn't gained many material items while in the forest. She carried her mother's handkerchief with her, tucked inside a small pocket in her tunic, unable to entrust its safety to the sack that held the rest of her belongings.

Brier spent the rest of the day wandering around the camp that she had called home for the last three years. She would miss this place. She hoped, one day, she would return. But there was no guarantee; she was learning that nothing in life was guaranteed.

Once she began this trip, there would be no going back.

CHAPTER 28

The sun was rising behind the mountains.

Brier watched it longingly, feeling its warm touch and wanting nothing more than to stay where she was, perched in the highest branches of her favorite tree. This could be the last time she watched the sunrise from this vantage. For so long the mountains had been the last remaining piece of her old home. Now, after three years, she was returning to Mac'tire.

Brier could no longer think of it as her home. The forest was where she belonged now and she had no desire to leave. She had grown accustomed to the way the leaves subtly changed color before burying the forest floor in their multi-colored blanket. And the feeling of the sun filtering through the trees, casting odd shadows on everything and everyone. The forest was her home but she could stay there no longer. She and her companions had to go before the duke to beg for his forgiveness like scared children. Beg for forgiveness that Brier didn't want. Her father had done nothing wrong. As far as Brier was concerned, this whole trip was a waste of time and a danger to them all. Walking into Mac'tire after being exiled was like asking for a death sentence. The duke had made it clear that they were never to return. Traveling to the castle was in direct defiance of that order. The elders seemed to believe that the duke would welcome them back after they offered proof of their innocence.

Brier doubted even the letter they'd found declaring the riot to be staged would ensure their safety.

Some said it was God's will for them to return, some just wanted a feeling of safety once again. Brier wasn't sure what to believe.

She closed her eyes, wishing she would wake up and find everything that had happened was just a dream. She'd lost everything because of the exile because the duke hadn't trusted her father. The thought of returning was disgusting. The thought of groveling at the duke's feet even more so. What she hated most was that she wouldn't have her father with her. This had always been his idea, returning to Mac'tire. If only he could be here to see it through. If she had to return, she wished he could be with her instead of the others.

The others. Brier supposed she should start thinking of them as her team, her comrades. After all, they were stuck together whether they liked it or not for this quest.

They were a ragtag group.

There was Flint, of course, the only bright spot of the trip. He had always been there for her and now Brier would be there for him. She only wished he had picked a less dramatic adventure for her to follow him on. He was a true friend, strong and dependable, much like her father had been. He was a strong Christian, who listened closely to God's instruction in the same vein his father had. As much as Brier dreaded the idea of returning to Mac'tire, she would do it for him.

Then there were the unknowns, Echo and Erin. Brier

suspected she would get to know them all too well soon enough, but for now, she knew very little.

They were siblings and their father had been killed during the attack. They both seemed eager to return to Mac'tire.

Other than that, Brier knew much less than she would have liked. With a lack of information came a lack of trust.

Which left Reid.

Too bad he was coming along.

Brier wanted desperately to escape from him but it seemed their lives were permanently entwined despite how much they both detested the fact. Or at least, Brier did. Reid was cold and distant and impossible to read. There was no way to know for sure how he felt. She had done little to hide her feelings and she was sure Reid must have picked up on them. She felt some sympathy for him; it was unavoidable after everything that had happened. Her sympathy battled with jealousy and envy that had grown and festered over the years and a strong distrust that was a more recent addition. Reid wasn't dependable unless you depended on him to look out for himself. He seemed to excel at that. Brier suspected that this would be a long trip indeed with Reid coming along.

She leaned against the cool bark of the tree and tried to savor the moment instead of thinking of what was to come. It was peaceful with the light breeze blowing through her hair and sending the shorter strands brushing against her cheeks. She would miss this place. She would miss the escape and freedom of sitting high in the branches of a tree.

I'm acting like I'll never return, Brier thought.

She wondered if she *would* ever come back to this place. If she did, she would be alone. Then again, wasn't she already alone? Her father was gone, her mother was gone, the only person left was Flint and he wouldn't come back with her.

She tried not to feel resentful about that. She knew that she would always have God by her side but she craved the human interaction that had become so scarce in her life.

After all they'd been through together, Flint was too consumed with his desire of becoming a knight to see how much Brier didn't want to return to Mac'tire.

Flint may have a future there, but Brier never would. She would never fit into society like she was supposed to. The forest had roughened her, changed her and she couldn't go back to the way she had been. Here she was free to be herself.

She ran her hand across the tree's rough bark. It scratched against her blistered and calloused fingers. They weren't a lady's hands. They were the hands of a forester. This is where she truly belonged.

She should be with the others, making the final preparations for the trip. Instead, she found herself in her tree, cherishing her final moments of peace, watching the sunrise streak across the sky. Soon, she would leave on the journey that would determine her fate, but, for now, she could admire this brief moment of peace.

She could have stayed there forever but eventually, the vibrant colors faded from the sky and she could put off her duties no longer. With the ease of an experienced climber, she swung down from her branch and started to descend the tree.

She landed catlike on the ground and bent to retrieve her bow. She took a long look around, trying to imprint every detail of the tree and the hill in her memory, then started the walk back to the outcasts' camp.

Brier took the long and secluded path.

She had only recently discovered this route and she felt it a shame to waste any opportunity to use it. It twisted through the forest before coming out at the bottom of the hill.

It was long but only had a slight incline as opposed to the treacherous trek Brier normally made. Not even Flint knew about this new path.

Brier had thought about telling him but it was too much fun watching him make the difficult climb. She didn't want to ruin her entertainment by implying that there was an easier way.

After three years, she was amazed at how much she was still learning about the forest. She was sad to leave so soon. She had the feeling that if she were to spend the rest of her life here, she still wouldn't learn all its secrets.

Brier stayed alert for any possible threats hidden amongst the trees. She had learned the hard way that there was always the possibility of an animal attack. A pair of eerie yellow eyes flashed through her mind reminding her just how dangerous the forest could be.

She shivered slightly despite the pleasant late-summer weather. The summers in the forest had always been comfortable.

The trees provided plenty of shade to chase away the sun's heat and without the constant threat that winter posed or the necessity of gathering food and supplies in the fall, summer boasted a time of relaxation for the outcasts. Well, as much relaxation as being in exile could give a person.

As Brier walked along the path, she tried to take in every detail of her surroundings, stamping the images into her memory.

Why must I leave? She asked.

She had selfishly prayed that the trip would be canceled but it had persevered regardless of her desires.

The path continued to curve until Brier came to a lookout. From the spot, she was able to see the modest little camp that the outcasts called home. A beam of light filtered through the trees behind her and illuminated the clearing below.

Children only a few years younger than herself were running between the rows of huts, playing in the sun. Their joyful laughter echoed through the forest. Brier envied their carefree attitudes. She couldn't remember the last time she had laughed so freely. It seemed like a long time ago. Before her father and mother had died before there was talk of returning to Mac'tire. Maybe she had never been so joyful. She had always looked at life with a more stoic view than other children. Maybe it was a result of her father being a forester.

The smell of roasting venison drifted through the air, making Brier's mouth water. She remembered her mother's delicious venison stew with a pang of sadness and regret that she would never taste it again.

The thought that she had eaten the last bowl of stew her mother would ever make without a second thought or care was like a jolt to her heart causing her to pause for a moment and close her eyes. Brier blinked a few times to clear the blurriness from her vision then continued.

As she descended the hill and entered the outcast's camp, she savored the feel of the summer sunshine on her skin. She took a deep breath of the forest air. It was so fresh, unlike the stale air in Mac'tire tainted with the smells and tastes of the town.

Brier took another deep breath, wishing she could bottle up this air and take it with her.

There were so many things she had taken for granted. Things that she would soon have to say goodbye to, perhaps forever. She had never spent much time thinking about it before, but now, this last day before she left, every little thing weighed on her. Several of the children waved to her before they continued in their games.

Brier hated that these children younger than her had been forced to live this rough and unforgiving life. The elders could excuse what the duke had done all they wanted but every time Brier saw these children who knew nothing different than this life, she saw what the duke's actions had done. Some of them were too young to remember life in the town. If by some miracle, they were accepted back, the children would face the judging looks and mistrust of being an outcast without ever doing anything to warrant such treatment. They would never fit in with their peers, not fully, not after everything they had experienced.

These children had grown up both boys and girls playing together in the forest, rough and unrestrained. Would they still play freely like this in Mac'tire?

Unlike the other outcasts, Brier maintained no hope of being accepted back. Even if the mission was successful, they would still be treated as outcasts, as criminals. Even the children would always be thought of as the sons and daughters of exiles.

Brier forced herself to keep walking. She couldn't dwell on such things now. Despite her feelings on the matter, she still had a trip to go on.

She had to cross through the entire camp to reach the little hut that she had once shared with her parents. Now it housed only her and Reid.

It was on the outskirts of the camp, just as her father had liked it. He always preferred to have some distance from the others. Likely so he could keep an eye on everyone and make sure they were all safe.

Brier took her time as she approached the hut, making a circuit around the outside perimeter and taking in every detail.

The walls, which had only been built up a few years ago were already worn from the weather taking its toll. The forest was a harsh environment, one that had battered the hut. Brier didn't see the rough wood walls though. What she saw were some of the happiest memories she'd ever had. She remembered the long hours where she and Reid had helped Leif build this hut. Working through the cold fall weather, Brier had learned more about survival in that short time than she probably would for the rest of her life.

Then, when the hut was finished, there had been many a night gathered around the fire where Leif told stories of his time as a forester or shared the word of God out of his ragged, leather-bound Bible, his most precious possession. Brier and Reid often recounted the events of that day's training to Rachel around that same fire. Brier had celebrated birthdays in that hut and other milestones. Her mother had taught her how to cook a warm meal and her father had taught her how to fletch arrows.

There were so many memories housed there. Somehow, leaving it was more painful than leaving her home in Mac'tire had ever been.

Brier forced herself to keep moving. If she stayed any longer it would be even harder to leave.

She stepped inside and grabbed her bag of belongings.

She didn't have much that she would take with her, only some clothes and supplies: extra arrow fletchings, a whetstone to sharpen her knife, a needle, and thread to patch up any holes in clothing, shoes, or blankets.

Brier stared at her father's Bible for a moment. She had planned on leaving it behind, not wanting to risk its safety on such a dangerous trip. Her hand brushed against the rough cover.

How her father had obtained such a treasure, she didn't know. He had shared the book with all of those who were close to him, letting Warren borrow it for days on end and encouraging Brier and Reid to read the pages at their leisure. Brier had learned how to read by studying the book with her father's help. Brier snatched the volume up and placed it carefully in her satchel, wrapped between layers of garments.

If nothing else, it would be a reminder of her father on the journey. She slung the sack over her shoulder and turned to leave. She couldn't bear to stay any longer. Hopefully one day she would return but for now, that day felt very far off.

When Brier stepped outside, she almost collided with Reid. His hair was disheveled and the dark circles under his eyes made it clear he hadn't slept well. Brier could relate; it had been weeks since she had gotten a good night's rest.

The sight of Reid made her already short temper spark. She groaned and pushed him aside so she could move past. She had been hoping to avoid him until the departure. She was still bitter that he was going along.

Reid took her annoyance in stride and, without a word, slipped into the hut. He returned a moment later before Brier could escape, holding his bag of belongings.

Apparently, she wasn't the only one who didn't want to linger.

Brier started to walk away, not bothering to see if Reid was following her. She could feel his presence beside her and she tried to ignore it. They stayed silent as they walked, not saying a word or even acknowledging each other. Brier hadn't expected anything else.

Reid wasn't the type to speak unless absolutely necessary. And Brier wasn't the type to start a conversation with Reid unless it was unavoidable.

They avoided eye contact until they reached the hut that was used by the elders and now the group returning to Mac'tire. Reid stepped forward and held open the canvas door for her.

She stepped inside, still not looking at him. The canvas fell into place behind Reid and Brier stood for a moment letting her eyes adjust to the sudden darkness.

The others were already present, hunched over the table inspecting a map. Echo looked up as they entered.

"Finally, you've arrived," he crossed his arms over his chest, "We've been waiting for you."

Flint gave her a grin from across the room.

Sure, you can smile, she thought, *I'm only doing this*

because of you.

Echo cleared his throat and Brier rolled her eyes in annoyance. Honestly, it wasn't like running a little late would kill him. She wasn't even that late anyway. If he was that worried about being punctual maybe Echo should have just left without her, she wouldn't have minded much.

Brier took her place beside Erin at the end of the table and glanced at the map.

She had seen it plenty of times before; it showed the surrounding areas of Mac'tire, their final destination.

"Echo was going over the plan one last time," Erin whispered, filling Brier in on what she had missed.

Brier raised an eyebrow in disbelief. They had already been over everything at least a dozen times. Apparently, Echo wasn't *that* worried about being late to leave. He probably just wanted another chance to admire the map.

"Is this necessary?" Brier whispered, not soft enough though because Echo heard her and turned to glare. Brier matched his glare with a look of complete disinterest and Echo turned away. Flint gave a muffled snort of laughter and Echo's face went red.

He cleared his throat again and spoke, "The whole trip will take at least five days on horseback. I assume you've already been shown your horses."

Each member of the group had been assigned a horse to ride. The equines were from a town not far away. They were stocky animals with rough coats but they weren't chosen for their appearance. They had large reserves of stamina and were surefooted, making them the ideal choice for the journey. They had also cost the outcasts a considerable amount of traded goods to purchase.

After the previous attempt to return to Mac'tire, it had been decided that horses would provide the extra speed necessary to make the journey safely. The horses' prey instincts should also warn them of any danger. It was a small comfort, but still more than the elders had when they went on the journey.

Brier had been paired with a buckskin mare named Sparrow.

Sparrow was a gentle horse by most counts, which was a comfort to Brier who until recently had never so much as sat atop a horse. The thought of riding all day instead of walking still made her nervous. They had all been shown how to care for the horses and had been given a crash course in riding them courtesy of Jacob, one of the outcasts and a former stable hand back in Mac'tire.

"If there are no setbacks, the trip should go smoothly," Echo said and Brier realized that she must have missed some of his lecture.

"Then, once we get to Mac'tire, we only have to get into the castle, gain an audience with the duke, and convince him to pardon a bunch of outcasts. That'll be easy," Flint remarked sarcastically.

"We do have a good chance," Echo insisted, "after all, we weren't the ones exiled, our parents were. What happened with the riot and exile was a huge misunderstanding. If we tell the duke our story, I'm sure he'll hear us out. The letter should do most of the talking for us."

Brier was about to voice her opinion on just how useful that letter was likely to be when Reid spoke, cutting her off, "What if the duke won't see us?"

Echo looked at Reid, seemingly shocked that he would speak up, "Well, we'll demand an audience with him. I don't see why he would turn us away when he hears that we have evidence to prove our innocence. I just hope he'll believe us when we tell him who our parents were."

Brier stiffened slightly at the "were". She was still getting used to thinking of her parents in the past tense. Judging by Erin's hung head, Brier guessed she wasn't the only one.

Erin and Echo's father had been killed by the wolf attack but their mother's death had also been a result of the exile. She had been one of the first casualties of the illness that had swept through the camp the first winter. Perhaps that was what had attracted Erin to becoming a healer in the first place.

"If the duke doesn't believe we are who we say we are, it will be difficult to convince him," Echo scratched his chin in thought.

"I might have something to help with that," Flint spoke up.

All eyes turned to him. Flint reached behind him and produced a long leather scabbard. Brier recognized it as Warren's sword. She looked away from the weapon, the memories associated with it making her uncomfortable. Everyone else's attention was immediately drawn to it. In her attempt to keep her focus elsewhere, Brier's gaze fell on Reid. He was as stiff as a board and had a sickly look on his face. She couldn't ponder over his ill-ease for long though because Flint started to speak.

"This was my father's sword," he explained with only a slight waver to his voice. Brier wondered if he was remembering the day of the burial when she had given the blade to him. He had worn his father's sword at his side for a week before returning to carrying his own weapon. When Brier asked him why his response was simple.

"I'm not worthy of wearing such a powerful weapon at my side, at least not yet."

There was a hiss as Flint drew the blade from the scabbard. The sword shined. Reid pushed away from the wall with a sudden movement and stepped outside.

Echo and Erin were too focused on Flint's sword to notice but Brier glared at Reid's back as he disappeared. *What was he doing?* She decided it would be best to ignore him and instead forced herself to pay attention to Flint.

"I um... I know I should have said something sooner, but I've been trying to build up the courage to see it again," he trailed off.

"It might prove to be just the thing to convince the duke to hear us out," Echo remarked.

Flint nodded and waved the sword around experimentally.

"It's wonderful," Erin exclaimed, her eyes shining.

Flint blushed and put the weapon away, attaching the scabbard to his belt.

"We should get going," Echo said, "Everyone gather your things. It's time."

CHAPTER 29

Brier looked back as the little camp that she had called home for three years started to disappear in the distance.

Farewells had been brief. They had a long journey ahead and few to say goodbye to. Brier wondered why they even bothered with the pleasantries. None of them had any family to send them off. *It's in case we don't come back,* she thought as she waved goodbye to people she hardly knew. The outcasts were a tight-knit group living in close proximity to each other but Brier had been so absorbed in her own life that she still felt like many of them were strangers. She wondered now if she would regret not being closer to this odd unit of people.

As they left the camp, Brier was plagued with more than just mental insecurities. She wondered if she was physically prepared for this trip. A matter of weeks ago, she hadn't so much as sat on a horse. Spending hours in the hot sun riding one was an unpleasant thought. Sure enough, after only an hour in the saddle, she could already feel a deep ache settling into her bones. She felt awkward and unbalanced, completely out of her element. Hopefully, she would never have to fire an arrow from her mounted position. *Lord, give me strength*, she found herself praying often as she swayed back and forth trying to match her horse's gait.

The terrain, at least, proved to be surprisingly flat. There were a few hills and dips but the path the elders had taken before was much rougher than this.

Brier was grateful that the remaining elders had deemed it safer to take an alternative route to reach Mac'tire. She didn't want to see the clearing where her life had fallen apart again.

The mild terrain wouldn't last. The lands between the outcast's camp and Mac'tire were rough and extensive. They were just putting off the worst for later. Brier could only hope she would be more accustomed to riding by then. Her horse Sparrow, unlike her namesake, had a rough gait that caused Brier to bounce in the saddle. There were several times when, if not for her grip on the reins, she would have fallen headfirst out of her seat. She tried to shift her position and move in synch but it took all her energy just to stay balanced. Strange, that she so easily scaled a fifty-foot tree, yet could hardly stay atop a slowly moving horse.

She turned her attention to Flint, trying to take her mind off her unstable position. She would have expected him to be shaking head to toe with excitement. Instead, she was surprised to find that she wasn't the only one unhappy. The atmosphere was somber and dreary, like a cloud of dread hung in the air between them. Brier might be the only one who didn't want to return but all of them were sad to leave the camp behind. Mixed with the fear of what they might face, the mood was dour. Brier didn't give herself much time to consider that aspect of their journey. She suspected the duke would be upset at their return and might not hear them out but she was more concerned about the dangers they would face on the trip there.

The possibility of another wolf attack hung heavy in the air.

They had all prayed for safety before departing and Brier found herself repeating the prayer often as they traveled.

There was silence, broken only by the stamping of the horses' hooves, as the group plodded along. It was so dull Brier almost wished something exciting would happen just to spark conversation. Almost.

She wasn't overly disappointed that things were a bit boring. Being bored was better than being dead.

The quiet was unnerving though. It gave Brier too much time to think of everything that could go wrong. She looked towards Flint once more, hoping he would say something, anything to break the silence. Flint was always eager to make conversation. Now, his serious, melancholy mood made her nervous.

Not everyone was as affected by the silence. While Brier found it unnerving, Reid seemed to enjoy it. He sat hunched in his saddle, comfortable and carefree. Brier wanted to wipe that relaxed expression from his face. If she had to be so uncomfortable, the least he could do would be to look a bit out of sorts.

Although this was not the first time Brier had made this journey, the path this time was different. They would make decent time on horseback and avoid the area where the wolf had attacked. None of them were familiar with the path so they had to rely on the map for directions. Eventually, they would find a known path, and Brier and Reid would take over leading the group to Mac'tire.

The trail gradually grew indistinct, the trees

thickening and the undergrowth becoming dense. They had to dismount several times to lead the horses over obstacles.

Fallen trees and thick bushes made the terrain difficult to traverse. The worst part though was the mud. Despite it being midsummer, there had been terrible rains lately causing the dirt to turn into a mucky mess.

At times, the horses would sink up to their knees in it and when the riders dismounted, they would be swallowed up as well.

The mud coated them in a thick layer from the knees down and then baked in the sun, solidifying into a plaster.

Brier detested the slow pace they were forced to move at. She felt like a hare stuck in brambles waiting to be attacked by some hungry beast. She listened keenly for growling and watched for yellow eyes peeking out from the shadows. She scoured the mud for tracks left by wolves or other creatures that might see half a dozen horses and people as a good lunch. She'd learned her lesson long ago and also looked at the foliage and trees for any animals lying in wait.

Before long, the sun appeared and dried the mud. The ground grew more stable but the sun posed its own problems. In less than an hour, both horses and riders were covered in sweat. They discarded their cloaks and kept moving. There was no time to waste, they couldn't let the sun stop them from moving forward.

Once it reached midday, the heat would be even more severe. However, Brier was eager to keep moving. The farther they moved, the closer they got to Mac'tire and the less time they spent traveling through the dangerous forest.

They were easy prey surrounded by trees on all sides and unfamiliar with the path they were taking.

Brier hadn't wanted to go on this quest but, now that she was committed, she certainly wasn't going to let anyone die because they were taking unnecessary risks.

They kept moving. Their clothes stuck to their backs and their legs rubbed uncomfortably against the hot leather of the saddles. Soft groans from riders and horses were the only complaints.

Breaks came in the form of watering the horses and Brier was grateful for any opportunity, however short it may be, to dismount and stretch her legs. Echo was relentless. He might not have trained as a forester like Brier and Reid but he was just as aware of the danger and perhaps even more eager to keep moving. When the sun reached its peak, the silence was finally broken and the real complaining began. "I don't think my muscles have ever been this sore," Flint said, "And I've trained as a knight."

"Echo, can't we stop for a break?" Erin asked, her voice dry.

Echo studied the sun's position in the sky, considered for a moment, then nodded.

"Fine, we'll stop for lunch."

Flint, Erin, and even Reid sighed in relief. Brier was too busy trying to unstick her legs from the leather saddle to comment. She swung down from her horse, hopping once to regain her balance as her legs swayed under her. She fiddled with the saddle girth and Sparrow let out a long grunt of contentment once the saddle was loosened.

Brier patted the horse's neck and her hand came away sticky with horse sweat and hair.
She made a face and wiped her hand on her tunic. It was time for everyone, horses included, to cool down.

CHAPTER 30

It had been a long day and Flint had a feeling it was only going to get longer. First, they had gone through their farewells at the camp, then trekked through that awful mud before the sun had come up and soaked them all through with sweat. Now Flint was wandering through the forest with Reid of all people and he was very, very lost.

It was supposed to be a simple errand, taking the horses to a nearby creek for water. Of course, it hadn't ended up being that simple. Right when a break was finally in sight too. It had been an exhausting day both physically and mentally and Flint was looking forward to a nice rest and lunch. His stomach growled at the thought. Echo's map specified that the stream they were heading towards was less than a half-mile away. It would be a quick trip, then he and Reid would be back and relaxing in no time. Or so Flint had thought.

At least he was with someone trained as a forester. The only problem was, that Reid looked just as lost as Flint felt. *Not good.* A prickle of sweat that had nothing to do with the heat dripped down Flint's neck.

"Uh, Reid?" He asked hesitantly.

Reid looked at him, one eyebrow raised.

"Shouldn't we have come across the creek by now?"

"Yes."

Flint gulped. That wasn't the response he was looking for. His eyes pleaded for a more detailed answer but Reid stayed silent.

He hated when Reid was like this. It made him impossible to understand. Flint was used to people who said what they meant, his father, his mother, Brier. Reid was wildly different.

When he did talk, which was not often, his words were filled with hidden meanings and changes in tone that, try as he might, Flint couldn't interpret.

"So, uh, do you think we're..."

"Lost?" Reid finished his thought, "Not yet, only off course."

Flint released a breath of relief. If Reid didn't think they were lost then that was at least reassuring. That small reassurance was not enough to put Flint completely at ease. The tall trees looming above him and the claustrophobic feeling of the darkness closing in put him on edge. He'd be relieved when they got out of this part of the forest. He listened for any sounds of wild animals but his senses were not as keen as those of Brier or Reid. He longed for the feeling of his sword grasped in his hand but he couldn't reach it with the reins of the three horses he was leading in the way. Hopefully, if there was danger Reid or the horses would detect it in time to give him a little warning. They must be in the clear for the moment. Reid walked calmly ahead and the horses made no noises of discontent. *Please, God, help us find the stream,* Flint prayed. His legs were throbbing as he walked and his stomach grumbled in protest. Most of all, he wanted to rejoin the others. Being this far away from the camp was unnerving and despite Reid's company, Flint still felt relatively alone.

The worst thing about the whole situation was the quiet.

Other than the heavy breathing of the horses and the faint clip-clopping of their hooves, there were no noises. It made Flint vastly uncomfortable.

He was used to noise and a lot of it. His parents had both talked often and Flint himself wasn't exactly reserved. Brier would raise her voice when excited or angry and there was a constant source of commotion back at the camp. Flint wished Reid would talk but he knew he would have no such luck. He glanced at the side of Reid's head but all he could see was his unkempt hair. An itchy sort of feeling came over Flint like his skin was crawling. It was much too quiet. He couldn't take it anymore.

"Do you think we should turn back?" he asked, hoping Reid would answer his question and break the silence.

Reid shook his head and for a moment Flint was afraid he would stay quiet, "I have a suspicion," he voiced instead.

Flint was given something other than his encroaching sense of doom to think about. He latched onto Reid's words like a lifeline. "What suspicion?"

Reid studied him critically. Flint could feel the judgment in that gaze. He lifted a hand awkwardly with the reins and rubbed at his crooked nose. Maybe he should let Reid stay silent. He didn't want to anger him and cause a fight. Brier wouldn't be there to break things up. Reid only shrugged and turned away.

"Maps aren't always accurate, especially inexpensive ones found in small villages."

"Are you saying that Echo's map might be what is getting us lost?"

Reid nodded, "It's possible and probable. However, I suspect the direction is probably accurate."

"Then why haven't we found the stream yet?"

"The map's distance is likely what's off."

Flint considered that for a moment. It could be possible and it would certainly explain why they were having difficulty finding the stream.

"So, we keep moving forward?"

This time Reid didn't grace him with a response.

Flint sighed and they lapsed into silence once again.

It lasted longer this time until Flint felt like he might explode from unease. He tried to keep his eyes on the path but his gaze kept flickering back to Reid, hoping he would say something, anything. Surely, they were getting close to the stream. It couldn't be far off now.

Flint wanted to break the silence and strike up a conversation, even if only with himself. There was a tension in the air that he couldn't ignore. An unspoken awkwardness between him and Reid. There was the memory of the fight between them. Flint still hadn't apologized for that and he probably never would. As far as he was concerned, he hadn't done anything wrong. Reid had thrown the first punch. Flint wasn't bitter about it, only unwilling to claim he was in the wrong. Then there was Brier. She and Reid hated each other and with Flint being Brier's best friend there would obviously be an uncomfortable air between him and Reid. Flint didn't dislike Reid but he did find him strange and that strangeness unnerved him a bit.

Eventually, Flint's unease over the quiet overruled

any awkwardness. He would rather take his chances with the latter.

"It doesn't seem like you to volunteer for something like this. I mean the trip to Mac'tire. Are you going back to become a forester for the duke?"

Reid stiffened, grinding to a halt. Slowly he turned towards Flint, his face white and drawn. Just as quickly Reid tore his gaze away and focused on the path in front of him. Flint wondered what he had said to upset him. He had hoped to break the tension in the air but his words had only seemed to make Reid more uncomfortable.

"Is something wrong?" Flint asked, concern creeping into his voice.

He tried to see Reid's face but Reid turned his head farther to the side. Reid's horse muzzled his shoulder, seemingly concerned also. Reid ignored the horse and Flint.

He should say something more. Try and understand why Reid was upset. But would that just make him more upset? What could he say? They weren't exactly friends. However, if something was bothering Reid, who else would he talk to about it? Flint may have lost his parents but he still had Brier. Reid didn't even have that. Flint took a deep breath and spoke before he could overthink things any further.

"You know Reid if something is bothering you, you can tell me. I know that things have been hard lately and if you want to talk…"

Reid laughed. It was a quiet, slightly crazed sound and it shocked Flint into silence. He watched Reid with concern as the laugh grew in pitch before subsided altogether.

"You ok, Reid?"

"Fine. I don't need to talk."

"Oh, ok. Well, the offer still stands."

"Sure."

Flint wasn't satisfied with that response but he didn't pry. He'd pushed his luck with Reid far enough today. It'd be better to keep the conversation open and not ask anything that required an answer.

"I think this quest will be good for all of us. Despite spending the last few years living in the forest, I haven't done much exploring. I'm looking forward to this opportunity to learn more. I know you and Brier will get us there safely, that is, if you don't kill each other before we get to Mac'tire."

At Reid's stiff shoulders, Flint knew immediately that he shouldn't have said that.

"I'm sorry," He started to say but Reid just shook his head.

"No, you're right. She really does hate me, doesn't she? I can imagine all of the terrible things she must say to you about me."

Flint wanted to deny it but he couldn't. Reid would know it was a lie. Brier's dislike for him was too plain to see.

He couldn't help defending her though, "You *did* leave her alone while her mother was dying."

Reid's eyes widened, "I guess I did." He was silent for a moment, "It was a mistake. I don't blame her for being mad."

"She has every right to be."

"I know."

"Why did you leave her? You two had just started to

get on better terms."

Reid shrugged, "I don't know."

Flint could tell that he was lying but he didn't call him out on it.

He squinted up ahead. There was a glimmering and a soft gurgling sound.

The stream. Flint and Reid exchanged a glance then both took off at a jog, horses trotting behind them. The beautiful view of sparkling water was laid out in front of them. They had made it.

CHAPTER 31

They waited for Flint and Reid to return with the horses before they ate. It took longer than anticipated and Brier felt unease wiggle its way into her chest when the boys had been gone for more than ten minutes. She glanced at the line of trees often, wondering what could be keeping them and silently praying for their safety.

After half an hour had passed, Brier was ready to go after them. She should have insisted on joining them. It was the reason she had come along on this trip, to begin with. She was supposed to keep an eye on everyone and make sure they were all safe. Despite trusting Flint and Reid's ability to protect themselves, she still couldn't shake the worry that they might be in trouble. After an hour she was set on going after them. She was pacing the clearing and praying fervently that they would show up. She pulled her bow over her shoulder and checked her quiver to make sure she had enough arrows, preparing to go after them. However, she wasn't given the chance. There was a rustling of bushes then Flint and Reid emerged from the trees leading the horses behind them.

Brier abruptly stopped pacing and faced the two boys, "Where have you been?" she demanded, hands on her hips. Silently she thanked God that they were safe.

Her heart still wouldn't stop beating wildly in her chest with worry.

Reid looked sheepish but Flint's face reddened with anger.

Brier thought he might yell at her but instead, he dropped the reins of one of the horses and pointed an accusatory finger at Echo, "We got lost thanks to that terrible map of yours."

"Lost?" Erin asked in shock.

Flint nodded roughly, "The stream was a good mile farther out than the map said it would be."

Echo pulled out his map and looked at it, "No, you must be mistaken. This map was made by a master cartographer, you can tell by the attention to detail. You and Reid must have gotten lost on your own."

Flint barred his teeth and took a step towards Echo, "Do you realize how long we were wandering around for thanks to your map's misdirection?"

"You *were* gone much too long; we'll have a lot of distance to make up thanks to you."

Flint fumed and Brier thought they might have a fight on their hands. Reid sighed in annoyance. Brier wasn't sure if that annoyance was directed towards Echo or Flint.

"Maybe the map was wrong, but the important thing is that you're back now. Let's just sit down and enjoy our lunches. We still have a long day of traveling left," Erin suggested, always the mediator.

Everyone grabbed their lunches and sprawled out on the cool grass under the shade to eat. Erin said the prayer over their food. Their meal was fairly unimpressive, dried meat and bread and cheese, but Brier didn't mind. The heat lessened her appetite anyway.

She took a long swig of water from her canteen, grateful that the leather exterior had kept the drink relatively cold.

She sighed in contentment and poured a little water into her hand so she could sprinkle it over her head.

The mood of the group improved vastly thanks to the meal. Even Flint let go of his anger and made some pleasant conversation.

He tried to tell a few jokes to make everyone laugh but it only succeeded in causing Erin to choke on her bread. Brier, far too accustomed to Flint's poor jokes, focused on eating. Reid wandered to sit by the horses the minute Flint started talking and Echo was too enthralled poring over his map for any inconsistencies to pay attention.

Once everyone was finished with their meal, Echo laid out the map. He probably slept with the thing, he kept it so close. Brier felt uneasy trusting it after Flint and Reid's experience. She would much rather rely on her sense of direction than a piece of paper that a stranger had drawn on. It seemed like Echo never deviated from the plan. Sometimes it was truly infuriating. Would he even listen to her and Reid's directions if they were remotely different from his map?

"Oh, no. I'm not trusting that thing again," Flint refused to even look at it.

"He has a point. If it was wrong before, it might be wrong again. If we rely on it too much, we could get lost," Brier backed Flint up, looking at the map with distaste.

"I told you all, the map could not have been

mistaken. Flint and Reid just wandered off from the path. It's an easy mistake given how dense the forest is."

Brier glanced at Reid; it was unlikely that he would wander off the path indicated.

After all, he had been trained by Leif and Leif had taught them better than that. Brier may not like him but she trusted his sense of direction perhaps more than anyone's. Reid shrugged noncommittedly, "We don't have much choice," he mumbled.

Flint sputtered.

"It's okay Flint, we all get lost occasionally. We shouldn't distrust the map so easily, it's our best chance of getting back to Mac'tire," Erin said.

Flint looked at her, blushed, and looked away, "Yeah, sure."

"We've been making good time so far," Echo told them, "Other than our brief setback this afternoon."

"Which was not our fault," Flint reminded.

"Of course not. I would like to make it to this creek before stopping for the night." Echo pointed to a small line on the map.

They remounted their horses and then set out once again. The promise of a good night's sleep awaiting them rejuvenated the energy of the small group. They sat straighter in their saddles and were more alert to their surroundings. The food had helped and being able to stop and stretch their legs for a while. Brier was grateful that Echo had chosen a place near a stream to stop for the night. She looked forward to being able to wash off the dried mud and dust she'd collected over the course of the day.

The path grew steadily more difficult as they progressed. The trees thinned but there was no trail, not even one forged by wildlife, for them to follow. The sun continued to beat down making it difficult to focus. The alertness of before dissipated the longer they sat in the saddle.

They stopped and walked the horses periodically, giving both horse and rider a chance to stretch their legs. They made slower time but they were careful not to overwork the horses and Echo insisted that if they stopped to walk, they would be less sore in the coming days.

Brier wondered how he would know such a thing. As far as she knew, he had no more experience with horses than she did.

Brier was thankful that being a tracker allowed her to get down from the saddle more often. Every couple of miles she and Reid would dismount and inspect the area for animal tracks or other signs of danger. They might be accused of being overly cautious but Brier didn't want to take any chances. The further they got from the camp, the less safe it would be. They were, in essence, in the middle of nowhere. There were no towns for several days' ride. They were wandering through untamed wilderness and it was incredibly likely they would run into danger. Brier looked closely at the tracks, determined to not miss anything. She enjoyed the time walking but it was always difficult to get back in the saddle again.

The day dragged on and Brier swore it to be the longest hours of her life. The repetition was excruciating.

Riding, walking, then riding again, all under the unbearable heat. Finally, they came to the creek. It was small and unimpressive but after the long day in the saddle, everyone sighed with satisfaction at the sight of the cool running water. Brier was especially grateful that it was where the map had said it would be.

Flint leaped from his horse, foot getting tangled in the stirrup.

He hopped once to dislodge it then ran to the water and jumped in, clothes and all. The water was shallow, only reaching his knees but that didn't stop him from flopping down and completely submerging himself in it. His antics elicited a giggle from Erin, an eye roll from Brier, and an angry shout from Echo.

"Get out of there before you drown yourself!" Echo demanded.

Flint gave a small pout and instead scooped up a handful of water flinging it in Echo's direction. Echo remained dry sitting atop his horse but Brier swore she could see a vein pulsing from his forehead.

"Come on, he's just having some fun," Erin told her brother.

Echo sighed and waved dismissively at the scene before dismounting and stalking away.

Brier, Erin, and Reid dismounted and released their horses to wander. Brier's legs quaked beneath her and threatened to give out. She clutched onto a tree for a moment to regain her balance. The earth still felt like it was moving beneath her. Flint sat in the water for a few minutes before rejoining them. He was dripping wet and Echo regarded him with distaste.

Brier shook her head in mock annoyance, "Really Flint? How old are you?"

Flint smirked, a mischievous glint in his eyes. Brier took a step back, not liking that look one bit. She realized what Flint was about to do a moment before he moved. She jumped backward.

"No. Flint don't!" she warned, a dangerous undertone lacing her words.

Flint ran forward, arms outstretched, trying to trap Brier in a wet hug.

"Don't. If you take one step closer..."

Flint kept coming and Brier decided enough was enough. She closed her eyes and kicked up a cloud of dust. When she opened her eyes again, she was met with the sight of a surprised-looking Flint covered head to toe in a layer of dirt.

He coughed and Brier couldn't stop herself from laughing. Soon, Erin was joining in and even Echo couldn't fully restrain his amusement.

"Oh, you're going to regret that," Flint teased.

This time Brier was a few steps too slow. Flint chased her between the trees and around the bank of the creek. She stumbled in her haste and Flint took his opportunity. He barreled into her at full speed. Brier swung her arms, trying to keep her balance but before she knew it the water was rising to meet her. She closed her eyes and gasped at the cold. She came up spluttering and coughing, trying to force the water from her lungs.

"Flint!" she yelled as soon as she caught her breath.

Flint laughed and, despite her best efforts, Brier was soon joining him.

She'd get back at him eventually when he least suspected it.

The two friends pulled themselves out of the creek, Brier giving Flint a playful shove as they went. Erin was laughing and Echo had his face in his hands, whether in embarrassment or to stifle his laughter Brier wasn't sure. Reid had already moved on to unsaddling his horse, not paying Brier or Flint any attention.

Brier was grateful for the change in mood. Where they had been somber, they were now relaxed and carefree. It was Flint's specialty to cheer people up and often in ways that hid his intention to do so.

There were plenty of trees and the group gathered gratefully under the shade. Their moment of peace was short-lived as Echo set them to work.

"Let's set up camp."

There were groans all around as they struggled to their feet.

"We can rest after the work is done," Echo insisted.

"Have I ever told you that you're too serious, brother?" Erin asked as she walked past him.

There was no arguing with the leader though so they all set about their tasks. Brier was in charge of gathering firewood and scouting out the area. Her feet ached in protest with every step but worse still were the aches from riding all day.

Still, she thought, *I don't have it so bad; the boys are stuck with the brunt of the work.*

Flint had to set up the tents and Reid had to haul water from the creek for cooking. Echo had set himself the task of trying to find some fresh food for them to eat for dinner.

Most likely the job would soon fall upon Reid, as he was easily the superior hunter. Although, Brier would argue she was just as capable.

Erin busied herself with creating a pit for the fire. She had volunteered early on to cook for the group.

Brier kept a constant watch over her surroundings as she scouted. The trees were too dense for her bow but she kept her knife close. If needed, she could call for help; she wasn't so far away that the others wouldn't hear her. She'd like to avoid that option if at all possible. She could take care of herself. Thankfully, there was no trouble. The forest was quiet and peaceful. A few small animals like birds and rodents darted across her path but nothing that would pose a threat.

When Brier finished gathering the firewood, she headed back to the others. Two tents were pitched by the time she returned; one for the girls and one for the boys. They were good-sized tents and for a while, it had been considered to only take one. But Brier appreciated the privacy two tents would offer.

She walked to the fire pit that Erin had constructed, impressed at the neat job. Erin didn't look like the type who would dirty her nails but she had managed to dig by hand a small pit and place large rocks around the edges to keep the fire from spreading. Erin watched her inspect the pit, smiling when Brier nodded in approval. Brier stacked her sticks inside and gathered some dry grass, pushing it into the cracks to act as kindling. It wouldn't be a big fire, but it would do. Brier reclined back when she was finished, waiting for Echo's return with some food.

She and Erin stared at each other awkwardly as they waited. Reid had left the buckets of water by the fire pit and gone off, presumably to do his own scouting of the area and Flint was inside one of the tents.

Brier realized it was the first time she and Erin were alone together. Brier wasn't sure what to do. She should say something, perhaps compliment the fire pit Erin had dug, but she had no idea what to say to another girl. She was used to living with her father and Reid and her only real friend was Flint. She was used to discussing hunting expeditions and weapons training, not whatever it was normal girls talked about. Thankfully, Erin spoke first.

"I hope Echo finds some food. He's never been the best hunter, too busy pouring over maps I suppose."

Brier smiled, still unsure what to say but hoping Erin would accept her silence as a response.

"I imagine you or Reid could do the job in half the time but Echo wants to prove that he's useful. He might be annoying at times, trust me, I would know, but he tries his best and he'll be a good leader."

"I'm sure he will," Brier said, though she was sure of no such thing. She hardly knew Echo and so far, she was not overly impressed by his leadership skills.

Before Brier could say anything else, Echo emerged from the trees carrying three medium-sized trout. Brier raised her eyebrows in surprise, it was an impressive haul considering the depth of the creek and the short amount of time Echo had been gone. He must have found a good fishing spot.

Brier wished she had time to investigate and perhaps do some fishing of her own but the promise of dinner was too tempting.

Brier started the fire, fanning it till its flames lapped hungrily at the wood. Echo handed the fish over to Erin who cleaned and gutted them with quick, expert strokes of her knife.

The fish went into a pan and some potatoes, brought from the camp, were placed near the fire to cook. It was one of the few things they grew in the forest and also one of their most useful resources. As the fish cooked, Brier's mouth watered at the smell. It would be nice to have some fresh food. Before long they would be stuck eating the smoked meat and hard bread they had brought with them. For now, Brier would enjoy the delicious aroma of sizzling fish.

As the fish cooked, Flint and Reid joined them around the fire. Flint's stomach growled loudly at the smell of food and Erin laughed.

Brier remembered the way she, her father, and Reid had always drifted to their hut after a long day as if the aroma of Rachel's cooking had drawn them in.

She closed her eyes for a minute and swallowed the lump in her throat. She let the laughter of the others wash over her and tried to push her memories away.

She'd done enough crying, enough mourning. It was time to move on. She knew her parents were in a better place, but that did nothing to alleviate the pain she felt. Brier felt a dull aching in her heart that refused to go away.

The hot meal lifted everyone's spirits and soon a steady conversation began. Compliments for Erin's cooking were shared liberally and Brier had to admit, despite her initial doubts, Erin was a valuable addition to their team.

Unfortunately, except for catching the fish, Brier could not say the same about Echo. After the food was regrettably gone, Erin brewed a pot of coffee and Echo turned the conversation to his plans for the following day.

With food in her stomach and the exhaustion that could only come from a long day of hard travel setting in, Brier's attention drifted. She only caught bits and pieces of Echo's speech. Phrases such as "Long hours ahead of us…" and "Stay focused on the mission…" were the most of what Brier garnered from the conversation.

Her eyes drifted shut a few times and she had to force herself to stay awake. Flint was less resilient. His snores caused Echo to break off from the lecture he had drifted into about the future of navigation.

Echo let out a dramatic sigh.

"Well, what are you all planning to do when we're accepted back?" he asked, changing the subject and effectively getting Brier's attention.

Brier elbowed Flint hard in the ribs and his head shot up as he was jostled awake.

"Huh," Flint mumbled as he tried to dispel the grogginess from his voice.

Echo mumbled something about remembering not to go off on any rabbit trails in the future. He cleared his throat and pronounced every word like he was addressing a child, "I *said,* do you have any plans if we are allowed to return to Mac'tire?"

"Oh, yeah, of course," Flint replied, stifling a yawn, "I'm going to be a knight just like my father." He puffed out his chest and Brier rolled her eyes.

"Well, I don't expect to achieve anything quite so astounding," Echo exclaimed, "I would be happy as a merchant or a craftsman."

Brier saw the common sense in Echo's statement. They were, after all, outcasts. Even if they were invited back into society, they would never be trusted or welcomed.

Living life as a merchant or craftsman would allow Echo to remain out of sight, out of mind. He could have a normal life without facing the townspeople's constant scrutiny.

"Though, I must admit," Echo continued, "I've always wanted to work as a scribe or maybe even a cartographer. I doubt that's in my future, though."

Brier studied Echo a little closer than before. Perhaps they were not so different. They were both realists. Echo knew that he wouldn't be able to fulfill his dream. He knew that they would all have to live careful, unnoticed lives when they returned to Mac'tire.

Erin's words proved that she thought along much the same lines, "I only hope to marry a kind and affectionate man who believes in God and can take care of me," she said, a slight blush creeping up her face.

Even if Erin had other dreams, it wasn't realistic for a woman to wish for anything more than an advantageous marriage or a respectable trade such as handiwork.

Another reason why Brier didn't want to go back.

Flint shuffled in his seat; his eyes focused on the ground in front of him. Brier studied him with confusion. His eyes lifted for a moment, focusing on Erin.

His cheeks reddened and he quickly looked away. *Oh, so it must be the change of tone in the conversation,* Brier thought.

Flint was probably embarrassed at stating his far-fetched ideals of becoming a knight, especially given the limited options that Erin had for her future.

"How about you, Brier?" Echo asked.

Brier, already uncomfortable with the topic at hand, wished she could avoid answering. The expectant stares of her companions left her feeling obligated to say something. After all, everyone else had shared their plans. She looked into her now empty cup of coffee and sighed.

"I'm not sure yet," she whispered, lying.

She knew exactly what she wanted to do, to be. She also knew that it was impossible. She had thought about it since she was chosen to take part in the quest, maybe even before. Maybe the thought had been in her mind the minute her father placed that bow in her hands.

She still felt the same revulsion at the idea of returning to Mac'tire but, if she did return, she knew what she would want to be.

She wanted to be a forester.

She wanted to deal with poachers and wild animals like her father had. She knew that she was capable of it, probably more capable than most, but being a girl, her dream was impossible.

I resent Flint for leaving the camp behind to follow in his father's footsteps, but I would do the same if I could, Brier thought bitterly.

Just another reason why she shouldn't stay. Living a calm, quiet life would never be enough for her. When her father had taught her the skills of forestry, he hadn't meant for her to follow in his footsteps.

What once had been a means of survival was now much more than that to Brier.

She hoped the others wouldn't require a further answer. Erin looked at her with understanding. Flint and Echo nodded in acceptance of her vague response. Brier let out a small breath of relief.

"What about you Reid?" Erin asked.

They all turned their attention towards where Reid had been sitting only to find that he was gone. Brier was glad she didn't have to listen to his answer to the question. She had no doubt that he would share her desire to become a forester. The only difference was, that he might stand a chance. Still, a tinge of annoyance came over her. If she had been forced to answer the question, why should Reid be able to avoid it? He might be standoffish but he could have at least told them he was leaving.

Reid's disappearance forced the conversation to an end and, freshly aware of their exhaustion, everyone started to consider heading to their tents for some sleep.

Brier dumped the dregs of her coffee into the fire and stood.

"I'll take first watch," she volunteered.

There were muttered agreements as the others stood up and cleaned their eating utensils. Yawning and stretching, Erin, Flint, and Echo headed for their respective tents.

Brier rubbed her eyes to chase the sleepiness away and made her way to a tree, sitting beneath it and stretching out her legs. The idea of keeping watch had come from Brier and Reid, though at the moment Brier was starting to regret her decision.

It was an important job, and one they could not afford to be slack on. The chance that a wild animal would sneak up on them and attack was too high to ignore.

Brier kept her bow and quiver by her side and her knife at her belt. Based on the uneventful occurrences of the journey thus far, she didn't expect anything exciting to happen.

She made herself relatively comfortable but stayed alert. She wouldn't let anything sneak up on her.

Brier scanned the whole horizon and then focused on certain spots for a few seconds at a time. It was starting to cool off as the night set in and Brier felt herself relaxing slightly. The cool breeze eased the nerves and tension from the long day of riding. She could hear the horses grazing nearby and the occasional sound of an owl or other nocturnal beast. All the sounds came from small, harmless animals.

After a few minutes of quiet, Brier allowed her mind to wander.

She thought about the conversation earlier. For so long she had never thought she would return to Mac'tire. She had never even considered what she would do if she did. Now that she was facing that decision, she felt overwhelmed.

Life in exile was so much easier. Brier had never considered how much things would change if they returned. Many of her favorite childhood memories would've never happened if they hadn't been exiled. In a way, the exile had not been all bad.

Though, as she had that thought, she remembered all the terrible things that had happened as a result of the exile.

Her mother had wanted her to return to Mac'tire to set things right. Brier intended to keep that promise. Perhaps she would return to the forest after all this was over. She could live her life freely there. The others deserved the chance to start over in Mac'tire if they so wished. Brier couldn't take that from them.

Snap!

She was startled out of her thoughts. The sound of a twig snapping, she recognized it immediately.

Some may have ignored such a small, insignificant sound, but after her years in the forest, Brier had learned never to ignore any warning of danger.

She rose slowly and reached for her bow. Quietly she placed an arrow to the string and scanned her surroundings. Nothing. Absolutely, nothing.

There was no animal in sight. Brier peered deeper into the darkness. Her heart was hammering wildly inside her chest. She scanned the area again. Nothing.

She waited for a wolf or other predator to jump out at her, but nothing came.

She glanced at the horses but they seemed perfectly content grazing on the grass and sleeping peacefully mere feet away. She listened for any other sound but none came. It must have been her imagination. She sat back down and continued to study the horizon. It may have been a false alarm this time but she wouldn't let herself get distracted again.

Before long, her watch was over and she went to wake Flint. She didn't bother telling him about the twig snapping. It had been a false alarm and Brier was a bit embarrassed at her panicked reaction. Flint, half-asleep, didn't notice Brier's nervous countenance.

Once he was settled for his watch, Brier headed to her tent. She laid down and tried to sleep but sleep evaded her. Instead, she lay awake. Thoughts of the twig snapping filled her head and haunted her dreams.

CHAPTER 32

Brier woke the next morning to a feeble streak of sunlight filtering through the tent flap and an awful ache in her back.

She lay still, trying to figure out when she had fallen asleep. She couldn't remember dosing off but she must have slept for at least several hours. Groaning softly, Brier rubbed her back. She dreaded the idea of another day spent in the saddle. Seeing that Erin was still asleep, she reached for her cloak. She needed to get up and stretch out the kinks in her spine. Slowly, quietly, she crept out of the tent.

Brier stood outside waiting for her eyes to adjust to the sudden brightness. No one else was awake. *Lucky her.* she always seemed to wake up sooner than she would have liked. *It must be a result of all the forester training,* she thought.

Letting out a yawn, she rubbed her hands together to warm them and stomped her feet a few times to regain feeling. No doubt it would be uncomfortably hot later in the day. For now, Brier didn't mind the cold. She made her way over to the tall tree where she had kept watch last night. Leaning against the rough bark reminded her of her tree back at the outcasts' camp and she had a twinge of homesickness. She shook her head.

She had only been gone for a day, why should she feel this way so soon after leaving? The damp grass soaked through her pants and Brier shivered.

She felt on edge. They'd already lasted longer than the last group but she worried they wouldn't make it to Mac'tire without some sort of trouble. There were too many things that could go wrong. She shoved the thought aside.

It was too beautiful a morning to worry. She pulled her knees to her chest and rested her chin against them. The yellow and pink of the sunrise danced across the horizon. No other moment displayed the majesty of God so clearly. Brier had always thought that the sunrise was God's gift to the early risers like her. It was as if God were saying, "Sorry you have to get up so early, but because you do here's a little present." Each day the sunrise was unique but still beautiful. *Thank you, God, your presence is all-powerful,* Brier prayed. However, she couldn't help but wonder how much more beautiful the sunrise would be if she were watching it from the branches of her favorite tree.

She'd always enjoyed sneaking up to her hill and watching the sunrise paint the forest in vibrant colors. It was the one upside of waking so early. She missed her tree. She missed the rough bark and the wide branches that could easily support her weight. She missed the leaves that would tickle her neck and arms as she climbed and the scratchiness of the bark beneath her hands. She even missed the little birds that had made their home in one of the highest branches.

As she was pondering these things, Brier suddenly became aware of something beside her, or more accurately, someone. There was no shadow because of the direction of the sun but the presence of a person was unmistakable.

Brier tensed, wishing she had thought to bring her bow and some arrows with her.

She looked up quickly, bracing to make a move in case she needed to attack. A wave of relief swept over her when she realized it was only Reid. The relief quickly turned to disappointment. *Reid.*

He was always sneaking up on people, specifically her. She was embarrassed that her forester training hadn't helped her detect his presence sooner. She huffed in annoyance, upset that he could still get the better of her even after all these years.

She would always remember the time Reid had snuck up on Flint, appearing like a wraith beside him and not saying a word. It had happened shortly after Reid and Flint had gotten in a fight.

Leif insisted on all of them going on another walk and Reid apologizing to Flint. Flint hadn't known that Reid would be tagging along. He'd come to meet Brier with his nose still bandaged and his face swollen. Reid hadn't met up with them right away, instead waiting until right before they left to join them.

Flint was talking to Brier, explaining that his nose wasn't as bad as it looked, though the nasally tone of his voice and the way he winced when he moved too much, contradicted his claims. Distracted, he didn't notice Reid coming up behind him. Reid stood there patiently until Flint stopped talking, then took a step forward so he was in Flint's peripheral vision. The silent figure, seeming to suddenly materialize out of nowhere, caused Flint to jump at least three feet in the air.

Reid had mumbled a pathetic apology, "Sorry I broke

your nose," then left just as quickly as he'd appeared. It wasn't lost on Brier that Reid only apologized for the damage inflicted and not for overreacting or starting the fight.

The experience had proved to her how impressive Reid's ability to remain undetected was.

Still, she resented the fact that he was able to sneak up on her. Reid was the last person she wanted to see. Was it too much to ask for to enjoy the sunrise alone? He had never cared enough to stick around before; why would he approach her now? She was tempted to tell him to go away. Instead, she didn't acknowledge his presence. Silence stretched between them until Brier thought that Reid must have left.

"Beautiful, isn't it?" Reid stated, breaking the silence. Brier jolted in shock, hand going to her heart. She turned to glare at him. Reid lowered himself to the ground, sitting beside her. He spread out his legs and surveyed the horizon.

"Yes... it is," she finally responded.

Reid kept his eyes on the sunrise, the light glinting off his face, brightening his grey eyes and illuminating the scar that ran down his cheek. He looked more at peace at that moment than she had ever seen him. For a second Brier thought she could have grown used to sitting there with Reid by her side. With Flint there was almost always a conversation, sometimes unwanted. With Reid, there was silence, peaceful silence. She could almost forget that he was next to her, almost. Eventually, she grew uncomfortable though. Unfortunately, her discomfort made her voice the first, completely irrelevant thought that came to mind.

"Reid?"

He raised an eyebrow, keeping part of his attention on the sunrise.

"Why are you always so quiet?"

As soon as the words left her mouth, Brier regretted asking.

Reid tensed and any sense of peace disappeared.

Brier cursed herself for her forthrightness. Why would she say such a thing? Reid looked away. His eyebrows furrowed and his lips curved into a frown. She had stuck her foot in it this time. Why was it such a sore subject though? Reid's fingers idly traced the scar on his cheek. His eyes were distant.

After a moment, he looked at her again, this time giving his full attention. His mouth opened but he paused. His eyes searched her face and Brier could read the uncertainty and distrust in his gaze. His eyes were so intense and full of turmoil that she had to look away. His mouth closed and he abruptly pushed himself up, struggling to his feet. Part of Brier wanted to reach out, seize his arm, and stop him. Whatever he had been about to say must have been important and her curiosity demanded an answer.

She watched him as he started to walk away. After a few steps, he stopped.

"Someone once warned me of the consequences of talking too much," he explained, looking pointedly at her.

Then he was gone, leaving Brier pondering why such a simple question had upset him so much.

I suppose that's the best I'll get out of him, she thought. She found that her moment of peace was ruined.

She couldn't stop thinking about what Reid had said and what he hadn't said. She pushed herself to her feet and headed back to the camp.

Brier walked slowly. She did not want to catch up with Reid. What would she say to him? Surely, things would be awkward. For once, Brier could admit that it'd be her fault. She tried to put off the confrontation for as long as possible.

Maybe she should apologize for her rude question. Maybe they could go on as if nothing had happened. Reid would likely be in favor of forgetting the entire thing. Avoidance was his approach to a great many problems. She walked the outskirts of the camp, thinking that she could use the excuse that she was scouting the area for danger to explain why she had been gone so long. When she knew she could put off the inevitable no longer, she walked back to the camp. Erin had started on breakfast while she was gone and Echo was studying his precious map.

"Good morning," Erin greeted cheerfully as Brier approached.

"Good morning," Brier responded a little distracted as she scanned the area for Reid. She didn't see him, but to make sure she asked Erin his whereabouts.

"Have you seen Reid?"

"Yes, he came just before you. He went straight to his tent. Why do you ask?"

Brier opened her mouth to come up with some excuse but Flint took that moment to step out of the boys' tent.

"Oh, probably argued with him and he got the last word. Now that she's thought of something, she's come to tell him," Flint teased.

Brier scowled. He would never pass up an opportunity to poke fun at her. Flint tried to keep a straight face as Brier glared at him but eventually, he let out a snort of laughter.

"Though, judging by Reid's face when he came into the tent, I'm guessing you at least got a few good jabs in."

Brier looked away. *Why are you so quiet?*

"Why *are* you looking for him?" Erin persisted.

"Well, I um... I saw him out this morning and wondered where he had gone," Brier stammered out the reply.

Erin looked unconvinced and gave Brier a hinting look, "Whatever you say. For now, you can help me with breakfast."

"Sure," Brier agreed, eager to change the subject.

Before long, the meal of bread, potatoes, and dried fruit was ready. Reid came out from his tent shortly after they had started eating and sat as far from Brier as possible. He ignored her altogether, acting as if nothing had happened. She wasn't sure whether to be relieved or annoyed.

The meal passed in relative silence. The only conversation was between Flint and Erin with occasional interjections by Echo. Flint talked about sword combinations and Erin asked questions about the practicality of each movement. Brier and Reid spent the meal without uttering a single word, only throwing occasional glances at each other when they thought no one was looking.

Once they'd finished eating, they packed up and set out. Brier was still sore from the last day's riding.

She groaned as she swung into the saddle. She didn't think she could take much more of this.

The day itself turned out to be uneventful, to say the

least. The minutes blended into hours with the same routine. Ride, dismount, walk and repeat with only brief breaks in between. At least the clouds in the sky protected against some of the sun's heat.

The only action came when a rabbit crossed their path and then scampered into the brush on the other side of the insignificant trail, startling both riders and horses.

Reid had thrown his knife before any of them realized what was going on, missed, and been forced to dismount to retrieve it.

Multiple times Brier tried to make eye contact with Reid. She didn't want to strike up a conversation but she felt that she should explain that she meant no offense by her earlier remark. Reid seemed to know exactly when she would turn to look at him and chose that moment to look at the trees to either side.

Once, Brier turned to look at him and saw that he was whispering something into his horse, Cobalt's ear. Strange how Reid had more social skills with animals than with humans. As she watched, the horse responded to whatever Reid said with a whinny. Realizing that she was turned in the saddle staring at Reid intently, Brier quickly turned around. *Too* quickly. She swayed in the saddle precariously and had to reach for Sparrow's mane to steady herself. She breathed a sigh of relief when she was firmly seated once again.

Flint chose that moment to lead his horse over to ride beside her.

She mentally prepared a comeback for whatever snide remark he'd make about her near fall from the saddle.

Or perhaps he would tease her for staring in Reid's

direction. Flint didn't so much as snicker. The distant look on his face made it obvious that he was thinking about something. Brier was struck with the realization that they hadn't had a chance to talk since they left the camp. There'd been casual conversation with the others but they hadn't talked alone. She hadn't even had the chance to ask him how he felt about the trip so far. She wondered if he was as nervous about making it back as she was.

"I still can't believe we're returning to Mac'tire," Flint broke the silence, "It's been years since the exile. I wonder how much has changed."

No doubt lots had changed in Mac'tire. After all, they had been gone for three years. When they had left, they were only children. They still were children. Yet, due to their circumstances, they had grown up fast.

"I think everything will be different now."

It was strange to think of what they might face after all those years away. Anything and everything could have changed. Brier glanced at Flint. When she had climbed down from the saddle yesterday, she'd quietly blamed him for her sore muscles and discomfort. It was because of him that she had gone on this quest in the first place.

Yet, she couldn't stay mad at him. It was his dream to return to Mac'tire and he hadn't forced her to come along.

Despite what she might tell herself, she had made that decision of her own accord.

She'd followed him not because he forced her to but because she wanted to protect him and have his back.

Looking at him now, she saw his determination. He looked so grown up. No longer was he the same boy who'd played with her in the forest or cried into her shoulder as he mourned his parents' deaths.

If they were accepted back, things would change between them. It was inevitable. The friendship they had shared over the years would be put under tremendous strain. Flint would try to become a knight and Brier would be faced with the choice to stay or return to the forest. She hated that after everything they had been through, their friendship could so easily come to an end.

If they were accepted back, their lives would lead to very different paths.

Brier shook her head, trying to clear it. She refused to worry about that now. She would take advantage of these last days before arriving in Mac'tire. Flint was still here, sitting beside her. He was still her friend, her best friend. For now, that much was set in stone. She wouldn't let worries of the future stop her from spending time with Flint now.

"What?" Flint asked noticing Brier's stare.

Brier looked away, embarrassed, "It's just, I've realized how much you've grown up."

Flint chuckled, "I think we all have."

CHAPTER 33

When they stopped for lunch, Echo brought out the map once again. He spread it on the grass as they ate, gesturing to certain markings.

"We should be passing through dense forest for the rest of the day. It'll be hard going but we're making good time so we should be able to make camp before it gets dark," Echo explained.

"And if the map is wrong?" Flint asked.

Echo's face reddened, "The map is not..."

"Yeah, yeah," Flint waved off the rest of Echo's statement, taking a bite of his bread in disinterest.

Echo glowered but didn't say anything else.

They were all tired and sore. Brier was certain disagreements like this one would become commonplace during the trip. She just hoped she could avoid any further disagreements with Reid.

They ate a hurried lunch, eager to get moving again. The idea of traveling through dense forest at night made Brier's stomach churn. She inspected her companions' progress as they ate their meal and encouraged Flint, by shoving a wad of bread in his mouth, to eat instead of making conversation. She hoped Echo was right about stopping before dark.

Unfortunately, the day did not go quite so according

to plan.

Brier kept an eye on the sun as she rode, fretting as it sunk in the sky.

Flint reached across and nudged her arm, "Relax," he murmured with a smile.

Brier rolled her eyes at him.

"Watching the sun won't move it backward in the sky," he teased.

"I just don't want to be riding in the dark."

"We won't be. There's plenty of time left in the day."

He was right. Yet, her nerves refused to be sated. When Reid pulled his horse to a stop ahead of her, Brier jumped. She yanked on Sparrow's reins, narrowly missing bumping into Reid's mount.

"What are you doing?" Brier asked.

Reid ignored her. He tilted his head back and forth as he looked around and trotted his horse around the area. Echo and Erin, riding up ahead noticed Reid's strange behavior and pulled their horses to a stop as well.

"Reid?" Erin asked.

Reid mumbled something under his breath then turned to face them.

"We're going the wrong direction," he stated.

"What?" Erin and Flint exclaimed in unison.

"No. No, that can't be right," Echo, rummaged through his satchel, "According to the map, we've been going in the right direction this entire time."

"Forget the map!" Flint yelled.

Echo pulled the map from his satchel and rolled it out across his lap.

"See, here," Echo pointed to a spot only he could see. "If we were going in the wrong direction, we would have passed a stream a little ways back. I didn't see any stream, so we must be going in the right direction."

"A stream could have dried up," Reid stated calmly.

Brier looked around. There weren't as many trees as Echo claimed there would be and Reid was right about the stream, it could have easily dried up especially given the hot weather they had been experiencing lately.

She scolded herself for not realizing sooner that something was wrong. She'd been so focused on the time, that she hadn't thought to pay attention to her surroundings. She swung down from her saddle and started to walk around. Reid seemed convinced that he was right and while Brier hated to agree with him, she did trust his sense of direction.

"Echo, I think Reid may be right," Erin murmured. "There aren't as many trees as we thought there would be. Are you sure the map couldn't have an error in it?"

"No," Echo insisted, "Reid must be mistaken."

Flint groaned, "The map has been wrong before, Echo. It could be wrong again."

Echo waved the map in Flint's direction, "Perhaps the distance was slightly off earlier, but I swear that the map is not wrong this time. Trees are hard to depict on paper, the cartographer probably drew the trees larger than scale, which would make the forest appear to be thicker when here it is actually thinner."

Erin nodded in agreement, "I suppose that makes sense."

Flint looked between them for a moment before sighing, "Yeah, ok, I guess that could be it."

Echo nodded in pride and started to roll the map back up, "Well, shall we keep moving?"

Brier made no move to return to her horse. She was more convinced than ever that Reid was right.

There weren't near enough trees and a stream could have dried out in this scorching summer heat.

A problem with scale would not have caused such an inconsistency between map and terrain.

"Brier?" Flint asked when he noticed that she hadn't moved.

Brier ignored him. She needed to make sure Reid was right. There was an easy way to see whether or not Echo's theory about scale was correct. She walked to a tall oak tree and reached for one of its lower branches. With a heave, she pulled herself up into the tree.

"What *are* you doing?" Echo sounded alarmed.

Reid understood though and he moved to stand beneath the tree, watching Brier's progress as she started to climb.

"I'm trying to get a good look at the area around us," Brier explained.

She reached for a branch high above her head and Erin gasped when Brier was forced to stand on her tiptoes to reach it. Brier smirked. She would always enjoy how nervous it made people to watch her climb. She looked down and saw that Reid was completely unfazed. After training together for so long, he was used to her agility and lack of self-preservation. He'd seen her climb taller trees than this and ones with far thinner branches. He waited for her to reach the top of the tree and call down any information she gathered.

Brier turned her attention back to the tree. The branches grew thinner and the ground more distant. She felt the usual thrill of adrenalin coursing through her veins. Once she was as high as she could go, she peeked out at the world around her.

She always enjoyed the view that could be gained

from a high tree. Everything around them for miles and miles was visible and clear.

A breeze was blowing, one that had been non-existent while on the ground but threatened her balance high in the tree.

From her perch, it was obvious that Reid was right. They were far off course. The trees looked sparse and there were too many clearings near them.

Then there was a long, thin line of nothing. No trees, no foliage, just dry land. That would be where the stream had been. It must have dried up in the heat but the signs of its presence were unmistakable. Far off in the distance, she could see the trees thicken into a dense forest, the forest they were supposed to be in right now.

Brier started her descent. She stopped when she reached the branch which she had used to swing up into the tree. She sat on it and faced her companions.

"We're definitely going the wrong way."

"But the map!" Echo exclaimed.

"The map must be wrong then," Brier's voice was harsh and left no room for argument. Her annoyance with Echo had only grown thus far and her respect for him as a leader was scarce. She realized after a moment though that her tone had been too harsh.

Echo looked at her in shock and Brier quickly tried to think of something to say to soften her earlier statement.

"Or maybe we read the map wrong, either way, we need to correct our direction. There *was* a stream a short distance away, it looks like it dried up. More concrete evidence though is that the dense part of the forest that we are supposed to be in right now is visible and is very far away."

"No," Echo shook his head, "The map must be right. You must be mistaken about the stream. We're going in the right direction."

"Look," Brier said leaning forward slightly, "You're perfectly welcome to climb up there and take a look around for yourself, or you can accept the word of your *trackers*."

Echo shook his head again, "I do accept your word, I just believe you are mistaken. We'll keep moving in our current direction for now."

Brier sighed and swung down from the tree. She could tell Echo wasn't going to let this go. As much as it annoyed her, there was little she could do to convince him otherwise. She shared a look with Reid, the first non-awkward one that day. They both knew this would be a time-consuming detour. Maybe it was what Echo needed in order to trust the trackers more than his precious map.

"Wait a second. This isn't the first time we've had a problem with the map. What if they're right?" Flint asked, coming to Brier's defense.

Echo kicked his horse forward. "I'm the leader of this trip, we'll do it my way."

Brier and Reid remounted their horses. Reid considered her with a strange look on his face.

"What?" Brier asked.

Reid looked away and Brier could have sworn that he was embarrassed, "Thank you," he said.

"For what?"

"For believing me."

CHAPTER 34

As predicted, it was a long day.

Brier swung down from her saddle, groaning and rubbing her back. They had never gotten back on course after Echo's map led them astray. It had only grown more obvious that they were going in the wrong direction the further they rode. More landmarks on the map were never found. Brier hadn't spoken another word about Echo's obvious mistake. If he chose to ignore the word of his trackers then that was his decision. It was clear he didn't want to accept his shortcomings. He kept pointing out small details that would prove his directions accurate. The trees had thickened and he argued that it must mean they were back on course. Then they would pass a landmark that was unrefutably miles from their intended destination. By the end of the day, acknowledging that Echo had been wrong was unavoidable. They'd wasted valuable time and were now hopelessly off course. They would pay for it with long hours in the saddle tomorrow.

They stopped for the night in a small clearing surrounded on three sides by thick foliage. The trees completely blocked out the late afternoon sun, casting the spot in eerie shadow. Brier didn't like the look of the place. It would be easy for something to sneak up on them. She wouldn't be able to relax as long as they were camped here.

There was a stream nearby but they wouldn't be afforded the luxury of bathing or hunting for fresh food.

Echo's refusal to listen had cost them too much time and energy.

They would drink the stale water from their canteens that night, waiting till morning to refill them. Brier had been hoping for a hot dinner along with some cold, fresh water. Instead, they were stuck with cold, stale rations.

They set about their delegated tasks right away, anxious to be finished so they could rest. As Brier scouted out the area, a sense of unease crept over her. Something about the trees looked vaguely familiar, distinct in a way Brier couldn't quite understand. It was a ridiculous feeling, yet one she couldn't shake. She thought of suggesting to Echo that they keep moving and find a better place to stop but Echo's foul mood deterred her.

She took extra care scouting the area instead. It wouldn't provide the peace of mind that moving on would but it was the best she could do. Brier prayed that their decision to spend the night here wouldn't be a mistake. Reid volunteered to inspect the other side of the forest since there was no water to be hauled and that at least put Brier at ease. Very few things escaped Reid's notice. If something was amiss, Reid would detect it.

The trees might not provide a good position defense-wise but they did provide plenty of deadfalls to use as firewood. Brier's muscles screamed in protest as she bent to gather the branches.

She wondered if the discomfort of riding a horse would ever disappear. At least the pain distracted her from her fears.

When she'd finished scouting and gathering wood, the unease hadn't faded.

She had seen nothing to instill a sense of concern but she couldn't shake the feeling that there was some unseen danger just beyond her awareness.

She returned to the camp exhausted, and collapsed to the ground, letting the soft grass cushion her fall. Brier leaned back and watched Erin prepare the dried meat and tough bread that would be their dinner. She tried to let Erin's actions distract her from her feelings of concern but the worry that had embedded itself in her stomach refused to go away. She must have closed her eyes for a moment because she was shocked to attention when Erin announced that dinner was ready. Brier pushed herself up and tried to shake the grogginess from her mind. Her hunger fought against her exhaustion and finally won out. Before she could reach the fire and food, Echo stepped in front of her, blocking her path.

Brier stared at him, a cold fury on her face. First, he had ignored her and Reid, now he was keeping her from her dinner. She moved to shove past him but Echo chose that moment to pull aside Reid. Brier and Reid exchanged a confused glance before turning their attention to Echo.

Echo sighed, "I was wrong."

"What was your first clue?" Reid mumbled.

Brier managed to hold back her snort of laughter. She reminded herself that she was supposed to be mad at both Echo and Reid.

Echo had the audacity to look annoyed.

"I'm sorry," he said roughly before lowering his gaze. He paused to take a deep breath before meeting Brier's eyes and then Reid's. When he spoke, his voice was sincere.

"I know that I was wrong and I know that mistake cost us valuable time. I should have listened to you. It won't happen again."

Brier studied Echo for a moment. His apology surprised her. His actions seemed to prove that he wasn't the type to admit when he was wrong. Yet, that was exactly what he was doing. He'd approached her and Reid of his own accord and tried to make amends for his mistake.

After a moment, Brier nodded. As long as Echo recognized that he had been wrong, then Brier could live with the knowledge of the time they had wasted.

"I'm sure I just misread the landmarks," Echo continued, finding a way to defend his precious map, "we shouldn't have any more problems."

Brier, not for the first time that day, considered finding Echo's map and throwing it into the fire when no one was watching.

"Again, sorry," Echo apologized, jerking Brier's mind away from any thoughts of revenge on parchment. "I hope we can all move past this."

"As long as you take into account what we say next time," Brier said.

"Understood."

"And Echo."

"Yes?"

"You should probably apologize to Flint too. I think

he's more put out about this than anyone."

Echo nodded then looked to Reid who was already walking towards the fire. He kept looking at his surroundings and his shoulders were stiff. He had scarcely said a word during Echo's apology, although that wasn't uncommon.

Maybe he was mad. Somehow, Brier doubted that. She had seen Reid mad before. Now he seemed more unsettled than anything.

One of his hands rested on his knife and he jerked occasionally in one direction peering intently into the trees as if he were expecting an attack.

The meal passed in quiet conversation. Flint told a few jokes and relayed stories from his training. Erin interjected with a few of her own stories of training as a healer, stories that Brier felt should not have been shared over a meal. Echo was uncharacteristically quiet, probably still stewing over his mistakes.

Brier couldn't find it in herself to relax or join the conversation. Echo's apology had distracted her momentarily but now the feeling of unease returned. She kept a close watch on the trees as she ate, half-expecting a set of gleaming yellow eyes to stare back at her from the shadows. Every time a shadow moved Brier's eyes darted in the direction of it. Every time there was the slightest sound she tensed, her fingers grasping for an invisible arrow. There was something off about this whole place. Stopping in this clearing had been a mistake. She should have voiced her concern to Echo. She should have demanded that they stop elsewhere for the night.

Brier's nerves only grew the further the sun sank in the sky. She couldn't finish her food and her hands shook too much to hold her plate.

A rock sat in the pit of her stomach making it difficult to swallow.

The feeling of familiarity she'd felt earlier returned stronger than before. The trees, the bushes, and even the grass struck a chord of memory. Yet, her mind couldn't make the connection that she so desperately sought.

That is until her eyes fell on a small splotch of red marring the bark of one of the trees.

She stared at it for a minute, her mind unable to identify what she was seeing. Whatever it was, it was faded. But it was undeniably there, staining the bark of the tree. *Blood.*

Brier gasped and glanced hurriedly at Reid. He was staring wide-eyed at the same spot. Their eyes met for a split second as they collectively realized where they were.

Brier jumped, reaching for her bow. However, her bow was gone, back in her tent, much too far to reach now. Reid lurched to his feet, hands fumbling to draw his knife. Brier's heart pounded trying to break free of her chest. Flint, Erin, and Echo watched their trackers in surprise and shock. Reid's breath came in short, erratic gasps and his eyes were as wide as a deer staring down an arrow. He was sweating too. Brier watched, mesmerized as the sweat dripped down his forehead, his nose, and splashed onto the ground at his feet. She felt sick. She clutched her stomach and fought to hold in the bile that threatened to escape.

Whose blood had that been?

Had it been her father's?

Warren's?

Or one of the others?

How had they gotten here? How could they have ended up in this clearing? In *the* clearing. How could they have gotten so far off course?

"Brier?" Flint asked, his voice full of concern.

Brier wanted to cry. She wanted to run away. She was frozen. Just like she had been then. She could practically feel the bow in her hand, the arrow on the string, her heart pounding and her hands hesitating.

If only she hadn't hesitated.

Reid slowly put away his knife. He looked like he was going to pass out. His face was pale and waxen. Brier brought a shaky hand up to her face wondering if she looked the same. Her hand came away slick with sweat. Reid was the first to move. He turned and ran, leaving without a word. Brier managed a weak "excuse me" before she ran off to her tent.

"What was that about," she heard Flint mumble before she closed the tent flap.

Brier collapsed to the ground and buried her face in her hands. She tried to still her uncontrollable shaking as horrid memories flashed before her. The wolf. The bow in her hands. Reid throwing the knife and missing. Leif being dragged off. The bodies. The *blood* from the bodies.

Brier choked on her sobs. She pressed her hand to her mouth, trying to quiet herself in case Erin came to check on her, but she soon gave up and let the tears flow.

It was *the clearing,* the same one where her life had been torn apart. How long ago was it? How long since everything had changed? It used to feel like an eternity. Now, standing in the clearing, it felt fresh, like an unhealed wound. Raw, festering.

She could see the wolf now. Its piercing yellow eyes and the calm efficiency with which it had murdered the elders and dragged her father's body away.

CHAPTER 35

They were on the trail again.

Brier couldn't remember leaving but there she was swaying back and forth in Sparrow's saddle in the hot mid-day sun.

It was almost unbearably hot. The horses moved at a drowsy pace and the simple back and forth motion made the scenery fuzzy and indistinct. Echo and Flint rode ahead of the others. Their quiet voices drifted back to Brier but she couldn't make out their words. No one else talked. It was too hot, too miserable. Brier was drenched in sweat, it dripped down her back and made her hair stick to her neck. She couldn't feel it. She knew it was there but there was no discomfort only the knowledge that she should feel some. Her legs rubbed against the hot leather of the saddle, a dull sensation. She should be sore from the riding but she didn't think about that. She could only think of the heat.

It was so unbearably hot.

She reached down to grab her canteen and brought it to her mouth to drink. A minuscule drop landed on her parched tongue. *Empty.* Strange, she thought she had filled it up before they left. She couldn't quite remember. She only had the strong feeling that she had done it but no recollection of the actual action.

Beneath her, Sparrow stumbled then continued on.

"Keep moving," Brier mumbled in a dreamy voice that sounded like it was coming from far away. Everything was buzzing, like the hum of mosquitoes. She wasn't sure if she was talking to the horse or herself. She repeated the line over and over as a sort of mantra.

It kept her moving forward but not focused. She wasn't sure how long she'd been repeating herself when suddenly Echo held out his hand for them to stop. Brier was relieved, she felt her eyelids drooping from exhaustion. Maybe Echo would let them stop early for the day.

Suddenly Brier was overcome with the feeling that something was very wrong. Everything was silent, unnaturally so. She could see the look of worry on her companions' faces. Brier tried to shake herself out of her daze. The heat was too intense, the buzzing too strong.

She heard hoof beats ringing in the distance, not of one horse but many. There were angry shouts too. They were muffled, but Brier could still hear them. She hung her head and tried to sort out what was happening. Her mind drew a blank.

Ahead of her, Flint drew his sword. Echo balled his hands into fists and Erin let out a gasp of fear. Reid held his bow at the ready.

The horses danced around nervously, kicking up a cloud of dust. The dirty particles choked Brier. They made her eyes feel dry and gritty. She rubbed at her face, then, through a great effort, lifted her head to look around.

There was a bend in the trail. That's where the horses started to appear.

All of them were warhorses, large, with coats glossy from sweat. They frothed at the mouth and their ears laid back against their heads.

The ground shook as they charged toward Brier. Time became sluggish and slow.

Brier watched the horses in awestruck wonder. Their muscles bulged with each long stride.

Her mouth was dry. Drier even than before. The dust was suffocating. The sound was deafening.

Men sat on top of the horses. They were dressed in full armor. The metal gleamed in the sun, blinding Brier and sending rays of light all around. They carried lances and broadswords hung from their belts as they charged in perfect unison. Their bodies lurched forward alongside the movements of their mounts in rhythmic harmony.

Brier registered all of this dully. It was what was behind the knights and horses that sent a thrill of fear through her chest. Wolves.

She could see their razor-sharp teeth, their raised hackles, and vicious yellow eyes. There was something different about them, something unnatural. They moved in a tight column. Each step was calm and calculated as if some invisible force was controlling them.

Brier tried to move, to do something, but she was paralyzed with fear.

The mounted knights and the wolves were nearly upon the little group. Each gallop of the horses and each stride of the wolves seemed to last an eternity. Flint tightened the grip on his sword. Reid placed an arrow on his bowstring. They waited.

Then the fighting broke out.

They didn't stand a chance.

The warriors were too strong and they outnumbered them three to one.

The sleek, black horses towered over their small mounts.

Brier took a breath then the line of horses and riders collided. The knights were ruthless, pushing forward and charging their horses straight into the group. Some drew swords, others held their lances at the ready.

Flint tried to block the strike of one of the knights but the man was too strong. Flint's attempt barely slowed the motion of the sword. The weapon was thrust into Flint's side. Brier watched in horror as he screamed in agony, grasping for his saddle. He couldn't keep his balance. His fingers searched fruitlessly for something to latch onto before he slipped, falling to the ground, arms still outstretched. As soon as his body hit the dirt, he was lost, trampled underfoot by the enemy horses.

Brier opened her mouth to scream but no sound came out. Her heart was pounding. She couldn't breathe. She couldn't move. She held her bow in her hand but was unable to draw the string back. Her hands trembled. She remembered another time, a time when her father had needed her to act and she had stood frozen.

Now Flint was gone. Buried beneath a pile of dust.

The enemy didn't notice Brier sitting there. Instead, they moved around her and attacked the others. The wolves prowled the outskirts of the fight. They watched Brier, daring her to shoot. She couldn't lift her bow. Her arms were weighted like lead. She could only sit by and watch.

They went after Echo next. One moment he was

yelling for them to retreat, the next, a lance was thrust through his chest and he was falling to the wolves.

Erin's screams filled the forest but Brier heard them as if they were coming from far away.

Horror like she had only felt once before flooded over her. Hot tears slid down her cheeks. She tried to scream but her mouth was too dry. She tried to pray for deliverance but she couldn't find the words. Why couldn't she do anything? Why couldn't she move?

She watched as Reid was struck repeatedly with a sword. Still, he continued to fight, growing weaker by the moment. There was blood everywhere and there was a fury like no other in his eyes. The armored men wouldn't die and with one more stroke of the sword, the fight finally went out of Reid. He turned in his saddle, eyes meeting Brier's for a split second before he fell from his horse. He lay ominously still on the dirt trail, eyes staring sightlessly at the sky above him.

Erin had no weapon to defend herself, still, she did not escape the brutality of the attack. Brier closed her eyes as Erin was pulled from her horse. She could only hear the screams and cries for help. Then there was silence.

Brier opened her eyes and all of her friends were gone. Dead at the hands of the enemy.

She was alone.

It was all her fault.

She had done nothing, just like before.

The men turned and urged their horses into a canter. They disappeared quickly. It was as if they had never been there. The only evidence of their presence was the bodies strewn on the ground. The wolves stayed behind and watched Brier. They waited for her to make the next move.

Brier couldn't breathe. She felt her chest constricting. Now, now that everything was over, now that the battle was lost, she was finally able to move.

Brier threw herself from the saddle and ran to Erin where she lay motionless. She could hear Erin's small breaths, the only evidence that she was still alive.

"Erin!" Brier cried out as tears fogged her vision. Everything had taken on a blurry, surreal quality.

Erin's hand latched onto Brier's wrist; her grip viselike. Brier gasped and looked at Erin's face.

"Why didn't you h... help us?" Erin croaked.

The wolves snarled and moved to charge forward, drawing up their hind legs and pouncing in for the kill.

Brier woke, drenched in a cold sweat.

She stifled a scream, gasping for breath as tears rolled freely down her face. She wiped her eyes, panting. The vision of her friends lying dead or dying was still firmly implanted in her mind. She could see their still, lifeless forms and hear their final cries for help. Brier shook with the force of her panic. She could hear voices outside, voices that proved it had all been a dream. It wasn't real. She reached blindly for something, anything to cling to. Her hand brushed against her saddlebag and she grabbed hold of it. The course leather was reassuring. Brier dug inside the bag, looking. She felt uneven pages and a thick cover, wrinkled with age. She pulled out her father's Bible. It was heavy and bulky and she set it in her lap instead of holding it. She fingered the pages but didn't open the book. She didn't think she would be able to read clearly with her heart hammering so wildly in her chest. It was enough to just hold the book and know that it had only been a dream.

CHAPTER 36

"You look awful," Flint announced cheerfully when Brier finally stepped outside.

It had taken her fifteen minutes to calm herself enough to pass for being all right. Once she'd stopped her tremors, she had spent several minutes trying to erase any sign of crying. Her eyes were still red and swollen but she hoped she could pass it off as exhaustion.

As soon as she stepped out of the tent, she realized all her effort had been for nothing. Flint was too perceptive. Making matters worse, when she looked around, she was reminded just where it was they had camped. She'd been so worked up from her dream that she had momentarily forgotten the clearing. Now, the memory hit hard bringing with it the nightmarish thought of wolves charging from the trees to attack her. Brier considered running back to her tent to hide.

Everyone's eyes were on her. They watched her curiously as they sat around the fire eating breakfast. The monotony of the picture made Brier feel sick. It was so normal, so peaceful, so unlike the nightmare she was still reliving in her head. She glanced back at the tent. If she retreated now, she would only draw more attention to herself and cause the others to worry. Brier twisted a strand of hair around her finger and chewed on her lip.

"Are you alright?" Erin asked, her gentle voice full of concern.

It was so like her mother's voice Brier wanted to cry. She felt anything but alright. Nausea crept up her throat and she felt dizzy and disoriented like she was still dreaming.

She prided herself on her iron constitution. She could gut a deer or trap a rabbit without hesitation. Yet, this dream, though she knew it wasn't real, stuck with her. Brier pushed herself forward.

"I... I'll be okay," she murmured, collapsing to the ground next to Flint.

Her statement didn't reassure the others. Looks of concern were etched on all of her friends' faces, even Reid's. *Friends*, the thought startled her. A few days ago, she had known next to nothing about Echo and Erin, and Reid drove her crazy. Yet, now she thought of them as her friends. When had she started to feel that way? After watching them all die, she couldn't pretend that she didn't see them as friends anymore. Even Reid's stoic face was a welcome sight. Just seeing him, distant as ever but still there, gave her a sense of relief. Brier dreaded to imagine what things would have been like had her dream been real. A shiver ran down her spine at the thought.

She forced her mind away from the thoughts of her dream. Instead, she turned her focus to Reid, wondering how he was faring. It appeared that he had mostly overcome his shock from the night before. He was acting normal again at least if a little on edge.

Brier was surprised to see the understanding in his expression. He probably thought that her poor composure this morning was because of the clearing.

She hated the look on his face, the softness of his eyes, his small frown. Any part of her that had been glad to see him was gone, replaced with annoyance.

He didn't understand. He never would. Her nightmare and what had happened in this spot, all of it, could have been avoided if only she hadn't hesitated. But Reid, Reid never hesitated.

Her friends, the word still felt foreign in her head, returned to their meals glancing at her with concern. Brier watched them eat, trying to cement the image in her mind. As she listened to the sounds of chewing and smelt the food she was suddenly overcome with nausea. The thought of eating was revolting. She couldn't help but remember her dream, the wolves, her friends falling from their horses and lying dead in the dust. Brier buried her face in her hands, trying her best not to retch. She inhaled a deep breath, then, despite her best efforts, started to tremble.

"She doesn't look well," Echo spoke to no one in particular.

"Maybe she's sick," Erin, added, "She was acting a bit strange last night."

"Yeah, but Reid was acting strange too, well, stranger than usual, and he seems fine," Flint argued.

Brier wanted to protest that she was okay, or at least ask them to stop talking about her as if she wasn't there. When she opened her mouth to speak no noise came out. She clenched her hands into fists, digging her nails into her palms. The sensation was enough to help her fight back her tears. She was so angry at that moment. Angry at herself for being so worked up by a dream, angry that she had done nothing.

She could tell without looking that everyone was staring at her.

"What's wrong, Brier?" Erin asked softly.

"N... nothing," Brier lied.

As she spoke another wave of nausea swept over her and she groaned.

"She looks like she's going to be sick," Flint exclaimed, hurriedly scooting away from her.

"I'm alright," Brier said, "Just need something to eat that's all."

She was afraid to tell the others about her dream. Maybe if she spoke of it, it would come true. Or maybe she was too ashamed that she hadn't been able to save anyone when it mattered most even in her dreams.

When Brier finally lifted her head, Reid was studying her with an odd expression. She couldn't decipher the look but it was different from before. Not pity or understanding. Maybe concern. After a moment he looked away, dragging his gaze back to his food.

Brier took another deep breath. She wanted to be out of this clearing as soon as possible. If that meant fooling the others into believing she was fine, then so be it. Being here made the dream seem more intense. It felt like the wolves might come at any moment.

Erin handed Brier a heaping plate of food which Brier looked at with distaste. If she ate anything it would be even more difficult to keep herself from getting sick. Bread and dried fruit were a bland meal but Brier's stomach turned just looking at it.

Feeling several sets of eyes focused on her, Brier took a bite of her bread. Unable to swallow it, she washed it down with some water instead.

She gave her companions a weak smile and then

stuffed another bite into her mouth. She just hoped the food would stay down.

Seemingly satisfied, Echo started to discuss their plans for the day.

Brier let out a breath of relief and then noticed that Reid was still watching her suspiciously. She gave him a half-hearted glare.

It was difficult to pay attention as Echo pointed out places on his map or when Erin discussed healing herbs they should look for as they traveled.

Brier only caught bits and pieces of the conversation. Echo apologized once again for leading them in the wrong direction and explained a shortcut he had found on the map that could make up for lost time.

Brier's mind kept drifting back to her dream. It had seemed so lifelike. She could still see Flint falling from his horse, Echo impaled with a lance, and Reid fighting a losing battle. She could still feel Erin's hand grasping her wrist. She feared the images would never fade. Why was it so difficult to forget about this dream? There had been something strange about the wolves. Maybe that was it. The wolves in her dream had been unnatural, seeming to possess human intelligence and intent. Yet, they had seemed so real.

Brier managed to eat half of her food, her stomach churning the entire time before she discreetly scraped the remaining bits off her plate into a shrub behind her. She was certain Reid had seen her do it but he didn't make any remark.

After the meal, Flint and Reid collapsed the tents and put out the fire while Brier, Erin, and Echo led the horses to the nearby creek.

They stopped to fill everyone's canteens then returned to the camp to find the tents packed neatly away and Flint and Reid waiting for them.

They set off without further notice leaving the clearing behind. Brier found it strange to be leaving that place again.

Before, it had been so difficult. She hadn't wanted to leave without finding her father's body and she hadn't wanted to abandon the bodies of the elders.

Reid had dragged her away that time. Now, he rode beside her and she was leaving as if nothing had happened. She felt an immediate comfort after the clearing faded from view. She wished she could dispel her thoughts of the dream that easily.

CHAPTER 37

The heat came early.

A headache started to form in Brier's temples and as she jolted with Sparrow's rocky gait, it only grew. She'd rather walk but that was impractical and time-consuming. They had already lost most of the day yesterday due to Echo's misdirection. They couldn't afford to be slowed down further due to Brier's headache.

Even as the clearing faded from view, Reid kept a constant lookout. Brier was grateful for his vigilance. She was too tired to focus; it was all she could do just to keep from falling asleep. The fear of reliving her nightmare was the only thing keeping her awake.

The heat certainly didn't help. Before long, it was unbearably hot. Brier's clothes stuck to her body and her legs chafed against the hot leather saddle. The group tried to stay in the shade as much as possible but the heat was persistent and it beat down on them even through the covering of trees. Brier still hadn't overcome her anxiety and she was constantly glancing at the shadows expecting a wolf to appear. If danger did present itself, she might be too tired to do anything.

She missed her father. He had always comforted her after nightmares and her mother would make a cup of tea and sit with her until she fell back to sleep. They had always prayed over her and reminded her that God was always with her.

Several tears slid down Brier's cheeks and she took a deep breath to try to compose herself.

She wiped the tears away, hoping no one had noticed.

By the time they stopped for lunch Brier had somehow convinced herself that the only reason she had the dream was the combination of nerves and stopping in that familiar clearing. She even managed to eat all of her food. By the time Echo called an end to their break, she had started to feel better.

The day dragged on with minutes feeling like hours. Still, they pushed on. Echo was determined to make up for lost time. Flint made sure to remind him who was responsible for their delay. Flint's nagging brought a smile to Brier's face and improved her mood a little.

Brier reached for her canteen for what felt like the millionth time. Her throat was parched from the heat. She lifted the canteen to her lips and tipped it back. *It was empty.* Her dream came rushing back with blinding clarity. She pulled harshly on the reins, pulling her horse to an abrupt stop. She listened with all her might for the sound of pounding hoof beats and shouts. The only noise came from their horses and murmured conversation.

Flint and his horse almost collided with Brier.

"Is everything alright?" he asked, wondering why she had suddenly stopped.

"Yeah," Brier said shaking her head to clear it, "it's... nothing."

She couldn't quite shake the feeling that something

was very wrong, that her dream was coming to fruition.

"Are you sure? You've been acting strange all day," Flint studied her closely.

"I'm sure. I'm fine. Everything's fine."

Flint gave her a look that said he wasn't convinced. He opened his mouth to say something further but then changed his mind and pushed his horse forward.

Brier was relieved to see that the others hadn't stopped. She didn't want to draw unnecessary attention to her strange behavior or explain that her anxiety was due to a ridiculous dream.

Brier paused for a moment longer. It was just a coincidence, not a foreshadowing of other events. Running out of water was a natural occurrence on a hot day like this. They would stop at the first available water source to refill their canteens. There was no reason for her to worry. It was fine, it was all fine.

Brier urged her horse forward.

The birds above were chirping and the heat made Brier's eyes droop with exhaustion. Her poor sleep finally started to catch up to her. Before long, her eyes were drifting closed and she had to keep jerking herself awake.

She'd nearly dozed off completely when her horse suddenly stopped. Brier didn't even notice until Sparrow reared up, making sounds of distress. She jerked awake, her eyes flying open. She almost fell from the saddle, only regaining her balance after seizing hold of Sparrow's mane.

The other horses were panicking too.

"What's going on?"

"Be quiet," Echo commanded.

A feeling of dread settled over Brier. Something was

very, very wrong. Despite her own racing heart, she managed to get Sparrow to settle down. Brier leaned forward in her saddle to try and get a better look at whatever was scaring the horses.

"I don't see anything," Brier exclaimed.

"Everyone into the bushes," Echo called from the front of the line.

For once, there was no argument, no challenge of Echo's authority. They all moved as one to direct their frightened horses into the underbrush. Once dismounted, Brier strained to keep Sparrow from running and it was nearly impossible to keep quiet. Between the horses and their frantic breathing, whatever was out there would surely hear them. Erin and Flint were breathing as heavily as she was. Echo muttered rapidly under his breath and Reid was as pale as a ghost. Brier listened carefully and could hear a faint growling noise. Her blood froze. It took only a moment to comprehend what she was hearing. It was the noise that had plagued her dreams for many months now, it was the noise that had woken her panting and drenched in sweat just that morning. The growling of a wolf.

The creature rounded a bend in the trail and suddenly it was visible. It was massive with a black coat and yellow eyes. Its lips curled back from its teeth in a snarl and it seemed to be looking directly at their hiding place. Could it smell them? Or maybe, it could sense their fear. Suddenly the patch of bushes seemed inadequate to protect them.

Brier prayed fervently for protection; she could hear Flint doing the same.

They were still close to where the last attack had happened. And the wolf... the wolf looked so similar.

It even had a scar on its face. Brier shivered at the implication. It couldn't be the same wolf. That was impossible.

What should she do? Should she kill it? Could she? Or maybe she could run away and find a better place to hide from that unyielding yellow gaze?

How could this be real? *Maybe it's not, maybe I'm still dreaming,* Brier thought. She squeezed her eyes shut then reopened them. The wolf was still there. It was still moving closer. It was going to attack them. Panic clawed its way up her chest. She felt the familiar sensation of being frozen in fear. Memories of the dream resurfaced. What if she couldn't save them? What if she stood by and watched her friends die? Brier wrapped her arms around herself to try and stop the shivers that ran through her. Flint moved beside her. Acting on impulse, he unsheathed his sword, his father's sword. Brier remembered Warren trying to unsheathe that very sword to kill this very wolf. She stared at Flint, uncomprehending. Then Flint roughly shoved his horse's reins into Erin's hand and took a step towards the wolf.

"Flint?" Erin questioned.

Flint ignored her.

"Stop!" Echo ordered in an urgent whisper.

Flint looked back and for a tense moment, Brier thought that he wasn't going to listen. Then, sword still raised, he sat back and waited. Brier let out a breath of relief. She saw in her mind Flint's broken body, falling from the saddle.

"What is it doing?" Erin whispered, drawing Brier's attention back to the wolf.

The wolf had turned away from them, head tilted to

the side as if listening to something. It looked in their direction once more before running into the bushes on the opposite side of the trail.

They huddled together, waiting for the wolf to return but nothing happened.

Echo was the first to stand up and take a cautious step forward. Nothing. He turned to look at the group with a smile.

"Looks like it's gone."

Brier let out a sigh of relief, the adrenalin quickly fading. The wolf must not have seen them after all. Or maybe it had just decided attacking them wasn't worth the effort. Brier didn't care, as long as it was gone.

"Why did it leave?" Erin asked no one in particular.

"Don't know," Flint replied, "I'm just glad it did."

Reid stayed silent, surveying the trees around them.

They led their horses out of the bushes and prepared to mount.

Brier had one foot in the stirrup when she turned back to look at the bushes and gave a start of surprise. Two shining yellow orbs stared at her from the shadows.

An incoherent whimper escaped from her mouth and she slowly lowered her foot to the ground. The wolf stared at her calmly as she reached for her quiver and nocked an arrow to her bowstring.

It had circled around to come behind them.

Flint followed Brier's gaze and saw the eyes too. He made a strangled sound of surprise. Brier held her bow ready, string taut with tension.

She wouldn't hesitate. She wouldn't let her friends die. Then the wolf started to move. Her heart leaped into her throat as it emerged from the bushes. She faltered.

The wolf took another step closer. Then another.

Brier couldn't breathe.

Then Flint was in front of her, sword raised at the beast. The wolf snarled but Flint's arms were steady, unwavering. He stood strong.

"Get back, Brier. I'll handle this."

Brier couldn't move.

"Flint," she croaked.

"It's alright, I'll be fine. This is what I've been training for."

They both knew that was a lie. Flint hadn't trained for this. He had trained to fight men, men who would fight with honor and integrity. He hadn't trained to battle a wolf that knew only savagery and death.

Brier glanced behind her, looking for help. Reid had his knife in hand and was poised to throw it as soon as he got the opportunity but Flint was in the way. If Reid released the knife now, he would risk hitting Flint instead of the wolf.

Erin had the good sense to grab the reigns of everyone's horses and she struggled to keep them from dashing into the woods. Echo stared at the wolf, frozen in much the same way Brier was. Even if they had been trained, they were too far away to help. Only Brier was close enough.

Flint grasped his sword so tightly that his knuckles turned white. A drop of sweat rolled down his forehead. He tried to look calm and in control. He was trying to be brave for her.

Brier could see his clenched jaw and shaking hands. He was nervous and afraid. Flint took a step toward the wolf.

Brier had to help him. She had to do something. First the heat, then the empty canteen, now the wolf. It was just like her dream. Except now, if she failed to act, the consequences would be permanent. Flint would die.

Flint closed the distance between himself and the wolf. Brier watched in horror as they sized each other up, circling around and looking for an opening. The wolf's movements were calm, calculating.

It was just like the wolf that had attacked her father and just like the wolves from her dream.

"That idiot's going to get himself killed," Reid murmured.

Brier tried to ignore Reid's words but she couldn't help but wonder if they were true. Flint couldn't fight that wolf. He was strong, yes, but strength and skill alone were no match for savagery. She watched with growing dread as Flint made his first attack.

He swung his sword in an overhead arc at the wolf's head. The creature easily evaded him. Its speed was as terrifying as its appearance. Flint was thrown off balance by the attack. He stumbled then regained his footing. A moment later, he charged at the wolf again. It backed up, avoiding the strike then leaped to the side. Flint spun around to face it. Brier realized with a shock what was happening. The wolf was toying with him.

Reid started to move closer in an attempt to get a clear shot. Every time an opening appeared, it just as quickly disappeared. Flint and the wolf were moving too much.

With the tremors shaking Reid's hand, he might miss and hit Flint instead.

As hopes for help from Reid were crushed, the wolf went on the offensive. It lifted one of its clawed paws and slashed at Flint who barely managed to deflect the strike with his sword.

Before Flint could make an attack of his own, the wolf sprung at him. It bared its teeth and slashed at Flint's shoulder. He yelled in agony and dropped his sword.

Brier tried to scream but her voice had disappeared. She watched Flint fall to his knees, clutching his shoulder. Blood seeped from between his fingers.

God, please, save us! Brier prayed.

The wolf started towards Flint again. However, before it could reach him an arrow pierced the wolf's heart, quickly followed by a razor-sharp knife. The wolf yelped in surprise and crumpled into a heap, dead.

Echo rushed to Flint. Brier pulled herself from her stupor and followed him. She dropped to her knees at Flint's side. Reid approached the wolf with an arrow nocked to the string of his bow. He watched the beast intently, poised to shoot at a moment's notice. When he was too close to use his bow, he reached for his knife instead. He nudged the wolf carefully with his foot and then stepped back quickly in case it attacked. When it stayed still, he knelt beside it and slid his knife across its throat to ensure that it was dead. Then, seemingly satisfied, he joined the others.

Flint was on the ground, groaning and clutching his arm. Echo tried to pry Flint's hand away from the wound to get a closer look but Flint refused to release his grip.

"No, no," he muttered when Echo pulled at his hand.

Flint's face had lost all color and Brier wondered if he would be able to stay conscious much longer. He grit his teeth as tears of pain gathered in his eyes.

Dust stuck to his face, his hair, his clothes. Brier looked away.

Erin, having handed the horses to Reid, pushed past them to kneel in front of Flint.

"Flint, listen, I'm going to move your hand," she said, her voice was kind but firm.

Flint tried to argue but he couldn't form a full sentence. Eventually, he broke off into a sob and Erin gently pried his hand loose from the wound.

She leaned close to examine it and sighed. A wave of nausea swept over Brier at the sight of the injury. A steady flow of blood streaked down Flint's arm but even so the claw marks were distinctly visible. Flint winced in pain and tried to yank his arm from Erin's grip. Erin maintained a firm hold. She wiped the sweat from Flint's forehead with the hem of her skirt then turned to face Echo.

"We'll have to set up camp here for the night."

They quickly set about their allotted chores, Brier taking over Reid's job of caring for the horses so he could set up the tents in Flint's stead. Brier numbly set about her task, wondering about Flint and blaming herself for not taking action and shooting the wolf when she had the chance. She'd already lost her father this way, was she doomed to lose her best friend also?

Erin claimed that Flint would be all right but there were plenty of things that could go wrong.

As Brier was finishing with the horses, Reid approached her. She tried to ignore him at first, not wanting to talk. His silent presence grated on her already frayed nerves. After a while, she could ignore him no longer.

"What do you want?" she asked, not bothering to

veil the aggression in her voice.

Reid ignored her anger and moved closer to pat her horse's neck. Sparrow whinnied happily and Brier glared at the horse. *Traitor.*

How could Reid act so calmly? He might not like Flint but even so, he should be a bit shaken up. She was too busy watching Reid's face to notice the way his hands shook as he patted Sparrow's neck. He stood there for a moment before he turned toward Brier, pulling something out of his quiver.

"This is yours isn't it," he said holding out an arrow. "Nice shot by the way."

Confusion filled Brier. She hadn't lost an arrow. "Where did you find that?"

"In the wolf. Didn't you shoot it?"

Brier shook her head, "I didn't shoot the wolf. I thought you did."

Reid's eyes widened and he lowered the arrow. The look of surprise was an unusual occurrence.

"I threw my knife," Reid responded. "If you didn't shoot it and I didn't shoot it then who did?"

Brier grabbed the arrow. It looked almost identical to hers except for one small difference. The fletching on this arrow was brown while hers were gray. It was common practice for archers to use different colored fletching so they wouldn't confuse their arrows with someone else's.

Brier and Reid had followed this practice ever since they started learning how to shoot.

Brier held the arrow in her hand, her mind racing. This changed everything. She felt a lump rising in her throat as she met Reid's eyes.

"This isn't my arrow."

Attention!

If you've made it this far, then first of all thank you! I truly hope you've enjoyed this book.

If you want to find out what happens next, check out the other books in the *Forest Dwellers* series also available on Amazon.

Also, please consider leaving a review of this book. Reviews help independently published authors like me more than you can imagine.

If you would like to learn more about me and my writing, please check out my website https://sgmorand.com or follow me on social media at sgmorand or S. G. Morand.

If you would like to receive newsletters and updates about future publications as well as a free Ebook, please subscribe to my email list by following this link: https://sgmorand.com/contact-me/

ACKNOWLEDGEMENT

    This book was a long time coming. Many years of perseverance and help were necessary to get where I am now. Thank you so much to everyone who has supported me along the way. Thank you to Bowen Greenwood, Leslie Redden, and Becky Hefty for information about self-publishing, promoting, and writing. This book would not be in print without you.
    Thank you to everyone at Capital City Kenpo for teaching me everything I know about self-defence, knife-fighting, etc. Thank you to Pastor Paul and Pastor Josh for teaching me the Bible and that everything should be done to God's glory because He gives us our gifts.
    Thank you to my mom who might have read this book more times than I did. Thank you for your encouragement, brainstorming sessions, and editing. Thank you to my dad who talked me through many plot holes and filled in the gaps along the way. Not to mention designed the cover for this book.
    Thank you to all of the family and friends who have supported me in my writing journey. There are too many to list. And lastly and most importantly. Thank you to God who is the inspiration of all things and who nothing would be possible without.

ABOUT THE AUTHOR

S. G. Morand

Sarah Morand lives in Montana where she loves archery, collecting sarcastic t-shirts, and her obnoxious rat terrier, Ivan. She has an eclectic taste in books and her ideal house would be a Victorian library. Sarah started writing in middle school and after writing a plethora of short stories, finished her first novel by her senior year of high school.

Find more information at:
https://sgmorand.com

And follow on social media at:
Instagram: sgmorand
Tiktok: sgmorand
Facebook: S. G. Morand - Author
Pinterest: S. G. Morand
Goodreads: S. G. Morand

Made in the USA
Monee, IL
13 March 2025